FOLLOW
THE
BUTTERFLY

'A brilliant game of cat and mouse between author and reader. The pieces of this psychological thriller fit together as ingeniously as those in a Chinese puzzle box'
MARK SANDERSON, *THE TIMES*

'A tense, unsettling, gripping serial killer narrative that takes some very unexpected turns... Such a clever book that juxtaposes serial killing with some very profound points—my favourite kind of crime fiction. Highly recommended!'
HARRIET TYCE, AUTHOR OF *BLOOD ORANGE*

'Surprising, fresh and almost indecently fun, with two brilliantly original female leads and a sinuous plot that keeps you guessing until the very last page'
TAMMY COHEN, AUTHOR OF *THE WEDDING PARTY*

'Dark, clever and hugely suspenseful, with vivid, intriguing characters and a masterfully constructed plotline. The ending blew me away'
A.A. CHAUDHURI, AUTHOR OF *THE LOYAL FRIEND*

'A fascinating study in guilt, shame, blame and the stories we tell ourselves to make life bearable... The ultimate revelation of what has been going on in all four lives is horribly convincing'
LITERARY REVIEW

'Breathlessly plotted, deviously constructed, and brought to vivid, twisted life by an antiheroine for the ages... An utterly beguiling debut. This isn't just a thriller you sink your teeth into—it's a thriller that sinks its teeth right back into you'
ELIZABETH LITTLE, AUTHOR OF *DEAR DAUGHTER*

'The premise is highly original and flawlessly executed, with an unexpected, ingenious twist at the end... An utterly compelling, gripping read with an explosive conclusion'
DANIELLE RAMSAY, AUTHOR OF *THE PERFECT HUSBAND*

MARTTA KAUKONEN lives in Helsinki. Before she became a full-time author, she was a film critic for Finland's biggest newspaper. Alongside writing, Martta loves psychological thrillers, film noir, flea markets, abandoned houses and travelling. *Follow the Butterfly* is her debut thriller – it was a critical and commercial hit in Finland, is being translated into twelve languages, has already made the *Spiegel* bestseller list in Germany and is being adapted for a TV series. A sequel, *Meet Me in the Darkness*, is coming soon from Pushkin Vertigo.

DAVID HACKSTON is a British translator of Finnish and Swedish literature and drama. He lives in Helsinki, where he works as a freelance translator. Notable publications include *Land of Snow and Ashes* by Petra Rautiainen, *My Cat Yugoslavia* and *Crossing* by Pajtim Statovci, all available from Pushkin Press.

FOLLOW THE BUTTERFLY

Translated
from the
Finnish by
David Hackston

Martta Kaukonen

PUSHKIN
VERTIGO

Pushkin Press
Somerset House, Strand
London WC2R 1LA

UK edition published by agreement with Martta Kaukonen, Elina Ahlbäck
at the Elina Ahlbäck Literary Agency, and Rhea Lyons at HG Literary

Follow the Butterfly was first published as Terapiassa by WSOY in Helsinki, 2021

First published by Pushkin Press in 2024
This edition published 2025

FINNISH
LITERATURE
EXCHANGE

This work has been published with the financial support
of FILI – Finnish Literature Exchange

1 3 5 7 9 8 6 4 2

ISBN 13: 978-1-78227-878-8

Designed and typeset by Tetragon, London
Printed and bound in the United Kingdom by Clays Ltd, Elcograf S.p.A.

www.pushkinpress.com

To K,
for a book dedicated to you is one that cannot be left
unread

Above all, be the heroine of your life, not the victim.

— NORA EPHRON

Part One

THE RORSCHACH TEST

Ida

There was too much blood in the room. No, I hadn't covered the walls with Beatles lyrics scrawled in my victim's gore like the Manson family. But there was an enormous stain on the rug. It wasn't heart-shaped but the kind of stain that anybody taking an ink-blot test would describe as a butterfly because they didn't have the guts to say it looked like a vulva.

I started examining the bloodstain more closely, but my attention was soon drawn to my socks. They were so sticky that they were glued to the soles of my feet. As I stepped closer to the stain, it felt like walking across grass wet from the rain. A set of bloody footprints followed me from the body to the rug. I felt a chill. The stain really did look like the first card in the Rorschach test.

What would Freud have said about this? Can a rug stained with the blood of someone you've freshly killed really describe the subconscious? Or should we try to interpret it like an augury? A butterfly means I'm rising into the air? Murder gives you *wiiings*? If I'd been the one lying on that misogynistic cokehead's couch in nineteenth-century Vienna, psychoanalytical theory would have turned out quite differently.

Don't go getting the wrong impression of me now. I'm actually quite meticulous. I don't usually make a mess. I torture them, then murder them—without leaving a trace. For me this is a matter of honour. The victims' families never have to splash out on an expensive crime-scene clean-up on my account. I couldn't understand why I'd been so sloppy this time.

I had planned the murder carefully; every last detail was perfectly fine-tuned. I'd spent days thinking about the murder weapon. I always want the weapon to give a clue as to why I chose this particular suit as a victim.

On this occasion, I'd plumped for a filleting knife.

Oh, come on! Do you really need me to spell it out? The knife is one of the classic phallic symbols. What better weapon to thrust into the chest of an incorrigible womanizer who'd been chasing skirt for decades?

So, you see, everything should have been in perfect order, right down to the last brushstroke, but then suddenly chaos took over. I behaved like the worst kind of amateur. I would have to spend considerably longer at the scene than I'd planned. How would I have time to dispose of the body?

I thought for a long time about where to lay my victim to rest. Then I remembered once taking the commuter train from Helsinki to Kerava; as I stared out of the dusty window at the dreary landscapes passing by, I'd noticed a small pond behind the station at Savio.

A quick online search told me that the pond was located on the site of an old rubber factory that had closed down back in 1985. It was so overgrown nowadays that nobody in their right mind would want to swim in it. If I dumped the body there, I could save myself the bother of digging a shallow grave.

I would transport my victim's body to the pond in the boot of his own car, then once at the shore I'd spread out a tarpaulin I'd rolled up inside a sports bag, lift the body onto the canvas sheet, cut it up with a saw, then sink the tarpaulin, the saw and the dismembered body parts into the pond, abandon the car outside Savio station and catch the commuter train back to Helsinki.

For me, disposing of the body was always the most difficult part of committing a murder. Luckily, adrenalin gives you the kind of superpowers that had allowed me to haul men much bigger than myself into the boot of a car and an early grave.

Now I had to battle against time, if I intended to carry out my plan before anyone noticed the victim was missing. For the first time on one of my murderous escapades, I had the feeling that I couldn't trust myself. My heart started to race. A panic attack was all I needed. I had to calm myself down. But fear had already consumed my mind. This kind of sloppiness could only lead to one thing: getting caught.

My victim's home was just as I'd expected. It was the kind of place you see featured in lifestyle shows. Even if you watched the whole show, you still wouldn't be able to describe the apartment. You'd just have a vague memory of all the white surfaces that the presenters swore were in fact ten different shades. A white rug, white sofa, white curtains, white bed, white bedside table, then, as a daring little contrast, a bookshelf verging on grey, but still white. Am I the only one that thinks of the padded cells at the psychiatric hospital when I see the colour white? That being said, right now my victim's clinical bedroom was more like an operating theatre. I looked at the mess I'd made and swore under my breath.

All of a sudden, my attention was drawn to a print hanging on the wall. *Live Laugh Love.* The only people who resort to fortune-cookie aphorisms like that are those who can't properly express their emotions unless someone else puts them into words on their behalf. I knew perfectly well how to process my emotions: by killing.

The print made me think of the Post-it notes that people leave around the house to remind demented relatives what different objects are called. I was convinced my victim hadn't chosen this print himself but that it must have been a gift from a mistress many years his junior.

I stared at the print, then gave a start. My heart skipped a beat. Inside the O of the word 'Love' was a red dot.

I hurried closer to the wall. Yes, it was blood. How could it have spattered this far?

Everything had been going so well at first, and now this: a total disaster!

Getting into the apartment was a piece of cake. I'd been watching my victim long enough that his breathtaking stupidity had become all too apparent. I'd learnt that he kept a spare key in the communal garden. Every time he left home, he hid it in among the sunflower seeds in the bird feeder. His naivety was almost touching.

My victim spent his nights on one of the status symbols of the 1980s. This bed must surely be one of the last of its kind. I can thank my lucky stars I leaned an elbow on it as I started wielding the filleting knife, because it was only then I noticed that it was in fact a waterbed. If I'd accidentally thrust the knife right through my victim's body and the tip of the blade had nicked the surface of the mattress, gallons of water would have flooded the downstairs apartment and the neighbours would have run upstairs and banged on the door.

My victim was so fast asleep that I was able to stand there watching him for minutes. What's the rush, I thought? I always like to make sure that I *need* to kill a particular victim. I don't want to have second thoughts once it's already too late.

But, if I'm honest, I've never regretted killing any of my victims. Not even when some of them have begged me to spare their lives. Least of all then. It's something to be proud of. My victims go through such a rigorous vetting process that all those who make it to the final round have well and truly earned their place.

I've heard it all, everything from faint whimpering and bestial screams to mumbled monologues that I couldn't understand a word of. I've had 'Our Father' and the Ten Commandments, particularly the fifth. But I've always stuck by my decision.

Then it's knife out, a one-two into the chest, and so on and so forth. I doubt you're as perverse as me, so you probably don't want to know any more than that. You're only thinking about the most important question: what does it feel like to take a life?

It feels like nothing.

And it felt like nothing now too.

Everything repeats in exactly the same way. Every time, I wish it was different, that I might burst into life, that I might suck the energy out of my victim. That I might find a reason to carry on living. That I could experience power, that all my problems would be solved, that everything would finally change, that my actions might have a meaning, any meaning at all. That I might experience a revelation, have the final word. Some kind of catharsis. Anything. But there is nothing.

Nothing.

But still I try, over and over again. This one will be different, I tell myself, because I killed him in the morning or because I killed him with an axe, because I killed him quickly, because I killed him without torturing him, because I killed him silently, or because I laughed as I killed him. Because he deserved to die. Because he wanted to die. Because he would have died anyway.

But nothing ever changes.

The feeling is always the same: there is no feeling.

Maybe that's why I decided to stop all the killing. Or maybe I was just bored.

This will be the last time. This one will be my last victim. Imagine, what an honour, though one for which he would never hear the fanfares.

I barely had time to think the matter through properly before I started laughing. Me, stop killing? Yeah, right! Then what would I do? Killing was the only thing I had left. Without it, I would be empty, adrift.

Every human being has an identity. I didn't even have the building blocks of a personality. I was a blank slate, a barrel, empty and echoing. I had to paint my own portrait.

Being a serial killer was my whole identity.

And no matter how much I wanted to, how could I ever bring myself to stop?

The bloody butterfly in front of me answered on my behalf.

I would go to therapy.

HELSINKI TODAY

FORMER MINISTER
DISAPPEARS IN KERAVA

Retired finance minister Uolevi Mäkisarja of the National Coalition Party disappeared last night from his home in the Kilta area of Kerava.

Mäkisarja served as chancellor of the exchequer in the government that steered the country through the recession of the early 1990s. In particular, he is remembered for keeping a tight rein on public finances and for having little sympathy for 'scroungers', as he often called the unemployed.

Mäkisarja was reported missing by his companion, the actress Mirri Kuuramo. Ms Kuuramo arrived at the former minister's residence for a prearranged visit, but Mäkisarja was nowhere to be found, at which point Ms Kuuramo contacted local police.

Mäkisarja's car was found on Sunday evening in the car park outside Savio train station.

80-year-old Mäkisarja is 5'7" tall and weighs around 11st. He has brown eyes, dark-brown hair and a moustache. He was last seen wearing a dark suit and grey tie.

'The police take the disappearance of an elderly man very seriously indeed, and we will be instigating a full search at the first opportunity,' commented Reija Jalkanen, commissioner of the Eastern Uusimaa Constabulary.

The police ask members of the public to report possible sightings of Mr Mäkisarja to the Eastern Uusimaa Constabulary by telephone.

Clarissa

It all started with a telephone call. It was the first time I heard Ida's voice, just a faint whisper, as though she were calling from beyond the grave.

It was a Wednesday, 2nd January 2019, almost eleven o'clock in the evening. I was sitting on the living-room sofa watching an episode of the current-affairs programme *Newsreel* that I'd recorded on the digibox the night before. I'd been a guest on the New Year's Day show, and I was excited to see how my performance had gone.

I'd had so much work to get on with that I hadn't had time to sit down and watch the recording, but now I finally got myself settled in front of the television in the living room and casually swung my feet up onto the coffee table to get comfy. Fifteen minutes into the show, I gave a sigh of relief: everything had gone perfectly.

Sitting on the sofa in that TV studio, I sounded like an expert.

We women always have to prove ourselves and show that we're competent, whereas for men this is always taken for granted. Right from the start I'd convinced the presenter of my authority. He was enthralled and nodded at my every word.

But, for women, expertise is a double-edged sword. Men are afraid of intelligent women. I'd realized long ago that I was just too much for them.

Too smart, too talented, too qualified, too competent.

Too threatening.

Luckily, there was one way of compensating all these men for the fact that my intelligence threatened their fragile self-esteem. I shrunk, made myself as tiny as Thumbelina, by dressing as sexily as I could.

A sexy look calmed most men. It reminded them that although they were no match for me intellectually, at the end of the day even I—like all women—was just a piece of meat.

In preparation for my appearance in the *Newsreel* studio, I had—as was my wont—trussed myself up in my best feminine armour. I was sporting a pink Versace miniskirt, which was so short it was almost lewd, and a tight rosé blouse by Chanel, its top buttons left undone so as not to leave anything to the imagination.

I stared at myself on the TV screen and gave a satisfied smile. I snatched up the bowl I'd placed on the coffee table, picked out the biggest barbeque-flavoured crisp I could find and stuffed it into my mouth. Whole.

My phone's ringtone made me start.

Slightly peeved at the interruption, I pressed Pause on the remote control and fumbled on the table for my phone. An unknown number. Probably telesales. But they didn't usually call this late. Perhaps it was a new client.

I crunched the crisp and hurriedly swallowed it.

'Clarissa Virtanen,' I said as I picked up.

Silence. Maybe there was a problem with the line or the caller hadn't heard my name. I tried again.

'Clarissa Virtanen.'

The silence continued. I was about to hang up when I heard that faint whisper.

'Hi. It's Ida.'

I didn't know anyone by that name.

'Hello,' I answered.

'I'm looking for a therapist. Got any free slots?'

'Thank you for reaching out to me. My first free slot is at nine o'clock tomorrow morning.'

Silence.

'Hello? Are you still there?'

'Yes. Tomorrow, nine o'clock. Suits me.'

I gave her my office address and said goodnight.

And that's how it all started.

The game whose rules she never told me.

What is worst of all?

The sleepless nights, the shame, my scolding conscience? The choir of self-accusations that even at night I can't quieten down? The thoughts endlessly spinning through my mind? The nagging regret, gnawing away at my soul? The voice in my head mocking me? The fear that this will continue forever, that I'll never be at peace again? The fact that I've lost everything?

No. The fact that I long for her day and night.

Arto

I've been racking my brains to think whether I'd ever heard the name Clarissa Virtanen before. It was highly likely, because she was always parading herself in public like some kind of latter-day Pussy Galore. Meanwhile, I'd been languishing in my own alcohol-fuelled bubble and hadn't paid her the slightest attention, though as a reporter I guess I'm supposed to keep up with current affairs and follow people in the public eye. But let's agree the first I officially heard about her was from Irmeli Lahjametsä, editor in chief at *Helsinki Today*.

I'm pretty sure it was the 3rd day of January 2019. I suppose you're wondering why the date stuck in my head so vividly. Well, it was six years to the day since my beloved wife Marja had passed away.

I was sitting at the Quill and Parchment, a pub in downtown Helsinki popular with the editorial staff at *Helsinki Today*, waiting for day to melt into night.

I don't believe in the spirit world any more than I believe in ghosts. But that afternoon I had the distinct feeling that Marja was trying to contact me from beyond the grave and tell me something. It wasn't a pleasant sensation; in fact, it was chilling.

Perhaps Marja had taken a secret with her to the grave, something she now wanted to share with me but that I didn't care to listen to.

And there was someone else tormenting my mind too, someone I would love forever but who I'd never meet again. Someone who gave my life its meaning.

The staccato clack of high heels woke me from my fit of nostalgic melancholy. My eyes were suddenly wide open, and I found myself instinctively looking for an escape route. Too late. A figure appeared in front of me and grabbed hold of me.

Her embrace was warm. After a moment's confusion, I saw that it was Irmeli, the same as ever, only now she was wearing a new wig; her long blonde locks had made way for a tangle of black curls.

An intense course of chemotherapy had taken Irmeli's hair, but the gravity of her illness hadn't affected her steadfast dedication to her work. The new look suited her better than the blonde one. Framed in dramatic black, her violet eyes seemed to light up.

Those eyes alighted on the collection of empty pint glasses in front of me on the counter. It wasn't hard to know what she was thinking.

I surreptitiously tried to catch my reflection in the mirror hanging behind the bar. It was hard to believe that people used to call me handsome when I was younger. My prominent cheekbones were nothing but a memory; now limp flesh sagged in their place. I'd broken my once noble nose in a drunken struggle with the fridge door, and the scar running along the left edge of my nose was a constant reminder of it. When I was younger, my hair was thick as a horse's. Now it had thinned so much that the straggly wisps I'd tied into a ponytail didn't so much resemble a lion's mane as a rat's tail. My green eyes, which used to have such a sparkle in them when I was a young man, were now as murky as ponds overgrown with algae.

This summer I would turn fifty, but my reflection showed there was little cause for celebration.

Irmeli looked up from the pint glasses. Our eyes met, and her initial irritation turned to pity. I'd avoided another lecture—this time.

Shortly after Marja's death, *Helsinki Today* had sacked me because of my drinking. Despite this, I'd been working for the paper as a freelance reporter, and Irmeli still gave me the occasional assignment.

'Arto, it's a good thing I bumped into you. There's a story I'd like you to work on. I'm about to meet an interviewee, but there's just enough time to brief you.'

I wasn't especially interested in work. Still, I had to keep Irmeli happy because she'd forgiven me for so much. Too much, in fact.

I tried to muster a little enthusiasm.

'It's just the kind of story you'll like.'

Irmeli used this same mantra to sell all her ideas to her poor unsuspecting victims.

'A focus piece on a really interesting character. This could be award-winning stuff.'

What else would it be? I hated doing interviews. To be honest, I loathed my work in general. I loathed my life too. And I had no aspirations of winning a Pulitzer any time soon.

'The front page for the new lifestyle supplement is still free.'

Irmeli was well ahead of schedule. The lifestyle supplement wasn't due to come out until the summer. She must have been thinking of someone whose interview would go on the inner pages, if they wanted someone else on the cover of the summer issue. On the plus side, at least I'd have plenty of time to conduct the actual interview.

'I want you to interview the therapist Clarissa Virtanen.'

Why did Irmeli want me of all people to interview a therapist?

She slipped a piece of paper into my hand. On it was a telephone number.

If I could travel back in time, I'd take my lighter out of the pocket of my leather jacket, crumple up that scrap of paper and burn it.

Ida

I should have warned you right away: I'm a liar. The compulsive, pathological kind. Even when I'm talking about something completely insignificant.

If you ask me whether I'm more of a cat person or a dog person, I'll tell you I prefer dogs, though in actual fact I love cats and can't stand dogs; they smell when their coats get wet, they bring grit indoors on their filthy paws, and their constant barking really gets on my nerves. But still I'll tell you I love dogs. Why? I've been lying for so long that I've forgotten how to tell the truth.

And when you lie long enough, truth and falsehood start to look very much alike. Most people agree it's a good idea to be able to tell the two apart. It's noble and morally upright. I'm not so sure. Lies are my truth.

Besides, I don't believe in honesty. Most people have lied to themselves so much that they're incapable of telling other people the truth. A divorce is always the other person's fault, problems at work are always the boss's fault, and if your daughter ends up a self-harming anorexic, whose fault is that? Not yours, that's for sure.

Besides, when you lie for a living, you get very good at it.

If I wanted to, I could make you believe anything at all.

Anything.

Well, now that you know my vices, you'd best be on your guard.

I told you I was going to stop killing people. Ha! I never had the slightest intention of that.

Humans are lazy creatures. Ask any passer-by whether they're good at their job, and the answer will undoubtedly be yes. Why would anybody carry on doing something that requires a concerted effort? People want everything to be as easy as possible. I'm only good at two things: torturing and killing. And when I say good, I mean damn good. So why would I stop now?

But there was another reason I wanted to start going to therapy. I was afraid of getting caught.

There's one thing that unites all male serial killers: they like playing cat and mouse with the police. They leave little clues scattered around the crime scene. For them, the act itself is only half the enjoyment. They get off on the thought that they're smarter than the police. The victims are nothing but pawns. The real battle of wills is between the murderer and the investigators.

I didn't give a shit about the cops and their theories. They should thank me—after all, I'd been providing them with fascinating cases for years now.

Somewhere in Finland, there must have been a cop who had dedicated her life to solving the murders I'd committed. Maybe she was running a latex-gloved finger across the evidence from the crime scene, maybe staring at the photos of suspects pinned to the wall in her office and trying to work out which of them was cold-blooded enough to be a serial killer. Or maybe she'd given up altogether, taken sick leave and already trained up her replacement.

But so what? She was just doing her job. I would never meet her, and it was just as well. She was just a figment of my imagination, a ghost in police uniform. But it was as I stood there staring at the bloodied butterfly fluttering across the rug on my victim's bedroom floor, that I first considered the very real possibility of being caught. The thought stuck in my mind like chewing gum.

I could already imagine myself in solitary confinement—yes, that's where I'd end up, again and again, because there's no way I'd get along with the other prisoners, and my fists, nails and teeth would make damn sure they knew it.

I would do anything to avoid such a terrible fate.

Finland is too small a country for serial killers. To start with, there aren't very many of us here. As soon as you've acquired a taste for murder, you get caught. Of course, I'd broken all the records long ago, but it was nothing to brag about. It was only a matter of time until someone at the National Bureau of Investigation worked it all out. Then my carelessly concocted alibis would be no use to me. That would be the end.

Luckily, we have a Get Out of Jail Free card in our country.

In court, I could demand that I be forced to undergo a psychological examination. Some poor psychiatrist would have the pleasure of digging around in the deepest recesses of my mind. This examination would then conclude that, at the time of the murders, I was non compos mentis and could not therefore be held criminally responsible for my actions—in layman's terms, that I was stark raving mad. Instead of going to jail, those found to be criminally insane are sent to a psychiatric unit. There I would experience a miracle recovery, be sent home and get straight back to my favourite activity.

And so, I'd decided to err on the side of caution; I would look for a therapist who was a gullible fool with too much empathy for their own good, and if I did get caught, this therapist would write me such a heart-rending character reference that the court couldn't possibly deem me criminally responsible.

Ingenious, don't you think?

There was just one flaw in my plan: how would I cope with the therapy?

People see their therapist like a messiah, as if therapists selflessly gave up their time to help their clients, though the very name 'professional guidance counsellor' should leave us in no doubt about what they're up to.

The therapist is sitting opposite you for one reason only. Try getting them to help if you haven't got 90 euros in your wallet to shell out or a referral from the benefits office covering expenses for psychotherapeutic rehabilitation. The soft couch, the sycophantic praise, the life guidance—all this will be taken away if you can't hand over the cash.

The empathetic eyes, the compassionate expressions and the warm, motherly body language are all the result of years, decades of practice. You shouldn't let this fool you and you shouldn't take it personally.

As you can see, I had no illusions that my therapist would actually be interested in my story. The main thing was that she could be easily led. She would have to believe in my innocence so profoundly that she was prepared to testify in court on my behalf, if I ever ended up in the dock.

Very well. I'll admit, I did hope to see at least some kind of genuine reaction on my therapist's face when I told my story, a flicker of anything at all. I wasn't looking for any particular emotion. It could have been disgust or admiration; I didn't care.

I'm always fascinated by my victims' reactions. Human emotions are only on full display when you have to fight for your life. I suppose there must be some residual humanity in me after all. I want to witness other people's emotions.

Besides, I thought, if my story touched my therapist, I was sure she would do anything for me.

Now, much later, I realize I've only got myself to blame. I thought I'd found just the right person, but I was to learn the hard way that I'd been gravely mistaken.

Clarissa Virtanen.

I first spotted that smarmy poodle on a TV talk show. She was sitting half-naked on the studio couch, writhing like a cobra dancing to a snake-charmer's melody.

No matter how stupid the jokes the presenter cracked, she smirked and giggled so much that I thought she might piss herself there and then.

What a bimbo. She was nothing but a ditzy airhead, a Barbie doll.

Just the kind of therapist I was looking for.

Nonetheless, I made an error of judgement for which I will never forgive myself.

I thought she would just listen and wouldn't want to get involved in the course of events.

I know she wants to tell her own side of the story too.

And she'll stop at nothing to try and shut me up.

Clarissa

If it weren't for my husband Pekka, I wouldn't have been able to relax after work. He always insisted that I leave work behind me when I closed the office door for the evening. There was no question of me even flicking through my papers after finishing work for the day.

In truth, I was happy with Pekka's rule. If he hadn't been there, I would have spent endless amounts of time wallowing in my clients' problems.

If you want to read things into my relationship with Pekka, meanings that simply aren't there, be my guest! But no, I never tried to analyse him.

However, Pekka didn't know that I often stayed up through the night, pondering my patients' difficulties over a glass of red wine. I would sit in the kitchen in my silk dressing gown and linen slippers sipping my wine until morning.

Her Highness kept me company. I'd taken in the mongrel cat a few winters ago. She'd started nudging my ankles as I was standing in the snow waiting for the bus. She had a bloody scratch across her face that looked like it had come from another cat's claw. When I picked her up, she started purring there and then. It was love at first sight.

Her Highness enjoyed being able to spend time alone with me in the wee hours of the morning. She paced between my legs and meowed.

I liked the way the wine relaxed me, until it was time to start the next day and face all the problems from which I'd managed to take a bottle of wine's distance during the night.

I know there's no use worrying about such things. It's unprofessional. I can't imagine any of my colleagues sitting up all night, ruminating over how to prevent a patient's divorce or how to help clients overcome their depression. A professional ought to be able to keep their work and private lives separate.

I was too empathetic for this profession.

Pekka

I admired Clarissa because she had dedicated her life to helping people who had run aground. It seemed she almost felt guilty that she had managed to stay afloat while her patients were still submerged, thrashing about in the murky water.

I wasn't brave enough to look darkness in the eye for a living.

I'm certain that most of Clarissa's patients recovered, or at least that their quality of life was dramatically improved, specifically because of her therapy.

How many of us can say we do a job that actually makes a difference?

Clarissa had a habit of popping open a bottle of champagne every time she successfully saw a patient through a course of therapy. She would stand out on our patio and spray the champagne into the air like a Formula 1 driver on the podium. The rest, she poured into crystal champagne flutes and savoured one sip at a time.

She kept all the champagne corks in a large wicker basket. At the beginning of her career, she had difficulty leaving work matters at work; she was constantly worrying about things. She tried a number of relaxation techniques to resolve this, until she realized that neither crochet nor origami gave her soul the respite it needed.

As a constant reminder of these ill-fated attempts, an unfinished macramé wall hanging lay in the corner of the living room where she had thrown it in frustration. Her only successful handcrafting project was the wicker basket reserved for her champagne corks, and the secret to that was that I had finished weaving it for her. It was already full to the brim with corks.

But the morning after, the party was over and there was already another client on her couch begging for help. What does it say about the supposed 'happiest country in the world' that there's always a queue of patients at the door? Clarissa couldn't possibly take on all the clients desperate for help, though she worked overtime without ever making a fuss.

Most people in the social-care sector work themselves to the bone on the minimum wage without ever hearing a word of thanks. Clarissa wasn't exactly making a fortune, but she was respected within her profession all the more.

She was the most acclaimed expert on sexual violence and abuse in Finland. She had given expert statements in countless newspaper articles, but it was the #MeToo movement that really made her name. Once the movement got underway, not a week passed without some media outlet asking for her views and opinions.

She genuinely cared about her patients, perhaps even a little too much. At home, we didn't discuss her patients. Of course, Clarissa was bound by a duty of confidentiality, so she would never tell me any of their personal details. Still, it was important to me that during her free time she was able to forget about her patients' problems and focus on her own life instead.

It never occurred to me that I ought to be jealous of her patients.

I believed in our marriage.

I trusted my wife.

Famous last words.

Arto

Irmeli's interviewee—a young visual artist who had just landed a private exhibition at Kiasma, the Museum of Contemporary Art—flounced up to the bar of the Quill and Parchment and gripped Irmeli in a tight embrace. She said a quick goodbye and hurried off to order herself and the artist a round of drinks.

I decided to do some background research on Clarissa Virtanen right away. I was always either drunk or hungover, so I wouldn't necessarily be in a better frame of mind later on than I was sitting there swaying on my bar stool.

I took out my laptop and started googling Clarissa.

Three-quarters of an hour later, I'd read everything there was to read about her. Two things became immediately apparent: she was only too happy to give interviews, but she never talked about her private life. Every reporter's nightmare.

Clarissa Cristal Virtanen, 50, had been working as a therapist for twenty-one years. She was happy to comment publicly, not only on her own field of expertise, but on other associated subjects too, such as bullying in the workplace, narcissism or divorce.

When she was interviewed in a professional capacity, Clarissa was analytical and to the point. Her train of thought was clear and insightful. She was a tireless defender of the rights of women and girls and didn't seem to care how people reacted to her views.

She wasn't afraid to present controversial opinions. Unlike most experts, Clarissa never tried to wriggle her way out of things or duck a difficult question; her answers were always direct and sometimes even deliberately provocative. For instance, in a recent essay for *Science Monthly*, she claimed that the authorities were reluctant to get involved in cases of the sexual abuse of minors.

'The Finnish state should officially apologize to all victims of paedophilia, just as it did in 2016 to those foster kids mistreated while in the care of the Child Protection Agency,' she argued.

'Instead of protecting victims, Finnish law protects paedophiles. Finland cannot claim to be a civilized welfare state until it takes responsibility for every act of sexual violence committed against a minor.

'The law should be amended so that other adults, who knew about these crimes but did not report them to the authorities, can be prosecuted as accessories.'

I remembered this essay had sparked heated public debate, but I didn't realize it was Clarissa who had written it.

This memory lapse didn't surprise me. Alcohol had flushed far more important things into the abyss of oblivion.

Clarissa's opinions were so incendiary that they were easy to turn into headlines and snappy soundbites. It was no wonder the journalistic profession seemed so enthralled by her.

Though Clarissa refused to talk about her private life in public, she would turn up to the opening of an envelope given half the chance. If the gossip columns were anything to go by, she was friends with a good many celebrities. She was a familiar sight at book launches and invitation-only screenings of new movies. She could regularly be spotted in women's lifestyle magazines, popping up behind some famous etiquette expert in an enormous sun hat or lurking behind a TV-presenter couple about to cut their wedding cake.

I wasn't surprised that Clarissa was so protective of her private life. In this respect, she was a typical celebrity expert. They never breathe a word about their personal affairs. Instead, interviews are supposed to list their merits and theories, and the reporter has to remember to mention all the prizes, accolades and honourable titles the interviewee has amassed over the span of their career.

But I was an old fox; I could pull the wool over her eyes.

Some reporters are nervous about interviewing psychologists, psychiatrists and therapists. I suppose they must be worried that one way or another they will end up on the therapist's couch and regress back to their childhood. I find these kinds of fears ridiculous.

I wondered whether Clarissa was a competent enough therapist to solve my problems too. How would she react if I told her I had ruined the most important relationship in my life?

Longing seemed to gnaw away at my bones.

She was so close, but still out of my reach. And she had no way of knowing that I still thought about her all the time.

Ida

There's one thing I've forgotten to tell you. The truth is, Clarissa wasn't my first therapist. I'd been sitting on threadbare couches, wooden stools and sagging armchairs ever since I was ten years old.

One day my behaviour simply changed, and my parents never worked out why.

At the age of ten, I was sent to see a child psychiatrist. He only agreed to see me once.

I was normal, apparently.

My parents were relieved that my treatment ended before it had even properly got going. The things we didn't talk about didn't exist.

The town where I grew up was so small that everybody knew everybody else's business. My parents were worried someone might start gossiping that their darling daughter had ended up in care.

I've already told you the colour white makes me think of the psychiatric ward, haven't I? At age fourteen, I ended up in the children's wing of the psychiatric hospital. I'd been suffering from anorexia for years.

My skeletal figure aroused horrified admiration wherever I went. 'If only I was that thin,' one of my classmates sighed enviously. 'Just not ill,' she clarified. After all, all women and girls want to be thin. But the difference is we anorexics don't count how many pounds we need to lose to get into bikini shape; we count how many it will take to kill us.

You know what the funniest thing is?

Everybody thinks they've had a relatively normal childhood. Always. Regardless of what it was actually like.

I defended my parents to the psychiatrists at the hospital too. They were only doing their best! Anybody would have done the same!

The fact that I was in such a bad way wasn't a reflection on my childhood or my parents; it was a reflection on me.

Once I was an adult, my father took me—against my will—to see a psychiatrist at a private clinic. He recommended a course of psychoanalysis. The traditional lying-on-the-couch kind, that is.

I wasn't remotely interested in any archaeological digging in the recesses of my mind.

The psychiatrist freely admitted that his competence wasn't up to solving my problems. He chose his words carefully, but I could read what he really meant between the lines.

He didn't want to take responsibility for my suicide.

Clarissa

I'm flailing around in the deepest recesses of my mind trying to recall our first meeting. Could I have prevented what happened? This might sound ludicrous, but I'm certain of it: the minute Ida walked into my surgery, my subconscious started trying to tell me exactly what was going on.

But I didn't listen.

I have a habit of taking notes on each patient's treatment programmes and keeping their documents in individual folders in the filing cabinet in my office.

Ida's folder contains only a few sheets of A4. Some of them are filled with notes; others only have a phrase here and there. On some occasions I didn't take any notes at all.

In other words, these papers are no use whatsoever. You try and remember the most important events of your life without notes!

I can only imagine how Ida would laugh if she knew of my plight.

I couldn't possibly have guessed that a run-of-the-mill patient record would become a valuable piece of evidence used to prove… well, what exactly?

Not my innocence, at any rate. There's no point in trying to deny it any more.

Maybe I'm not trying to prove anything. Explain, more like. All I can ask is that you try to understand me. I fear even that might be impossible.

I'll remember that gaze forever. Ida reached out her hand and looked me in the eyes. Her eyes were dark blue, so dark that in the dim light of my surgery, they looked almost black. If you'll allow me to wax lyrical for a moment, they reminded me of a murky ocean with unimaginable riddles concealed in its depths.

Her gaze was defiant. It was as though she was challenging me to a childish staring contest to see which of us blinked first.

Ida saw right through me. To my other clients, I was first and foremost a mirror. In that mirror, they saw whatever they wanted to see. To some of them, I was a mother who had never valued them but showed disdain through her every gesture; to others I was a father who had abandoned them at the very moment they needed his paternal protection. But with Ida, I couldn't fall back on my usual professional role.

When we shook hands for the first time, I felt as though countless things happened in that one fleeting instant. They say a person's life flashes in front of their eyes at the moment of death. I had that exact feeling.

I was ready to sacrifice everything. How ridiculous is that!

This must all feel a bit confusing to you. I've done nothing but rack my brains to think what went wrong. Now I know the answer. It was all because of a misunderstanding, because things weren't quite as I'd imagined.

I'd understood everything wrong, right from the outset. Nothing was what it seemed at first glance. Neither that first glance nor anything else.

Ida always had the upper hand, though I thought I had everything under control. She was pulling my strings like a marionette.

I thought the same rules applied to her as applied to all my other clients.

Therapy is all about the art of illusion. Clients must come to believe that the ball is in their court, while in truth the therapist is always responsible.

Ida turned this paradigm upside down. I was in her grip and couldn't wriggle free.

In fact, I didn't even realize I was her prisoner.

Arto

Once I decided I'd spent enough time rummaging through Clarissa's past, I turned my attention to the drink again. I ordered a pint and nursed it at the bar, which I'd been propping up from the moment the Quill and Parchment had opened that morning. All day I'd been trying to keep my grief at bay, but now it was forcing its way into my mind so powerfully that I couldn't fight it off.

I decided to continue Marja's memorial celebration at home.

I popped into the shop to buy myself a twelve-pack of lager to keep me company on the sofa. I tried to convince myself that I wasn't actually very drunk—it was a weeknight, after all—and to prove this, I decided to watch *Newsreel*, like all good journalists should. This episode was a repeat from New Year's Day.

Clarissa's face appeared on my TV screen. Assuming I understood the discussion correctly, the subject was feminism. Apparently Clarissa's expertise allowed her to comment on this too.

'We will never achieve equality without quotas. This is the simple truth,' she said emphatically.

Clarissa was perfectly at home in the TV studio. She sat on the sofa, her back straight and her expression perfectly calm. The situation didn't seem to faze her in the least.

She spoke in a clear, steady voice, she chose her words carefully and presented her arguments in an easily digestible way. She didn't resort to jargon to make herself sound clever, but instead made sure that even a simpleton could understand what she meant.

I had switched the television on too late. The interview was already coming to an end. The host seemed every bit as smitten with Clarissa as I was. He stammered his words and fluffed his lines. Finally, the show moved on to the topic of Russia and Putin's penchant for hunting.

The following morning, I woke up with a headache. *Plus ça change.*

I decided to start the day by calling Clarissa and setting up a meeting with her.

I keyed her number into my phone.

'Clarissa Virtanen,' she said as she picked up.

Her voice was soft and mellifluous. I wondered whether it would turn to honey when she heard that I wanted to interview her.

'Hello. This is Arto Haaleajärvi from *Helsinki Today*. We're putting together a new lifestyle supplement, and we'd like to put you on the cover of the first issue.'

'How flattering! I'd be only too happy to appear, but on one condition. I won't talk about my private life in public.'

'Understood. Instead of your private life, I thought we could focus on the numerous achievements through the course of your career. I saw your interview on *Newsreel* last night, and what you said about equality was fascinating.'

'Quite. We women could certainly teach you men a thing or two.'

Was I about to get a lecture from the word go? I didn't want to discuss equality with someone who thought every interaction was an existential battle of the sexes, that I was from Mars and she was from Venus and never the twain shall meet. Clarissa probably believed that all men harbour a certain nostalgia for the caveman life; a time when men were men and went out hunting and gathering while women knew their place and gratefully understood it was best to stay at home between the fist and the fireplace.

42

'Would you have time for an interview next Monday evening?'

'I try to reserve Mondays for my family. This is off the record, but I doubt my husband and I would still be together if we didn't work on our marriage.'

I'd never worked on my marriage—if you believe Marja, that is. 'Words of wisdom.'

'Well, *this* time! Next Monday at 7 p.m. How about the Coffee Bean on Mannerheimintie?'

I hadn't visited the Coffee Bean since Marja's death, and I'd sworn I never would. She and I used to sit there all the time in the early days of our relationship; we'd look deep into each other's eyes and tell each other our secrets.

I noticed I had momentarily slipped into a swamp of melancholy. I clambered out again and replied to Clarissa.

'Of course. That's settled then. See you next Monday.'

Little did I know what I'd just unwittingly got myself mixed up in.

Ida

When I rang the therapist's doorbell, I knew what to expect when I got inside. I knew there'd be an opened box of tissues on the table. She would offer me them when she saw tears glistening in my eyes. Or perhaps she would just discreetly slide the box across the table and pretend she hadn't actually noticed I was crying.

Maybe she would measure my progress by the number of tissues I'd used. My tears were a sign of trust.

Next to the box of tissues there would be a clock turned to face the therapist. Our session would last forty-five minutes, not a moment longer. No matter how important the topic, the therapist's attention would always turn to the clock during the last minutes of each session.

Every therapist has their own phrase to round things off: 'That's all we've got time for today', 'We can pick up here next time', 'I'm afraid we'll have to wrap up for now'. Then the client gathers up their belongings, leaves and is left to their own devices once again.

What was it I said about therapists' selfless desire to help others?

Therapists' surgeries were always decorated in surprisingly uniform fashion. I guess their training must include an introductory course on interior design.

There's always an art print on one of the walls. Nothing realistic like von Wright's *Fighting Capercaillies*. The more analytical the training, the more symbolism in the print.

The melting clocks in Dalí's *The Persistence of Memory* served to remind any therapist with a penchant for masochism how painfully slowly the hands on the clock on the table between us edged forwards. Sexologists seemed to prefer Georgia O'Keeffe's lewd calla lilies. You know what I'm getting at.

And as for expressions of thanks by recovered patients—they were a world unto their own. Drawings, paintings, collages heaping praise on the therapist, thanking the therapist because the patient has finally seen the light.

I must mention the colour of the walls. Yellow is a hopeful colour. You can do it! If you just stare at these walls, you'll start to believe that everything will be better tomorrow. It's almost as though the sun were shining right through the walls, and before you know it, it'll start shining into your life too!

In my therapist's office, everything was just right. Van Gogh's sunflowers hung on the wall. Sellotaped to the door on the desk was a rainbow painted in watercolours, probably a creation by one of her former patients.

Only the colour of the walls took me by surprise. Light blue. That suited me; after all, I was looking for help with my aggression. I felt much calmer right from the outset.

There was even a glimmer of hope: the rug was bright yellow.

I sat down and looked her in the eye. What did she see in me? Was I nothing but another tragic young woman among many? Anorexic. Neurotic. Omniphobic.

My eyes wandered back to the sunflowers on the office wall. I tried to imagine the other women who had sat on this same couch staring at that same poster. What were they like?

I saw them weeping inconsolably, anxiously tearing tissue after tissue to shreds.

45

They were immature moaning minnies who didn't know how to solve their problems by themselves, crybabies used to someone else always doing everything on their behalf. I hadn't cried since I was a child.

I didn't have a shred of sympathy for the other patients. I had nothing in common with them.

I wasn't helpless.

I'd been looking after myself since I was ten years old.

My therapist's other patients were Fortune's favourites; people who had no idea what suffering really was. What they needed was a good shake and a hard slap in the face. Someone needed to knock some sense into them—preferably with a hammer. They'd come here looking for an answer to their problems, shopping for a diagnosis, as if you could just pick one off a shelf.

All of a sudden, I felt a burning jealousy towards these other clients. My therapist's brain was wasted thinking through other patients' problems when it could have focused all its attention on my case.

What if my plan went awry for the simple reason that my therapist didn't have enough energy to focus on me? What if I took out the other patients? That would stop them stealing her time. I could hang around after our session, hide around the corner and wait for the next patient to leave my therapist's office. Then I could attack her and drag her by the hair into the nearby woods.

The patient would try to shout for help, but I'd press a hand over her mouth and batter her over the head with a rock.

Thump. Thump. Thump.

Silence.

The thought made me chuckle out loud.

Sadly, I'd have to make do with forty-five-minute sessions every now and then. It was too little.

What if my therapist put me on medication? She was only a trained psychologist, so she didn't have any medical qualifications. But she could still refer me to a shrink. I could never accept that.

All psychiatrists agree that humans are the sum total of their brain chemistry. To their mind, my problems could be solved in one way and one way only: by stuffing me full of pills.

My brain was untouched. I was protective of its natural state. Until now, I've only messed myself up with drink, and I wasn't planning on changing my habits any time soon.

Suddenly, I heard a loud beeping sound. I snapped out of my tangle of thoughts and returned to reality. My therapist had set the alarm clock to go off to show that our time was up. So much for subtlety. No awkward platitudes or fake apologies, just the cruel, merciless beep of the clock.

For three-quarters of an hour, we'd sat in perfect silence. I'm sure nobody else made a living as easily as my therapist. Without further ado, she stood up.

Neither of us said anything.

I held out my hand.

We looked each other in the eyes.

The game had begun.

Clarissa

There was nothing particularly out of the ordinary in the fact that Ida and I didn't say a word to each other during our first session. Some people just want to sound out the situation in silence. They're trying to work out whether I will be a suitable therapist for them. If I didn't allow them to settle into the situation in their own time, I wouldn't see them again.

If the client doesn't want to talk, I don't try to force them. My patients have been trampled on so many times in the past that I don't want to become yet another person to walk all over them. I trust that the subconscious is always at work, whether we put our thoughts into words or not.

It's all about building trust. Especially at the beginning, it's important that the client sets the pace. That way, the psyche won't be forcibly ripped open.

The therapist has to wait until the patient is ready to move on. I think I'm good at gauging this right. I can sense my client's state of mind and I know when a certain subject has been dealt with and when it's time to move on to the next. I'm not in a hurry.

Despite the silence, Ida's presence filled the space.

As though there wasn't room for anything else, not even words.

I should have asked her to give her basic details: age, profession, parents' professions, number of siblings, any previous diagnoses and prescriptions.

I should have tried to establish, at least in general terms, what had motivated her to seek a course of therapy.

Ida sat on the couch like a little child, as though her entire being was now my responsibility. Everything about her was crying for help.

My intuition told me that something significant was going to happen between us. But what? There was no way of knowing.

I nervously gripped my pencil and notebook. I think I even pretended to write down a few observations just to hide my bewilderment.

I needed to chew something to let out my nervousness—gum, my nails, my pencil—but I didn't want to show Ida quite how agitated I was.

She was staring at me intensely, her full attention focused solely on me.

She had obviously decided that I would have to make the first move. I tried to think of something prudent to say, but my mind was a blank. I scrambled for the right words, but the thought kept slipping out of reach.

I didn't want to breathe so as not to take any oxygen away from her.

When I turned to look at the clock, it was a quarter to ten. The last time I'd looked, it was quarter past nine. The half hour that had elapsed since then I had spent in something akin to a trance. I had no recollection of it whatsoever.

I was afraid to think of what might have happened. Surely, Ida hadn't taken advantage of my weakened consciousness—and rummaged through my filing cabinet? I only locked the cabinet while I wasn't in the room. She could have accessed my papers without a care in the world.

Suppose she started to blackmail me! Or sent those documents to the tabloids and told everyone how carelessly I stored them!

It suddenly felt as though my survival depended on getting Ida out of my office as quickly as possible. She, meanwhile, didn't seem to be in a hurry to go anywhere. Once she had finally put her coat on, I hurriedly ushered her towards the office door. Her black velvet-and-lace dress was far too big for her; its hem rustled across the floorboards. I pressed the door shut behind her.

I felt like screaming.

I tried to convince myself that my behaviour was not indicative of a psychological breakdown. Nothing like this had ever happened to me before. There had to be a rational explanation for it. Perhaps every therapist felt something like this from time to time.

In a mild panic, I ran through my colleagues' experiences of nightmarish patients: violence, stalking, unpaid bills. But none of them had ever mentioned anything like this. This might be because nobody dared talk about professional failure of this kind. I wasn't surprised.

I dashed to the toilet. I didn't quite make it to the bowl and threw up over the bathroom floor. The coral-red stripes and squares on the black bathroom tiles danced in my eyes.

For a moment, I tried to take stock of my condition. The nausea had subsided, but I still felt weak.

Stuck to the side of the sink was a dyed black hair. Ida's hair. The sight disgusted me so much that I ran the tap and frantically washed it down the plughole.

My files! Had she touched them?

I hurried back to my office, gripped the handle of the upper drawer of the filing cabinet and yanked it open.

I went through everything one drawer at a time. The brown cardboard binders were in meticulous order, as always, and the folders piled neatly beneath them.

Only once I had fully calmed down did I think of Ida again. I had to take full responsibility for her. It was clear she couldn't do so herself. I couldn't have her suicide on my conscience. For that, I would never be able to forgive myself.

I hadn't forgiven myself for Riku's death either.

My dear, sweet Riku.

My little punk rocker, whose Mohican was always shining in garish blues and greens. Riku was finally at peace.

That's what I wanted to believe, at least, but I'd seen everything in this profession, and that's why I couldn't believe in anything any more.

Pekka

Clarissa received her patients at our shared home. We had lived in our detached house since the early years of our marriage. In my twenties, I had inherited my godmother Mirjami's home, a detached house originally built to house veterans in the 1950s. Clarissa and I had only just met, but even then we were already planning a life together. Mirjami's inheritance sped things up a little.

We don't have children, so our house felt rather deserted during Clarissa's holidays when there wasn't a constant stream of patients coming through the front door.

There was no use in my trying to avoid the patients. I was always bumping into them because I was self-employed, and I too worked from an office at home.

I'm an engineer by profession, specializing in the maintenance of old databases. During my student days at the university of technology, almost on a whim I'd taught myself the downright archaic programming language Cobol that insurance companies had once used to create their databases. Nobody else was interested in writing code commands in an ancient programming language, so my position was secure. It was a routine, boring job, but the pay was good.

When we first got married, I didn't know how to behave around the patients. Nowadays I can see that they too are just regular people.

To some extent, we are all ill. Every one of us. But some of us are better at hiding it than others.

We call these patients mentally unstable, delusional, paranoid or even crazy, though any of us could become ill, and it could happen at any moment.

For some patients, seeking help was a big deal to start with, so it was important that they felt welcome when they arrived at the house. Clarissa had painted the porch and the hallway, which served as her waiting room, in a beautiful shade of light blue. On the hallway ceiling, she had installed a speaker playing whale songs on repeat. The first time I heard this on a CD that she had bought, I thought I'd never get used to all that moaning. Nowadays I barely notice it.

On the coat stand there were woollen cardigans that the patients could wrap around themselves during their sessions. They were able to wait for their session in comfortable recliners, and in case the armchairs didn't pamper the clients' sensitive backsides quite enough, Clarissa had lined the furniture with soft white lambskins too. Next to the chairs was a small rococo table. The silver platter placed on top of it always offered the patients lapsang souchong tea and Arabica coffee and Clarissa's very own organic brownies.

I took pride in treating the patients with dignity. I usually made sure to look them in the eye and give them a curt nod before quickly disappearing into my office. Some of them muttered a pained hello and sometimes even feigned a smile. Nothing more.

With some of them, I had to watch my step. Sometimes you could tell just by looking at them that they were incapable of any kind of normal human interaction. Looking at me would have been completely out of the question. I didn't want to torment them by saying hello, as it was clear this would only have exacerbated their anxieties. In such cases, I just marched past them and pretended I hadn't seen them.

Clarissa and I had been together for so long that I always noticed when a patient really caught her attention.

I called these patients Clarissa's princesses, the children she couldn't have. She wasn't suited to being their therapist either because she always wanted more. She wanted to be their mother.

Thin, pale young women who avoided eye contact and slipped into Clarissa's office like ghosts. They left a sickly-sweet smell behind them which revealed that they had just thrown up the *bébé* pastries they had eaten before the session. The pink debris floating in the toilet would have brought me to the same conclusion.

To think of all the pain and depression resting on their shoulders!

These were grown women, yet somehow not. They tiptoed around as though they were still wearing the same ballet shoes, the same pink tutu they had worn as children.

If I ever managed to make eye contact with them, looking back at me was always a little girl whose childhood hadn't even properly started before it was cut short. These were the teachers' pets who should have gone on to become lawyers, company directors, doctors and engineers. But instead they amounted to nothing.

And they would never amount to anything.

All those expectations placed on them, all for nothing. All those doors standing wide open, ready for these girls to walk through them, only then to be slammed in their faces.

They had been promised the world, but they had ended up with nothing. Imagine the anger! Where could they possibly direct it?

At themselves, of course.

But nobody was interested.

They should have had their whole lives in front of them, but their story had already been written.

Clarissa was the only person who cared about them. She used to be one of them: a miserable slip of a girl who had nobody but herself.

But whereas most of them spent the rest of their lives closely guarding the ruins of their childhood, Clarissa had succeeded in putting her past behind her—the violence, the nightmares, the fear, the anguish.

Very few people were capable of such a feat.

How had Clarissa managed to buck the odds, to do the impossible—simply so she could save all the others—when the one person she couldn't save was herself?

Clarissa

When Ida gripped my hand at the end of our first session, there were no longer any tears in her eyes. Now her eyes were oozing defiance. The emotion lingered there for only a fleeting moment, then she regressed back to being a young child again.

Only in hindsight do I fully appreciate the meaning of that gaze, but it's too late now. At the time, I completely misinterpreted it. I thought the aggression was an attempt to conceal her fragility.

We are all prisoners of our first impressions. These always shape our understanding of other people. Sensitive. Vulnerable. Helpless. That's how I would have described her after our first meeting. And I relied on this impression later on too, though everything that happened subsequently seemed to contradict that reading.

You probably find it inconceivable that I didn't recognize her true motives. I am a therapist, after all, an expert on the human condition!

What can I say in my defence?

I might arrogantly say that any other therapist would have walked into her trap too. My colleagues would have floundered just as I did. I certainly believe so. And yet, this was something very personal.

The whole subterfuge was designed for me and me alone.

Pekka

The first time I saw her was from my office window. It was early morning, and I'd just started work. Clarissa had visited my office the previous evening to tidy up and closed the Venetian blinds. When I opened them again, I saw a young woman walking across the garden to our front door. A new patient.

My instinct told me she would soon become one of Clarissa's princesses.

This princess was dressed entirely in black. She glowered around distrustfully, as though the meadowsweet bushes had been planted simply so that an attacker could hide there and lie in wait for her.

I hurriedly closed the blinds again so as not to startle her. This princess was definitely one of Clarissa's patients who wanted nothing whatsoever to do with me.

Very carefully, I peered out between the slats. The princess had crouched down to tie her shoelace.

She hadn't noticed me.

Only now do I realize I was blind. If I'd been a little more on the ball, I would have noticed that everything changed once Clarissa became burdened with that girl.

Clarissa had had plenty of favourites in the past. Sometimes it seemed as though there was always one patient who was more important than the others, a princess who required her undivided attention.

The princesses always received special treatment. They were allowed to call her whenever they wanted, even in the middle of the night. They could ring our doorbell at any time, even outside regular office hours. Their sessions often lasted much longer than the standard forty-five minutes. Once, one of the princesses stayed in Clarissa's office for two normal sessions—the length of a full football match!

Clarissa's colleagues would have raised an eyebrow if they'd heard that she treated the princesses on credit and sometimes even for free.

To Clarissa, the princesses weren't just patients; she genuinely cared about them. Perhaps she was too attached to some of them— but who was I to judge? I'm not jealous, but surely every husband wants to believe he is the most important person in his wife's life.

Luckily, Clarissa seemed aware that her relationship with the princesses was too close for comfort.

Maybe we should put the question the other way round: how could I possibly have known what was going on between Clarissa and her new patient? I had no reason to suspect Clarissa of anything untoward.

Could there be a more trustworthy spouse than a psychotherapist?

Arto

A ghost hung over the Coffee Bean on Mannerheimintie. When I nervously stepped inside the café, I found myself automatically looking around for Marja, then scoffing at my own stupidity. Instinctively, I headed for our regular table at the far end of the café. It was free. I threw my coat and scarf over the back of a chair and walked to the counter to order coffee for myself and Clarissa.

The atmosphere in the café felt suddenly electric. I glanced around, bewildered, and wondered why the other customers all seemed so excited.

Clarissa had just stepped inside.

I saw her standing in the doorway. People were trying not to look, but curiosity got the better of them.

I strode over.

'You must be Clarissa Virtanen. Arto Haaleajärvi from *Helsinki Today*. Nice to meet you.'

I held out my hand, but she gave me a warm embrace instead.

'How lovely to meet in person! I must admit, I've long admired your sharp pen. I always used to read your columns in the paper. What a shame you quit!'

I muttered something bland in reply. It was humiliating to be reminded that I'd flushed my own career down the toilet.

The smell of Chanel N°5 caught my nose. I tried to hold my breath. I felt possessive of that perfume. It had always been Marja's favourite fragrance. Nobody else should have been allowed to use it. The scent hung around Clarissa, intoxicating me, and it was all I could do to resist its appeal.

We sat down at the table. I looked Clarissa in the eyes. She tried to avoid my intrigued gaze and began instead examining her artificial nails, which were painted pink and decorated with golden flecks like Christmas baubles.

'Do you mind if I record our chat? Just so I don't have to rely on my memory.'

I couldn't remember the last time an interviewee had refused a request to record an interview. Most people understood that I could quote them more accurately if I was able to consult a recording. And even those who didn't understand this right away soon got the point when I explained it to them.

'Of course. Psychological research has proven quite categorically that people shouldn't trust their memories,' she said and winked at me.

I dug my old Dictaphone out of my bag. My colleagues had long since abandoned these recording devices and switched to using an app on their phones. But even in this respect, I was a bit old school. I placed the device on the tray and pressed record.

We sat there opposite each other, and at the time neither of us thought remotely ill of the other.

Ida

The night after my first therapy session, I found myself standing in front of the bathroom mirror, yet again. The mirror was dangling on the wall, held in place by a single screw. It was only a matter of time before the screw would give way and the mirror would fall, shattering into pieces against the mousey-grey floor tiles.

I was living in a small studio flat in Töölö, in a block built in the 1920s. I hadn't bothered decorating. I didn't even own a bed; only a mattress, a bookcase, a desk and a chair. My bedside table was simply a cardboard box I'd used to carry my few belongings up to the flat from my childhood home. I wasn't short of money, but I suffered from an acute case of apathetic disinterest.

The clock on my phone confirmed my fears. I'd been standing staring at my own reflection for over half an hour, but I had no recollection of what had happened in that time.

I didn't want to think about it at all, but I couldn't *not* think about it. These days I often had memory lapses, and now they were lasting longer and longer.

I walked back to the little alcove where I'd put my mattress. Perhaps 'stepped' would be a more appropriate word. My flat was so small that it didn't take many steps to cross it.

I made the mistake of glancing at the window. The heavy rusted bars had appeared there again, locking me inside.

I wondered what to do about the bars. Should I let them stay on the windows overnight or would it be better to try and get rid of them right away?

I plumped for the latter. I couldn't bear the sickening stench of flaking rust a second longer. The rust stank of iron, like a sanitary towel discarded at the bottom of the bin and forgotten about.

Almost gagging, I bounded towards the window. The stench was insufferable. I grabbed the iron bars firmly with both hands. They started melting, as though instantly heated by my red-hot hands.

I gripped the bars as tightly as I could. Flakes of rust shimmered to the floor. I pressed my palms flat against the windowpane. The bars began to ripple in my field of vision until eventually I couldn't see them any more.

For a moment longer, I stood looking out through the window at an old pine tree swaying in the yard outside, to make sure the bars didn't return.

How I wished that one day I'd be able to put these delusions behind me.

But I didn't think I'd ever manage to control them. On the contrary, my grip on reality felt like it was loosening, slipping further away by the day.

I'd resorted to dangerous ways of trying to control my life. I challenged myself not to eat for a day, then two days at a time, and so on. Even if I couldn't make decisions about anything else in my life, at least I could decide what and when I ate. I imagined that by torturing myself I'd be able to rein in the pain and the anxiety, but starving myself only made me feel worse.

Sometimes I would slash my skin, though even physical pain couldn't smother my mental anguish.

For the first time, I started to appreciate why people felt the need to talk about their business with someone else. In the past,

I'd always found this incomprehensible. How could anybody else possibly understand me?

Talking is only meant for normal people. All of a sudden, I felt a glimmer of empathy for them. I tried to imagine what it would feel like to flagellate myself over something as immaterial as a divorce or cheating on someone. If I ever breathed a word about my life, I'd have to live in constant fear of the police.

But you don't need anyone else just to talk, right? Wouldn't talking to the wall do the trick just as well? I'd get just as much sympathy and understanding.

Besides, I did everything else by myself too. I only needed other people for one thing.

To kill them.

Clarissa

From the very first time I met him, I had a strange feeling about Arto Haaleajärvi. We had barely sat down in the uncomfortable chairs at the Coffee Bean when he started gushing about how much he admired me and valued my work on the sexual abuse of women and girls.

He called himself a feminist.

I'd met plenty of men who praised this noble cause—mostly in an attempt to get into bed with me.

Arto didn't have a ring on his left hand, but this didn't necessarily mean he was unmarried. He seemed like the kind of man who might be only too happy to let women think he was a bachelor, even if he wasn't.

He was a typical example of the kind of man who doesn't get on well with women more intelligent than him.

His dishevelled appearance didn't inspire much confidence either. I could diagnose him a mile off. His alcoholism was so advanced that it wouldn't have surprised me if his liver had given up right there in the middle of our interview and I'd have to call him an ambulance. His face was pallid, his cheeks sagged like a chicken's wattle, and his brow glistened with cold beads of hungover sweat.

Arto seemed such a lost cause that it was a wonder he was able to take care of his work at all. Still, I had a curious feeling that he could see right through me and would tell his readers all my secrets.

He had such a long career behind him that the professional touch was still in his DNA.

Why had I got myself caught up in this charade? What was I going to get out of this?

Maybe I was afraid I might confess all my sins to him, that I would be overcome with a sudden uncontrollable fit of honesty.

The greater the secret, the more the temptation to spill the beans.

In preparation for the interview, I'd noted down some of my thoughts so I would remember all the salient points. Of course, I understood my specialist subjects so thoroughly that I could have talked about them for hours without any notes at all.

Once we got onto the main topic of conversation, I pulled the violet leather-bound notebook from my rose-red Chanel handbag. I smirked as I noticed that Pekka had left me another little Post-it note on the cover. 'You show him who's boss!' Pekka knew that although my appearance gave the impression of implacable calm, interviews always made me nervous. I'd given dozens if not hundreds of interviews over the years, but this did nothing to alleviate my fears.

We women can never fully enjoy the fruits of our achievements; we're always worried that our success will eventually be ripped away from us, as though we didn't really deserve it.

I repeated Pekka's mantra over and over to myself: 'You show him! You show him! You show him!'

Arto Haaleajärvi had better have his wits about him.

Ida

On my way to our second session, I wondered whether I'd actually chosen a therapist that suited my purposes after all. Was Clarissa Virtanen stupid and naïve enough to set me up with the Get Out of Jail Free card I needed?

I hoped my therapist suffered from a sense of guilt. People wallowing in guilt are easy to manipulate. They're desperate to make amends for their very existence, whether they have any reason to feel guilty or not.

But I wouldn't go too hard on her. Clemency works much better with people like that. I would give my therapist the impression that I was the only person in the world willing to forgive her sins.

It all depended on whether she was able to save me. If my therapist could successfully make this happen, she could prove to herself that deep down she was a good person.

But what if my therapist didn't agree to write me the character reference I needed?

I'd never killed a woman.

Yet.

Arto

As soon as I'd woken up and knocked back a finger of whisky to steady my nerves, I decided to call Irmeli and tell her I'd already met Clarissa and interviewed her.

I didn't even bother getting dressed but sat on the edge of the bed in a ragged old pair of boxer shorts and scrolled down to Irmeli's number on my contacts list. This time I had the kind of material that would really knock her for six! I'd forgotten what it felt like to be proud of my work.

Irmeli managed to sound both encouraging and doubtful all at once.

'You're positively bubbling with enthusiasm, Arto! That's wonderful! But remember, the lifestyle supplement isn't coming out until the summer, so there's plenty of time to fine-tune the piece. Only send it to me once you've polished it into a real gem.'

Irmeli at least seemed to believe in my abilities—or maybe she didn't. One thing was certain: I couldn't afford to let her down again.

I hung up, took out the recorder from my bag's side pocket, pressed Play and started listening to the interview.

An hour later, I was seriously considering shutting myself away in my apartment for the rest of my life. The whole interview was a textbook example of wishful thinking on my part. At the time, I thought I'd managed to get Clarissa to open up. It's a good job I hadn't gone and bragged about it to Irmeli, telling her the interview was pure journalistic gold, because the Dictaphone revealed the whole sorry truth.

As long as we stuck to the subject of Clarissa's career and her long list of achievements, the interview seemed to go smoothly. Clarissa wasn't backwards in coming forwards and she had plenty of interesting anecdotes to tell. But once I tried to steer things onto the subject of her private life, she managed to deflect every one of my questions. The interview was an unmitigated disaster, but there was worse to come.

Suddenly, the only person talking was me.

I heard myself telling her about events that I didn't realize I even remembered.

'It was when I was in high school,' I said. 'My friends and I decided to hold a séance.'

My S's hissed on the tape the way they always did when I'd had some Dutch courage the morning after a heavy night propping up the bar.

I wound the tape back and forth in despair. A séance? I had no recollection of anything like that. Yet there I was, describing it down to the last detail.

And then—without any warning—my apartment was suddenly filled with the smell of lavender.

My mind hurtled back through the decades.

My high-school friend Lari had bought a Ouija board as a souvenir from his school exchange in New Orleans. The board smelt mouldy, as if it had been stored in an old basement with water damage. The decorations on it were childish, almost involuntarily comical. I remember when Lari showed it to me for the first time, and the two of us laughed at its stupid pictures. Maybe that's why they stuck in my mind so well that I still remembered them all these years later.

In the upper right-hand corner of the board was a witch, her nose covered in warts, gazing into a crystal ball to predict the future. She looked just like the wicked queen in the Disney animation of *Snow White*, who turned herself into an old hag to trick Snow White and make her eat the poisoned apple. In the lower left-hand corner, meanwhile, a wizard was waving a magic wand, his black cloak trailing along the ground.

It was obvious the board wasn't intended for genuine witchcraft, let alone black magic. It was just a harmless parlour game.

But we had to try it out.

Lari was so excited about our séance that he'd started preparing for it very carefully. He wanted the group to meet at my house while my parents were spending the weekend at our summer cottage. It was to be held in my parents' cramped bedroom to make the atmosphere as intense as possible.

Word about our spiritualist meeting quickly spread around the school. At break time, boys from another class, whom we didn't even know, approached us and asked if they could join us—even a few of the girls expressed an interest. However, Lari only invited his best friends to the meeting: that meant me and a couple of other boys whom he had known since childhood. If I remember, there were six of us in total.

When I woke up that weekend, it was raining. I was worried my parents might decide not to go to the cottage after all. Luckily, the weather cleared up before we'd finished breakfast. My mother made me promise to behave myself while they were away.

'No parties, and if you do have a party, don't let anyone trash the place.'

Lari arrived at around six o'clock in the evening. He was so excited he could barely speak. He had a plastic carrier bag in one hand. With the other, he clenched the Ouija board to his chest, caressing it like Gollum with his precious ring.

He hurried into my parents' bedroom to set everything up and closed the door behind him. Apparently even I wasn't allowed to know what he had in store before it was time.

The other boys soon turned up. Once the whole gang was assembled, Lari opened the door with a curious smile. One by one we walked into the room. Lari closed the door behind us like a true master of ceremonies.

I knew my friends well, and I knew that none of us took this spiritualist meeting very seriously, not even Lari.

We all thought it was just a game.

I hurried to the windows and pulled the curtains almost shut. The room became dim, and the boys' expressions turned serious.

We sat down in a circle on my parents' bed.

Lari took a lavender-scented candle from his plastic bag, placed it on the bedside table and lit it. This was the only detail in our séance that even remotely suggested black magic.

The atmosphere was tense. Lari had brought us only one can of beer each, but luckily my friends had come prepared and produced more drinks from their bags. We tried to conceal our nerves with lewd banter, but the speed with which we knocked back the beers revealed our true feelings.

Back then, nobody cared for craft ales, and it didn't matter whether the beer was lukewarm or flat. Nowadays, one sip of room-temperature beer and I can feel the vomit rising up into my gullet. Thankfully, there is no shortage of alcoholic drinks in the world to choose from.

We were already a little drunk, but we hadn't got to the main event yet. Nobody dared to start. Eventually, Lari had enough of our talk and was the first one who tried to make contact with the spirit world.

My memories of this particular moment are quite sketchy. Everybody else had tried, and now it was my turn.

I gripped the board and pulled it closer. I can't remember what I asked the spirits, but the answer was clear to everyone present.

A chilling draft rippled through the room and blew out the candle.

My friends looked at one another in shock. I couldn't help myself and fell about laughing.

Over the course of the evening, we went through what had happened many times, trying to come up with a plausible explanation. I went along with their excitement because I didn't want the others to realize the practical joke I'd played on them.

I had deliberately left the bedroom window open a fraction, just enough for the wind to blow through it at some point during the evening. When the window started to creak, I gripped the board and asked my question.

The following Monday I decided to put my friends out of their misery. Luckily, the boys had enough of a sense of humour to deal with my trick, though they were embarrassed that I'd pranked them so successfully.

We finished high school and our group of friends split up as we all moved elsewhere, and as the years passed, I forgot all about the séance. Marja was lying in hospital, and I knew she could die at any moment. She was already so tired that she could only stay awake for a few moments at a time, and even then her mind was long gone.

One evening, after a quick trip to the supermarket, I returned to Marja's side and sat on the edge of the bed. I brushed a strand of hair from her cheek and tucked it behind her ear, and all of a sudden I caught the sickly scent of lavender and the smell of a burning candlewick.

I turned to find the source of the smell. While I'd been at the shop, an ugly violet candle had appeared on the windowsill. I stood up to blow it out, but before I could reach it, the open window let in a long, bleak sigh of wind and the flame went out.

I'm not superstitious, but I can't help thinking back to my arrogant little joke at the séance. It's as if the spirits had the last word after all.

Clarissa

A full hour before Ida's appointment, I was standing in the garden outside the office, waiting for her. I needed some Dutch courage. Having a drink before a session would have gone against my professional ethics, but instead I imagined myself taking a little sip of red wine and savouring the sensation of it caressing my throat.

I pushed the pleasant image of that full-bodied wine to one side and tried to relax by looking at the statue guarding our front door.

It was a copy of Edvard Eriksen's famous *Little Mermaid* in Copenhagen. Pekka had carved it with a chainsaw and given it to me as a present on our anniversary.

Naturally, a chainsaw doesn't give quite the same finish as a statue cast in bronze, but Pekka's creation still had a charm all of its own. The mermaid's face was ferocious but still somehow beautiful. Some of my patients were terrified of it. They gave it a wide berth as though it might come to life at any moment, grab them by the wrist and pull them into its arms.

The Little Mermaid's story is a tragic one: she sacrificed her own happiness for her prince.

It was my job to make sure my patients' stories always had a happy ending. I was responsible for them. But what if this time I failed? What if I betrayed Ida's trust and couldn't help her?

I knew there was always a chance this could happen. I'd failed in the past.

With devastating consequences.

I shouldn't dwell on these failures, because then I'd start thinking about Riku. And if I started thinking about Riku, my soul would get caught up in all the swirling emotions I'd been trying to suppress: shame, guilt and regret.

I had no other option but to believe I could save Ida.

I needed a cigarette. I was so nervous that I smoked three in a row. I craved a fourth, but I was already starting to feel woozy.

I picked up the cigarette ends, went indoors and flushed them down the toilet. Pekka strongly disapproved of women smoking, so I tried to hide it from him, though only half-heartedly. He had never berated me for it. It was as though my pretending was enough for him.

Don't all couples play sadistic power games with each other without even realizing they are doing it?

I couldn't sit still in my office but started nervously pacing around the rug in a circle. The diamond pattern on the rug flickered hypnotically in my eyes and seemed to suggest I might have a migraine coming on. I was worried that seeing Ida might make me clam up again.

Finally, the doorbell rang.

I ushered Ida from the porch through into the office. She looked so brittle that I almost felt like leading her by the hand, as if that way I could make sure she didn't crack and break into small pieces.

All the same, I was determined to maintain the professional distance that our patient–therapist relationship required. In truth, I was afraid I wouldn't be able to take my hand from hers again. I settled for keeping my hand a few centimetres from her back as she walked along the corridor.

I doubt she even noticed it.

I took control of things right from the outset. Ida had barely taken off her raincoat, folded it and placed it next to her on the couch. I began.

'Why don't you start by telling me about your family. Do you have any siblings? What is your relationship with your parents like?'

I ought to have asked her these questions at our first meeting. I was still annoyed at myself for not taking care of this properly.

'I haven't got any brothers or sisters. My parents... our relationship... it's complicated... No... I don't want to talk about them because... No, I'm not going to talk about them...'

Almost without noticing, I gave a deep sigh.

I hoped she would be more talkative in future. Therapy sessions can be like pulling teeth, if getting an answer to each and every question is like trying to tug free the hem of a skirt caught in a doorway. It's one of the downsides of my work, but over the years I've become used to it.

Ida's stony-faced stubbornness was starting to irritate me. I'm good at analysing myself; I've been through my own long course of psychoanalysis. My irritation stemmed from my disappointment. Why wouldn't she yield to my desire to help her?

I felt as though I hadn't got anything out of our meeting.

I showed Ida to the door. Once I'd closed the door behind her, I cursed under my breath.

I returned to my office and noticed she'd left the cushions on the couch all higgledy-piggledy. As if I didn't have enough to worry about!

I didn't like messy people. It was quite enough that I had to clear up after my beloved husband, picking up the dirty underwear and sweaty socks he left strewn across the floor.

I started plumping up the cushions, then noticed that stuffed underneath one of them was a sheet of paper, folded many times. I unfolded it and straightened it out. On the other side of the paper was a charcoal sketch. My heart lurched in my chest.

Ida

Whereas at our first session my therapist seemed to retreat into a cloud of mist, at our second session she marched right up to me.

She reached out her hand to shake mine before I'd even stepped through the front door and into the hallway. She was standing all too close to me and exhaled a fug of smoky breath in my face. Her fingertips were stained with nicotine, and I didn't want to touch them because I was afraid my hands would start to stink. My bracelets jangled as I jerkily shook her hand as quickly as possible.

The therapist walked behind me along the hall and into the surgery, keeping her hand only a few centimetres from the small of my back like a proud mother watching her toddler take its first doddery steps. She didn't notice how unpleasant I found her closeness.

Given her line of work, you'd think she would have understood that everybody has their own personal space that shouldn't be violated.

She looked impatient when I stopped in the office doorway and tried to undo my tangled shoelaces so I could take off my army boots and pull on a pair of pink slippers from the basket with the sign on top of it insisting: 'No outdoor shoes in here!!!'

I was just starting to take off my raincoat when she hit me with a barrage of questions. To express my annoyance at her enthusiasm, I folded my coat, still dripping with rain, as slowly as possible into a neat square and carefully placed it next to me on the couch. Only then did I agree to answer her questions.

Her dour expression told me exactly what she thought of the decision to keep my wet raincoat on her couch throughout our session. But she refrained from commenting on this little stunt.

I could have written my answers to the therapist's questions at home and handed them to her on a piece of paper. It was always the same: therapists came along one after the other, and you always had to start again from the beginning, always answer the same old questions: parents, siblings, diagnoses, medication? I stifled a yawn.

I managed to control myself just when I was about to start lying. The truth is boring, especially if you have to rake over it time after time. Still, if there was anything that could be verified in my official records, I would have to be honest. I comforted myself with the thought that I'd have plenty of time to spin her a yarn.

The therapist seemed content after establishing my background details, though I refused to tell her anything about my parents. She licked her lips like the cat that got the cream.

I could almost hear the cogs turning in her mind as she tried to get a picture of my clinical condition.

Her expression promised sympathy.

Everything was just as it should be.

Next, I had to come up with a plausible reason for why I wanted to start a course of therapy in the first place. Luckily, I had an answer ready.

I tried to catch my therapist's eye, but she seemed to be gazing out at a grey sparrow nervously pecking at some grains on the window ledge.

'I feel like I've never been able to let go of my childhood. It's like my childhood still defines me. I want to put it behind me.

Now, for the first time, I feel like I'm ready to do it. But I can't do it by myself. I'm not sure I'll be able to do it with the help of a therapist either.'

My therapist nodded, a faint smile on her lips. You've got to admire these professional shrinks and their Oscar-winning acting skills!

'Therapy is a brave choice. People rarely have the courage to take responsibility for their life. Most of them shift the blame onto their parents instead. They think, this is just the way my life is and there's nothing I can do about it,' she replied, her voice now serious.

This didn't sound good. Whose responsibility was my life if not my parents'? It certainly wasn't mine!

Did she think I was going to take responsibility for my crimes too? No, this didn't sound good at all.

I tried to take a slight detour in order to find out what she thought about the matter.

'Sometimes people can't help the situation they find themselves in.'

A deep furrow appeared across her brow.

'There's always something you can do to help yourself. Always.'

How sanctimonious! Rage bubbled up inside me. I would have to kill her.

I couldn't take this fervent drivel a moment longer. What kind of narcissism makes her think that only her patients will be able to survive one trauma after another? Her smugness was unbearable!

I imagined my fingers around my therapist's pale neck. I'd choke her to death.

I pushed the image from my mind and forced my thoughts back to the here and now.

'But, you can cure me, right?'

My therapist writhed in her chair and gave a self-satisfied pout.

'I don't like it when people refer to gardening as therapy. Therapy isn't a hobby; it's hard work. You're going to have to do all the work yourself. I'm only here to support you. It's up to you whether these sessions are a success or not. But the good thing is, when you recover, you can take all the credit for it yourself.'

She seemed genuine. I could hardly believe that someone would do a crappy job like this and not want a feather in their cap for their troubles.

Clarissa

After our second session, I was restless. I had to get some air and let my mind breathe. Ida's sketch had brought me out in goose bumps, and I wanted to dispel the dreadful image from my head.

I couldn't afford gloominess, because whenever I succumbed to that, I started thinking about Riku.

I'd tried to abandon Riku's memory in the furthest recesses of my subconscious, but he refused to be rejected like that. He pushed his way into my mind like a stalker that not even a restraining order could keep at arm's length.

I decided to go for a walk around Töölö Bay. I called Harri and asked if he would like to join me.

The psychoanalyst and emeritus professor of psychiatry Harri Kuikkasuo had been my mentor for five years. We'd first met when I was attending one of his lectures about sexual violence.

After the lecture, I went to speak to him. We had so much to talk about that we ended up continuing the conversation at a local bar. My passion for the therapeutic profession must have made an impression on him because he took me on as a protégé. When, soon after that lecture, he retired and gave up his unofficial position as resident media expert in psychiatry and psychology, I assumed his mantle.

Harri and I had a habit of going through my professional problems on informal walks like this. He hadn't billed me for his mentoring services in a long time.

We agreed to meet outside the main entrance to the city library.

As I waited for Harri, I was puzzled to see a queue of teenage girls dressed in black queuing outside the library in the snow.

Riku never told me whether he was dating anyone, and I never asked. The girls standing in the queue would probably have appealed to him. I imagined him walking past them, the girls casting him admiring glances. Riku was such a beautiful boy.

What was left of his body?

How could such a grotesque question pop into my consciousness? I would have to rein in these unruly thoughts.

I forced myself to push Riku from my mind.

Harri interrupted my musings. He waved at me from afar, and when he reached me he gave me a gentle hug. We set off on our walk around the bay.

'You see? There you go again!' Harri enjoyed teasing me, saying I had taken his place in the headlines. Whenever a passer-by recognized me on our walks, he gave me an encouraging nudge with his elbow.

'And who's going to interview you next?' Harri couldn't contain his curiosity.

'I've just done an interview for *Helsinki Today*, actually. Not in a professional capacity, though; this was more of a feature.'

Harri raised his eyebrows in surprise but said nothing.

'Don't worry, I didn't say anything about my private life!'

Harri and I had spoken on countless occasions about how therapists should behave in the public sphere. He had very rigid views on the subject.

'Clarissa, remember this. Appearing on the covers of women's magazines diminishes a woman's professional credibility, whereas for a man it makes him seem more approachable.'

We turned as we approached the square outside the library. I said goodbye and headed inside. I wanted to borrow some light reading, a novel I could delve into, with a dreamy world I could lose myself in.

I pushed the library door open. A chime of laughter came from the direction of the café. I froze on the spot and felt a chill ripple along my skin. I forced myself onwards and strode towards the café with steps as long as the hem of my skirt would allow.

I looked around in all directions, but Riku was nowhere to be seen.

Ida

I closed the surgery door behind me. Everything had gone according to plan—so far, at least. I'd cried grateful tears when my therapist promised I would get better. She offered me a tissue and assured me that I'd made an excellent start. Acknowledging my problems was the first step to solving them.

I hoped I wouldn't have to listen to banalities like this every time we met. I could just as well go to the library and read Paulo Coelho.

Still, the therapist's determination was a good sign. She was ready to roll up her sleeves and get her hands dirty!

I smiled, satisfied that I'd carried out my brilliant plan. As if by accident, I'd dropped one of my drawings from my coat pocket and left it on the couch.

I had decided to leave my therapist a small memento after every session. That way, she wouldn't get the impression that the drawing had been left on the couch by accident. Instead, she could read it as a desire to communicate with her but an inability to put things into words. Regardless of their different schools of thought, all psychologists seemed agreed on the notion that drawings represented a more direct channel into the human mind than verbal communication.

When I got home, I pulled an old shoebox out from under my bed.

Inside the box was a small wooden doll, the length of my middle finger.

I rubbed the doll with my thumb. It was sanded so impeccably that its surface felt almost as smooth as plastic.

It was wearing a grey suit and a black tie with white spots. Its clothes had been carefully painted with a fine brush.

The doll was perfect.

Almost.

Someone had sawn its head off.

Once I had looked at the doll for a while, I propped it on the edge of my desk. Then I returned my attention to the contents of the box.

It was full of drawings showing the cage—and the Bastard. I'd drawn them at the age of ten when I was trying to convince myself that my kidnapping wasn't just a figment of my imagination. Thirty drawings in total. One every day for a month after being released from the cage; drawings full of rage, hatred, anxiety. Then I'd given up.

The drawings were very detailed. How was I able to record so much of what had happened to me at such a tender age?

The Bastard's figure was so distinct that he would have been instantly recognizable from the portrait. I'd managed to incorporate not only his appearance but his nature too. Nobody who'd seen his sadistic smile and sneering eyes would ever be able to forget them.

I'd never have guessed how looking at these drawings ten years on would affect me. Memories came crashing over me in powerful, shocking waves.

Flashbacks are a symptom of post-traumatic stress disorder. A memory of something I had experienced in the cage could flash through my mind at any moment, while I was queuing at the supermarket, sitting on the bus or in any other safe, everyday situation. The flashbacks felt so real that often I ended up having an uncontrollable panic attack. Sometimes the wave of nausea took me by surprise and appeared so suddenly that I didn't make it to the bathroom. When I looked at the first portrait of the Bastard, I threw up over it. Thankfully, I'd drawn many portraits of him.

Why bother making new drawings of him? The pictures I'd drawn as a child were authentic and supported my story far more robustly.

In the old drawings, my emotions were still raw, like a fresh wound cut in the skin. There was no way I could replicate the atavistic terror I'd felt back then. An adult can't express the feelings of a child.

It didn't even occur to me that anyone other than my therapist would gain access to my drawings.

That evening, while I lay in bed, frustratedly tossing and turning, waiting to fall asleep, I recalled my therapist's front door. Attached to it was a neon-pink Post-it note bearing, in beautiful handwriting, the words: *You are on the journey to your inner self.*

I couldn't think of a worse destination.

Arto

It's a good thing Irmeli had given me enough leeway that I was able to put off editing Clarissa's interview for weeks before deciding to put the final touches to it.

I sent the interview so that Irmeli could read through it, though if I'm honest the whole thing belonged in the bin.

Barely fifteen minutes later, Irmeli sent me a message, the tone of which was, to put it mildly, abrupt.

My office. Now.

Half an hour later I arrived at the *Helsinki Today* building. Irmeli was waiting for me in the foyer and beckoned me into her office.

Her face was dripping with disappointment. If you asked the women in my life what emotion best described their relationship with me, disappointment would surely be top of the list.

'Arto Haaleajärvi. How on earth is this possible?'

Irmeli flicked back and forth between the two sheets of A4 in her hands and gave a weary sigh. She'd had enough of me. On bad days, she called me by my full name. She hardly ever called me plain old Arto these days.

'Perhaps Clarissa hypnotized me?'

Irmeli's lips, clenched and tight, told me now was not the time for jokes.

I'd written up Clarissa's interview as best I could. That is to say, I'd tried to conjure something out of nothing. Irmeli could hardly believe I'd wasted my time on an article that was unpublishable.

This sort of thing happens to beginners, not to an old journeyman like me.

'A word of advice.'

An opening line like that didn't bode well. I was expecting her to revoke my associate contract, for everything to be over. Finally.

'When I fired you, you were at rock bottom. There aren't many people who would have dared to rehire someone they'd just dismissed for alcoholism—even as a freelancer. And I didn't do it out of pity. I've always known that if I just gave you another chance, one day you would reward me for it.'

What Irmeli said about pity was a lie. Pity was the only reason she had offered me the associate contract right after firing me from my old job.

And why did she pity me? For one very simple reason: I was the widower of her best friend. Marja.

Irmeli hadn't finished yet.

'You can drink all the whisky in the world, but you won't find Marja at the bottom of the glass.'

As if I didn't know that already. It didn't stop me trying.

'Right, this is what we're going to do. I want you to meet Clarissa again. And this time you're going to get a personal story out of her, even if you have to wring her neck to get it.'

Her tone was harsher now.

'Your drinking stops now. Do you hear? Now!'

Could it be any clearer? The interview with Clarissa Virtanen was my last chance.

Irmeli chivvied me out of her office like a headmistress dismissing a grubby little urchin after giving him a good dressing down. All I could think of was the worn-out old cliché *every cloud has a silver lining*. Clarissa had edified our readers with this particular platitude too.

But how would I get her to agree to another meeting after the fiasco last time?

Interviewing the therapist had brought my old traumas to the surface.

I forgot all about Irmeli and Clarissa and thought instead about her—who else?

I'm sure she didn't spare me a second thought these days. She probably imagined I didn't think about her either—and she was relieved.

But she was wrong.

She hadn't got rid of me.

And she never would.

Ida

I was sitting on the bus on the way to our third session. I wondered what my therapist would say about the drawing I'd stashed in her couch last time.

There was a rare, genuine sensitivity about my therapist. I was sure my drawing would have touched her profoundly. You remember *The Scream* by Edvard Munch, right? Well, multiply the horror on that face by a hundred, a thousand.

Who knows, my sketch might even be used in court to confirm that I couldn't be held criminally responsible.

Impatiently, I sat down on the couch in my therapist's office. Now we were getting somewhere! But no! She started churning out platitudes again. I squirmed uncomfortably on the couch, chewed my cuticles and waited, wondering when she would finally steer the conversation towards my drawing.

I could feel myself getting angry as our session was coming to an end and I realized she had no intention of talking about my artistic creation. Was this some kind of sick power game?

I knew how to play that game too! I was convinced that even though my therapist hadn't taken the bait this time, there was no way she'd be able to resist commenting on the drawings showing the cage and the Bastard. I was offering her secrets from the deepest recesses of my psyche on a silver platter!

What did she do with these drawings?

I don't know, but sometimes I imagine her looking at them and thinking of me.

Nothing too flattering, but she's still thinking about me.

Clarissa

It was hard to sit opposite Ida as if nothing had happened, as if the sketches she had drawn didn't exist or as if I had never laid eyes on them.

We never mentioned the sketches, not once. Yet Ida kept bringing them to every session. Maybe she thought if she wore me out, I would yield to her will.

Do give me a chance to defend myself! It was nothing but an accident—at first, that is—that I didn't bring up the subject of the sketches.

After recovering from the initial shock, originally I decided that at our third session we would talk about the sketch and nothing else. We would analyse it together and try to work out what it revealed about her.

Because Ida had such a unique character, I thought I might be able to incorporate a few more creative methods in her treatment. I don't have any qualifications in art therapy, but I thought it might be a good idea to use the drawings to our benefit. If I could just use the drawings to connect with her, that connection would hopefully strengthen so much that later on I would be able to use methods with which I was more familiar, such as dream analysis.

I'd even come up with a list of questions that we could think about together. Did the drawing represent an event from Ida's childhood or did it depict something from her present life? What was she thinking about when she drew those things? Did it remind her of a particular event? If it could talk, what would the drawing say? What did she see in the drawing herself? Was her mother trying to oppress her? Had she sketched an image of her own death?

When it came to the crunch, however, I found I couldn't follow through with my plan. How can I explain this? Everything feels so illogical.

The truth is, I pitied her.

The drawing was so violent, so grotesque, that it felt almost cruel to bring it up. I wanted her to have at least one place in the world where she felt safe, perhaps for the first time in her life. Don't we all deserve a place like that?

I wanted to shut all the evil in that drawing outside my office. Now, don't laugh, but I thought of my office as a womb. It was as though, if I could just keep all that evil on the other side of the door, I could control it.

As you know, Ida brought evil into my office by herself.

According to my favourite philosopher Ludwig Wittgenstein, whereof one cannot speak, thereof one must be silent. I came to realize that that whereof I could not speak was constantly on my mind. One way or another, everything we said referred back to the subject whereof we were supposed to remain silent.

All of our conversations were charged with meanings that were reflected in our silence. This brought a certain energy to our exchanges; nobody but us could understand the true meanings behind our words.

All those references, the symbols and footnotes… Did I really know what they meant after all? Perhaps Ida had planned this too.

What if she was using those drawings to manipulate me? My attention was drawn to them so forcefully that I didn't see what I should have been concentrating on instead.

Were the drawings yet another way of distracting me? Would everything have become clear if I hadn't been so spellbound by them? Was Ida trying to drown me in a world of murky symbolism because she thought I enjoyed analysing it?

I was trying to solve the riddle of the drawings, while all the while the truth was somewhere else altogether.

Ida

After our third session, I was consumed by a murderous rage. I was infuriated that she hadn't afforded a thought to my drawings.

Once the session ended, I hopped onto the bus and cursed under my breath. A man who got on after me almost came and sat next to me, but when he heard me swearing, he gave me an understanding nod and continued to the back of the bus.

I'd already decided what trinket I wanted to steal from my therapist as a souvenir if I ended up having to kill her. She wore a thin silver chain round her neck with her name in gold lettering. The dot above the 'I' was decorated with a small diamond. I imagined how the stone would sparkle in the light from my lamp as I lay in bed reminiscing about our moments together.

My emotions were swirling so much that I didn't even notice I'd got off the bus and started wandering into the Kamppi shopping mall. I normally gave the place a wide berth. As soon as I realized where I was, I started feeling even worse.

I hated shopping malls. I was repulsed at the thought that every single person walking past me was experiencing some kind of emotion at that moment. All that rage, love, uncertainty, fear, happiness, envy, anxiety, crammed into one place! And I was supposed to wade through all those emotions like an ant caught in a jam jar—as if I didn't have enough emotions of my own.

The worst of it was that you couldn't tell what they were feeling just by looking at them, and I had no way of interpreting their emotions. A teenage girl's disinterested scowl might convey passion as much as contempt.

The churning of people's brains seemed to echo along the corridors even louder than the inane ambient background music. Though nobody was saying anything, it still felt as though my head was about to explode. All those plans, those hopes and dreams, the selfish notion that *I*, of all people, had some special meaning, that *my* life had a greater significance, that the whole world revolved around *me*.

The immaterial thoughts of the people marching through the shopping mall pierced my skull, pressed into my brain and yelled in chorus. Hundreds, thousands of emotions forced their way through my skin, each trying to stand out from the cacophony.

The emotions of these strange passers-by shoved my own emotions to one side and flickered in my subconscious as though they were my own. My persona wasn't strong enough to withstand an attack like this. It felt as though my sense of self was evaporating into thin air.

I darted into a panicked run. Luckily, there was no queue at the women's toilets. I yanked my trousers and pants down to my ankles and sat on the toilet for a pee, all the while trying to calm myself down by taking deep breaths, though I knew it was no use.

I stood up, tugged up my pants and trousers, and noticed that the toilet bowl looked as though someone had just slaughtered a small animal in there. I flushed, but the water started flooding over the bowl. The toilet floor would soon be swimming in my menstrual blood. I slammed the lid shut and dashed outside.

A queue had formed outside the toilet. People gave me a curious look as I came staggering out of the cubicle, bashing into the person at the front of the queue as I went.

I didn't even stop to wash my hands but rushed out into the corridor and quickened my steps further still as I turned the corner and headed towards the escalators.

I knew I had to get out of the building immediately. Otherwise, I wouldn't know who I was any more.

A little girl walked towards me, a picture of a pink butterfly on her T-shirt. All of a sudden, the butterfly emerged from the T-shirt and flew off. It fluttered in front of my face, as if waiting to make sure I'd seen it. After this, it headed towards the front doors of the shopping mall, as though it were leading me to salvation.

I tried to dodge the people walking towards me without knocking into anyone, but it was impossible because there was such a cram of shoppers. I almost fell over on the escalators but managed to grab the handrail at the last minute.

People stared at me. Their quizzical expressions only increased my panic levels. I could feel sweat gluing my hair to my temples and running down my back.

As I was running, I accidentally bit my tongue. The rusty taste of blood triggered my delusions again. I could see the bars of the cage. They appeared in front of me, blocking my way. I had to walk around them. The people walking towards me looked at me in confusion as I swerved to the left, though they couldn't see any obstacles in front of me.

It felt as though my mouth was full of rust flaking from the bars instead of my own blood. I couldn't control myself; I had to spit on the floor as I ran. Two unusually keen security guards saw me and started heading in my direction. Thankfully, I could see the mall's front doors looming up ahead. The guards realized I was heading outside and let me go on my way.

Once outside, I continued running another few steps, and only then dared to stop. It took a moment to steady my breathing. I carefully shook off all the thoughts and emotions that had invaded my head and left them on the pavement outside the mall.

I finally managed to regain my grip on reality. The blood dripping from my tongue tasted like blood again instead of rust.

HELSINKI TODAY

MINISTER REPORTED MISSING IN KERAVA LAST MONTH FOUND DEAD

Former chancellor of the exchequer Uolevi Mäkisarja, reported missing in the Kilta area of Kerava a month ago, has been found dead. Mäkisarja's body was found in a pond located on the premises of the old rubber factory at Savio.

Mäkisarja's body was discovered by a dog walker who wishes to remain anonymous.

'I just can't believe it. I voted for him several times. I'm so shocked that I doubt I'll ever be able to walk my dog by the pond again,' said the woman who discovered the body.

Police remain tight-lipped about the details of the investigation but have given a short statement.

'Mäkisarja's death is being investigated as a homicide,' said Inspector Jaana Taivaskivi of the violent-crimes unit of the Eastern Uusimaa Constabulary.

Arto

I left the paper's head office and returned home, deflated. On the way, I desperately tried to think of different pretences I could use to justify to Clarissa why we had to meet again.

Eventually, though, I plumped for honesty. As a psychotherapist, Clarissa would see right through any attempt to pull the wool over her eyes. I took a deep breath and picked up my mobile.

'Hi, Arto! Thanks again for such a lovely evening!'

What? *What* lovely evening? Did she think it was 'lovely' watching me make a total fool out of myself?

'No, thank *you*! Listen, the paper's editor in chief thinks the interview is still missing that little something. Do you think we could meet up again so I can ask a few follow-up questions?'

Please, please, please, I found myself thinking, the way I did as a child when I wanted something really badly.

It seemed to work, as Clarissa agreed to my request.

'By all means! We had such a nice time! Am I right in saying the interview won't be published until the summer?'

She didn't wait for me to respond but continued right away.

'I'm rather busy in the near future. I'll call you when I have time in my diary for another meeting.'

A little bewildered, I agreed. Mission accomplished. Well, half, at least. I'd convinced Clarissa to agree to another interview, but the most difficult part of the task still lay ahead: how could I make her spill all her darkest secrets? Did she even have any to spill?

Just because my closet was full of skeletons didn't mean everybody else's was too.

Clarissa's curious behaviour irritated me. I imagined her laughing behind my back, as if she found my alcohol problem somehow amusing. As a therapist, how did she have the nerve to behave so rudely towards me?

There was only one way to calm my mind—a way that was both forbidden and unlawful. I pulled on my coat, wrapped a scarf around my neck, took my bag and umbrella from the stand and left the apartment.

I'd managed to force myself not to visit her for weeks now. Four weeks to the day, to be precise.

My mood was like that of an alcoholic celebrating three weeks of sobriety by coming crashing off the wagon. I imagined her standing by the window of her studio flat, blissfully unaware of everything, just like always before, those mournful eyes staring out through the windowpane.

During the daytime she looked out at the children playing in the yard, and in the evenings she watched the dog walkers and their mutts. She kept her curtains open at night too, and even then she stood at her window. Was she gazing up at the stars?

But she never noticed me, never. I was able to watch her in peace. I didn't dare hope for more.

I walked to the bus stop as slowly as I could, as if trying to give myself a little extra time to come to my senses, though I knew I'd never be able to convince myself to change my mind. Every step took me a little closer to her. She pulled me in like an unopened bottle of Scotch.

Even as I stood at the bus stop and waved to the driver to make him pull over, I tried to force myself to turn around and head home. But it was futile. I stepped on board the bus, chose a seat near the window and sat down.

The bus driver made an announcement that he would have to take a diversion because the city marathon route cut across the start of Mannerheimintie.

I looked through the window at the darkness outside. I couldn't remember the last time I'd seen daylight. A crowd of undernourished-looking waifs ran joylessly past the bus. One of the runners was sucking water from a sports bottle, though his body was so emaciated that an intravenous drip might have been more appropriate.

During the Middle Ages, these people's masochism would have made them climb to the top of a tall column to proselytize and flagellate themselves with thorns.

I was glad when the bus finally reached the right stop, as I had no desire to watch the marathon runners a second longer than necessary.

Right next to her building, like a godsend, there was a park. I sat down at my regular spot, a bench that allowed me to glance up to her apartment.

And I wasn't disappointed. There she was, standing at the window, stock-still, in the same position as always. In her right hand she was holding a mug, and every now and then she took a tiny sip from it, like a sparrow dipping its beak into a puddle. She was watching the children running around the park, and I was watching her.

It wasn't supposed to be like this, but it was.

It started sleeting, but I tried not to let it bother me. I'd sat here in worse weather than this; once I even sat through a hailstorm. The hailstones struck me in the face as though someone was throwing little stones at me, and as they melted, the water trickled down inside my jacket collar. But all I wanted was to see her, that was enough, and then I could convince myself that nothing else mattered, neither the hailstones nor the fact that I'd never be able to touch her ever again.

The wooden bench was uncomfortable; I could feel it pressing painfully into the small of my back.

I propped my black umbrella against the bench to protect me, then took that morning's edition of *Helsinki Today* out of my bag and pretended to read it, though in truth I was following her every move.

What was she thinking as she stood there by the window? What if she was thinking about me after all? If only sporadically?

Or had she managed to forget all about me?

She couldn't deny the impact I'd had on her life.

There was a bond between us, one that she could never forget.

All those precious moments in the cellar, just the two of us.

Me and her.

Part Two

THE BECK DEPRESSION INVENTORY

Clarissa

I think where I was most mistaken was in the assumption that Ida would eventually kill herself. Still, I believe that any professional treating Ida would have reached the same erroneous conclusion. All the red flags were there. The eating disorder and self-harm were the most obvious examples of her turning the aggression that her trauma had caused onto herself instead of channelling it outwards.

I know what this must sound like. But I had no reason to draw any other conclusion. Ida's suicidal tendencies were so glaringly obvious that it was impossible to dismiss them out of hand.

My mistake was to dismiss everything else instead.

Nonetheless, Ida's symptoms weren't a bluff. I still believe they deserved attention. I'm worried you won't take my word for it any more. You've already decided that my professional skills can't be trusted. But I have some weighty evidence to show you!

At our fourth session, I asked Ida to complete a BDI test, that is the Beck Depression Inventory. This is a multiple-choice test used to establish a diagnosis of depression and to measure the severity of that depression.

The test consists of twenty-one questions. These describe the most typical symptoms of depression, including loss of appetite or a dwindling sex drive. Each question has four possible answers, from minimal to severe.

Ida's test results were alarming. Judging by her responses, she was suffering from very acute depression. Her answers included:

'I have no appetite at all any more', 'I feel I am a complete failure as a person', and, most critical of all, 'I would kill myself if I had the chance.'

I understand if you think I'm just trying to put a positive spin on things. But why would I do that? I wouldn't get back anything I've already lost. I had to accept that long ago.

Let me remind you of therapists' professional ethics. It was my duty to protect Ida. Though we therapists are not legally responsible for our patients' actions, we are responsible for their lives and well-being. If someone sees a drunk passed out in a snowdrift and does not stop to help and call an ambulance, that person can be held legally responsible for any harm that comes to the drunk. But the therapist's duty of care is weightier still. I knew about Ida's suicide plans. My job was to make sure she never followed through on them.

So, why didn't I have her sectioned in a psychiatric unit? Her clinical depression would have been grounds enough for this. We are approaching that foggy zone again, the place where nobody can see clearly—neither me nor you.

I'm not going to wait for someone to cast the first stone; that happened long ago. I'll be perfectly honest with you.

I was jealous of Ida.

I mean it when I say there was nothing more important to me than making sure Ida recovered. But nobody else was allowed to help her recover but me.

Ida answered the test questions so quickly that it was as though she had practised completing the test in advance.

It wasn't long before I noticed the way she focused all her attention on her fingers. She had an infuriating habit of biting her cuticles. She scratched and scraped her fingers so much that it made me want to scream.

Was I the only one, or did all therapists find that their patients had an unpleasant neurotic tic that it was pointless trying to coax them out of? It disgusted me. Sometimes a cigar really is just a cigar, but sucking your fingers certainly suggests acute problems during the oral phase.

Once I had interpreted the test results, I told Ida I was very concerned about her.

We didn't talk about medication because I didn't think it would benefit her. A cocktail of beta-blockers and antidepressants would have left her so doped up that she would have been walking around in a fog like a zombie, and our therapy sessions would have been useless.

As a psychologist, I didn't have the competence to make such an assessment. But I didn't consult my trusted mentor Harri either.

I won't even try to defend myself.

The results of the Beck test often take the patient by surprise. This is a demanding test because it reveals things about the patient that they might never have considered before.

Moderately depressed patients might not be aware that their symptoms are a sign of depression; rather they often think they are tired because they are stressed. Severely depressed patients, meanwhile, often make light of their symptoms. The test results can shake the patient into a realization of quite how advanced their psychological quandary really is.

I didn't ask her, though I assumed from her reaction that Ida was already familiar with this test. I didn't have to explain to her what her responses told me. She was only interested in her points score. 'Fuck the rest,' she muttered almost inaudibly. She noticed the way I flinched at her coarse language, as if she'd slapped me across the face with the flat of her hand, and when she apologized, it sounded sincere.

This was the first time I'd heard Ida swear. At first I was so taken aback that I didn't pay any attention to the change in her. Only later did I notice that, when she swore, she almost became a different person, aggressive and cruel.

After this, I regularly found myself on the receiving end of Ida's sarcasm. Just as I was complimenting her out loud, saying how encouraging it was to see the progress she was making, she would give me a smarmy smile and bring me crashing back to earth: 'You're starting to sound like a therapist.'

When we become angry, we let our guard down. Some people are able to control their aggression better than others. The change in Ida was like Dr Jekyll and Mr Hyde. The nice girl disappeared, only to be replaced by her evil doppelgänger.

It's only now that I really understand which of these was the real Ida.

Ida

I've got a solution to all your relationship problems.

I know. The bond between murderer and victim can hardly be considered a relationship, but I didn't have any other kinds of relationships. Except the relationship with my therapist. Although, to be fair, that one encompasses all our human relationships from childhood to the present day. A therapist is by turns a mother, a father and a partner.

You really should take this advice seriously. Listening is the key to everything else.

And I don't mean just any old psychobabble. I mean, people tell you the truth about themselves at the beginning of a relationship, but nobody listens.

Unfaithfulness, fear of commitment, you name it. Nothing is a better predictor of people's behaviour than their previous behaviour.

On the first date, a man tells you that none of his previous relationships lasted more than a few weeks. What makes you think you'll be any different? Early on in a relationship, a man drunkenly admits that he's betrayed all his previous girlfriends. What makes you think he won't do the same to you? And when, in a moment of candour, he whispers in your ear that he would never hurt you, you know he's planning to do exactly that.

When I told you I was a pathological liar, you should have believed me.

That doesn't mean that I can't tell the truth, sometimes, when the truth is more useful than lying.

Over the years I've taken all kinds of psychological tests, everything from ink-blot tests onwards, so I'd guessed my therapist would want to test me again and I'd been mentally preparing myself. I guessed right. The first test she gave me was Beck's depression inventory—one that I knew all too well. The first time I'd had to fill it out was as a teenager in the paediatric unit of the psychiatric hospital.

This time I had a very clear objective. The test result had to look good, if I ever ended up having to take criminal responsibility for my actions in a court of law. I had to give the impression of being as depressed as possible, preferably completely catatonic. A result like that would fit my defence like a glove. Someone who is severely depressed doesn't even have the energy to get out of bed, let alone murder people.

Why wasn't I trying to avoid repercussions completely, you might ask? I could try and convince the jury I was innocent. That way I might avoid a stay at the loony bin too.

But sadly, it wasn't that simple. If my test result indicated severe depression, my therapist would probably want to put me on medication. Antidepressants have pretty unfortunate side effects, you know. Before they start having the desired effect, they ease the patient's condition just enough that she regains a little of her own initiative. Just enough that she might have the wherewithal to kill herself. Or, in my case, to slaughter complete strangers.

So, either way I'd end up in the dock.

I'd already given my dilemma a good deal of thought when my therapist handed me the test: depressed, but not too depressed?

Most people appreciate the truth. You've probably already noticed my case isn't exactly a statistical average. Honesty is emotional weakness. Nothing speaks to a fundamental lack of imagination and creativity more than honesty. Lying shows that I'm prepared to go the extra mile in communicating with people. As a rule, I lie whenever possible.

But this time you've got to believe me. I answered that test with complete honesty. This time I didn't have to stretch the truth.

The truth was already brutal enough.

Pekka

I had a good reason to go in there, into the forbidden area, the inner sanctum. Clarissa was attending a seminar in Kuopio, and I'd agreed to move her filing cabinet while she was away to hold down the corner of the rug. Only a few days earlier, she'd tripped on the rug and banged her elbow against the edge of her desk.

I opened the door to Clarissa's office. Her Highness slipped inside and darted in and out between my legs like a child on a sugar rush. I couldn't stand the creature.

Clarissa should have trained the thing better. Instead, I'd noticed that the worse the cat behaved, the more she thought it sweet and adorable, as though a cat too can have traumas that it needs to work through by acting out.

It wasn't my intention to snoop around. Even when I found a folder lying on top of the filing cabinet, it didn't occur to me to look at the documents inside it.

I want to stress how serious a matter this is.

I could not be held accountable for my actions. Clarissa, however, could have got into a lot of trouble if it ever came to light that she didn't keep her patients' documents safe and out of other people's reach.

If I were to rummage through Clarissa's papers and the authorities ever found out about it, she could say goodbye to her career.

I decided to leave the folder on her desk, so it didn't fall on the floor while I was moving the cabinet. I picked up the folder: the Princess's papers.

Clarissa was in the habit of drawing a pencil sketch of each patient on the front of their folder. Though I'd only seen the Princess from a distance, I recognized her instantly. Clarissa had highlighted precisely the features that had caught my attention when I first saw her. Now that same haggard young woman stared back at me from the cover of the folder.

I guessed the Princess's tragic story before I opened the folder: she'd been sexually abused as a child.

What else?

Poor girl.

I hadn't the faintest idea what kind of game she was playing with my wife.

Ida

I remember the first time best of all. I was fourteen. I had every reason to kill myself, all of them totally rational. I hated myself. It was no accident that I'd ended up falling victim to the Bastard. He chose me. Everything that happened to me happened because I was me. Otherwise it would have happened to someone else. Everything was my fault and mine alone, nobody else's. I deserved all the evil that was done to me. That was clear.

I didn't settle for just one method of committing suicide. I decided to take my father's diazepam and to slit my wrists.

That day, my father wasn't working late, the way he often did. Instead, he came straight home, as I lay almost unconscious in the bloody bathtub and realized I'd forgotten to write a suicide note. The next morning I woke up in the paediatric ward of the psychiatric hospital. Another reason to feel like an utter failure.

My father sat by my sickbed and talked with the psychiatrist. He asked how soon my wounds would heal and whether we could remove my bandages before I was due to go back to school. It was important to him that my schoolfriends never found out what I'd done. Not to worry, the psychiatrist replied, I had a long spell in hospital to look forward to. On top of my suicidal tendencies, I was in acute need of treatment for my anorexia too.

I started to feel sorry for my father. I decided to keep trying, for his sake, so he wouldn't have to bear any guilt for my death.

But my willpower wasn't strong enough, and I attempted suicide again. I'm still ashamed of how I totally bungled my second attempt. I must be the only person in history who screwed up trying to hang herself. I was already an adult by this point, so I can't very well claim that age was a mitigating factor.

Everything was going well until I had to kick the chair away from under my feet. My toes got caught between the smoothly sanded pins at the back of the chair, meaning I couldn't make the chair fall over. I kicked and kicked and kicked, but my toes wouldn't come loose. I felt like a complete idiot as I clambered down and wrenched the noose from around my neck.

I got quite close on the third attempt. I managed to put myself in a coma for a full day. A combination of pills and booze, then I walked off into the nearby woodland to die like a wounded animal. That way, I thought, there was no way anyone would find me before it was too late. I was wrong. A keen blueberry picker strayed from the path and spotted me lying under a pine tree.

That time, nobody came and sat by my sickbed.

As I lay in the hospital, I started thinking there must have been a reason for my survival. It probably sounds like I'd found Jesus or something. Maybe that was it. It felt as though my life must have a greater meaning, something bigger than me. People have died for less. I, on the other hand, had already survived three times. It was then that I realized I wasn't meant to kill myself.

All the rage that I'd been focusing on myself ought to have killed me. But I was still alive. What if I redirected that rage, channelled it outwards? I could avenge everything that had been done to me, force all the self-loathing out of myself, regurgitate it over other people. I would do it in such a way that I'd never have to be ashamed again.

Now there would be bodies.

Pekka

I was standing in Clarissa's office, alone, gripping the Princess's folder. I swear, I'd never snooped in Clarissa's paperwork before.

In the past I'd never had any recourse to do so. Clarissa's work didn't interest me. I was more fed up that my wife's career impinged on my life so much. The atmosphere in our house was always somehow morose, as though the anguish oozing from Clarissa's patients lingered the air long after they had left.

The Princess stared at me from the cover of the folder, an accusatory look in her eyes.

I don't know where I got the impulse to open it. The sudden inclination took me completely off guard, and I couldn't resist.

A voice in my head shouted at the top of its lungs, telling me not to touch the folder. Another voice shouted louder still: *Nobody will ever know.* True. Clarissa wouldn't notice a thing. She wasn't exactly going to test the folder for fingerprints.

The things we don't know can't hurt us, right?

My hands were trembling. Is this what criminals feel like at the point of breaking the law? Nobody was watching me, were they? I glanced out of the window. There was nobody in sight.

Though I couldn't see our neighbours and their old orange banger wasn't parked in its usual place in front of their garage and in all likelihood they weren't even at home, I rushed to the window and pulled the curtains shut. As if my neighbours would give a damn if they saw me standing in my own house with a folder in my hand.

I opened the folder. It was empty.

I conceded defeat.

Before leaving the office, I decided to surprise Clarissa by giving the room the once over with the vacuum cleaner. Nothing pleased my wife more than when I cleared up. I peered under the couch to see whether there was any need to hoover the room. There wasn't a speck of dust. Clarissa must have vacuumed just before leaving.

My eyes were drawn to two pieces of papers stuffed under the couch. It wasn't like Clarissa to hide papers under the couch and forget all about them. This looked like a secret stash. My wife was so pedantic about cleanliness that even a paperclip dropped down the back of the sofa was enough to set her off.

I carefully removed the papers from their hiding place. Her Highness watched me with soulless eyes and started meowing. Maybe Clarissa had told her to keep an eye on me while she was at the seminar and to report back on everything I got up to.

I swiftly snatched up the cat, dropped her in the hallway and shut the door in front of her curious, twitching nose. She started impatiently scratching the door, now meowing all the more. I didn't pay her any attention and started examining the papers instead.

The uppermost paper was a mess of charcoal smudges. Perplexed, I turned the paper in my hands. I couldn't work out what it was supposed to represent. I tried looking at it from all angles but couldn't make head nor tail of it.

If I'm honest, it looked like it had been daubed by a nursery-school kid. Not just any kid, but a deeply disturbed one.

The kind of kid whose childhood had been dramatically cut short.

I picked up the next sheet. This one had a charcoal sketch on it too, but I could make it out much better than the previous one.

A dark figure stared back at me. A man dressed in a suit, a grotesque smirk on his face.

The man's expression startled me. He exuded evil. I wouldn't want to run into him in a dark alleyway.

He looked like the sort of man who took pleasure in other people's suffering.

These pictures could only be described as 'sick' and 'twisted'. I'm no art expert, but they reminded me of Hugo Simberg's representations of death, particularly his painting *The Garden of Death*, of which he made several different versions, all showing skeletons dressed in black tending to a garden. That being said, compared to this artist, Simberg seemed positively cheerful.

I felt bewildered. Didn't I have anything better to do than scrutinize drawings that shouldn't interest me in the first place? What the hell was wrong with me?

In my frustration, I stuffed the drawings back under the couch, as if to prove to myself that I didn't intend to have anything further to do with them.

I was consumed by a strange sense of foreboding. My stomach was churning, and my throat was so tight that I found it hard to breathe.

It was as though the drawings were trying to tell me something.

Me specifically.

Arto

I arrived at the Coffee Bean a little early, but this time Clarissa was there before me. She gave me a breezy wave from the same table where Marja and I used to sit and hugged me again as though we were old friends. I had readied myself for the scent of Chanel N°5 and scrunched my nose as we embraced. Clarissa must have read my thoughts and taken them into consideration because this time she had dabbed on a little Opium by Yves Saint Laurent instead. I recognized the perfume instantly because I'd once bought it for Marja at the duty-free shop on the boat to Sweden. Marja didn't think much of it, and for years the bottle stood gathering dust on her bedside table.

Now Marja's bedside table was like a shrine. All her personal effects were exactly where she had left them when she died. I'd been meaning to go through these things for ages, to keep a few items to remember her by and throw the rest in the bin, but even this felt too final, as if after that I would no longer be able to kid myself that Marja hadn't actually died.

I went to the counter and ordered coffee for Clarissa and myself.

Her friendly smile turned to concern when I sat down opposite her.

'What's the matter, Arto?'

Women always seemed to fret about me, and to be honest it was getting a bit tedious. It's not like Clarissa was my therapist!

'Well, where should I start? Work is a nightmare, and everything else is a nightmare too, so in summation you could say my whole life is a bit of a nightmare.'

Clarissa looked at me, trying to decide whether I needed a padded cell or whether a straitjacket would be enough.

'Arto. You won't get help unless you ask for it.'

Right now, the only thing I needed from Clarissa was a few tasty quotations for the interview. Something like: 'I'll never forgive myself for not having kids' or 'My husband is jealous of my success' or preferably something a bit shocking, like 'I've forgiven my husband for cheating on me.' Stuff that would make the headlines.

There was something genuine in Clarissa's expression, something you can't fake. The same warmth that flowed from Irmeli's voice when she was trying to get me back on my feet. The warmth I used to see glowing in Marja's eyes before our relationship started going downhill.

'If this interview doesn't make the front page, *Helsinki Today* is going to end my associate contract. And in order to get you on the front page, I need a little glimpse into your private life. I'm sorry.'

Now all my cards were on the table for her to see; and I didn't even have a five up my sleeve, let alone an ace.

I was worried she might storm out of the café without so much as a goodbye. And before I knew it, she was on her feet, hurriedly pulling her coat over her shoulders.

'You're a frightful worrywart, Arto! We'll get you your headline, mark my words! But on one condition: you and I are going to go to my regular, the Watering Hole, and have a glass of red.'

I was dumbfounded. Clarissa's behaviour was completely reckless. Where was the forensic, analytical expert whose interviews were professional to the point of being dull as dishwater?

She crouched down to pick up her handbag, and with that I got the answer to my question. She stumbled, gripped the table for support, her coat sleeve dangled in my coffee cup, she knocked the cup to the floor, giggled and kicked the shards of broken porcelain under the table.

Clarissa was drunk. At ten past five on a Monday evening.

I wasn't aware I'd been looking for one, but I'd finally found a kindred spirit.

Pekka

That evening, I lay under the duvet in bed, trying to count the flowers on the rose-patterned wallpaper that my wife had chosen for our bedroom. I couldn't get the drawings I'd found under her office couch from my mind.

When I glanced at the alarm clock and realized I'd spent half an hour wondering whether I should count the rosebuds too or only those that had fully opened, I decided to use my time more effectively and concentrate on the mystery of the drawings.

I tried to think how Clarissa—or any other professional psycho-analyst—might have interpreted them. As an amateur, I couldn't even say whether there was anything in them to interpret or whether they were simply harmless scribbles. Had someone picked up a stick of charcoal and sketched those disturbed images just for the fun of it? Or did they have a deeper meaning?

I was becoming increasingly convinced that the drawings must contain some kind of hidden message intended for me. I realize quite how bizarre this notion was, but intuition smothered my common sense.

How could I get to the bottom of this puzzle? I hadn't the faintest idea. I didn't know what to latch on to.

I decided to approach it as though it were any normal logical conundrum that could be taken to pieces and solved using rational thinking. I created an Excel file and wrote down in the different columns everything I knew about the drawings. In the first column,

I wrote the date I had discovered them; in the next column, the total number of drawings. There were two: the black smudge that I couldn't fathom at all and the smirking man in the suit.

I thought about it for a long while but couldn't come up with anything else to write down. But this was just the start. All stories have to start somewhere.

But, I thought, I was in no rush to work out what the drawings were all about.

At the time, I didn't know that my life would depend on solving this mystery.

Arto

'Arto, I'm so terribly sorry.'

Clarissa's phone call woke me from my coma. Her voice was dripping with guilt. An apology! What on earth for?

Our meeting yesterday crept back into my mind, though I would rather not have thought about it at all. We had hurried out of the Coffee Bean as though Clarissa wouldn't have survived another minute without a glass of wine. She looked like she already had quite enough alcohol in her system, but who am I to talk?

When we arrived at the Watering Hole, I could barely hide my shock. I don't think I've ever stepped foot inside such a dump. I couldn't understand how a sophisticated woman like Clarissa could enjoy herself in a dive like this.

I sat down at the bar and ordered a whisky for myself and a glass of red wine for Clarissa. She visited the bathroom, then joined me. On the way, she had picked up the karaoke list and started excitedly waving it in front of my face like a lottery ticket with the winning numbers.

'Arto, you and I will make a fantastic duo!'

Oh, God, no, I thought to myself. Over my dead body. But only half an hour later I found myself with Clarissa on the Watering Hole's rickety stage, singing Tom Jones's eternally awful *She's a Lady*.

I was terrified at the thought that some prankster might have immortalized our advanced state of intoxication on camera and uploaded it to YouTube to be mocked by everyone and his dog.

'Can you forgive me?' Clarissa implored me on the phone.

This was the first time I'd been able to absolve a drunken woman of her shame. I recalled all the times I'd asked Irmeli and Marja to forgive my drunken escapades. I knew what it felt like to wallow in guilt, so I wanted to let Clarissa off the hook as quickly as possible.

'It's okay, take it easy. Let's forget about yesterday.'

'But… you're not going to…'

Clarissa sounded like she might burst into tears at any moment. I couldn't deal with women crying. Their tears always rendered me powerless.

'You won't write about this, will you? My reputation…'

Clarissa spluttered on the other end of the phone, and I imagined her reaching into her pocket for a tissue. I needed to stop her crying before she got properly started.

'Let's make one thing absolutely clear: I won't be writing a word about last night.'

I was serious too. We alcoholics have to look out for each other. Maybe this would bring me some good karma. Maybe Clarissa or someone else would save my skin the next time I well and truly screwed things up.

'Thank you! I owe you one. Let's meet up again, and this time we'll come up with a good headline for you. How about I ask Pekka—my husband, that is—if he'll allow me to tell you something about our marriage.'

'That sounds like a plan!'

'I… I'm not an alcoholic, by the way.'

No. Neither am I.

'We don't have to talk about that.'

'It's just, I'm having a terrible time at work. One of my patients is a young woman with a very debilitating eating disorder. If you ask me, I believe she was sexually abused as a child…'

I didn't want to hear another word. I could feel a headache coming on, and it wasn't just because I was hungover.

'I thought you had a duty of confidentiality to your patients.'

I hadn't intended this as sarcasm, but that's what it sounded like. And apparently that's how Clarissa took it.

'I'll check my diary and send you a time by text message.'

All of a sudden, her voice was cold. It looked like I might not get that sensational headline after all.

Clarissa

I could have died of embarrassment. Arto's voice on the other end of the phone was thick with disdain. I tried to calm myself down. Everybody can go over the top from time to time. It's not for nothing they call wine the drink of the wise. Nice try, but it didn't work. Shame flushed my cheeks.

If Arto was so inclined, the whole of Finland would soon hear about my drunken shenanigans. He'd promised me he wouldn't write about what had happened last night—but can you ever trust a reporter? Surely a great scoop like this supersedes all journalistic ethics.

I didn't really want to think about what happened, but I had to. I had to try and remember exactly what I'd done before I read about it in Arto's sensational tell-all interview.

There were gaping holes in my memory. I remembered us sitting at the Coffee Bean for a while, but I didn't remember what happened there. My only memory was the sound of smashing porcelain, as though a coffee cup had been knocked from the table and smashed on the floor. Who was it—Arto or me?

My next recollection is of the karaoke at the Watering Hole. How did we end up there?

I felt so utterly ashamed that I wanted to dig a hole in the garden and hide. If my patchy memories were anything to go by, after the karaoke we moved back to the bar. What on earth had we talked about?

At some point in the evening, I found out that Arto was a widower. A whole string of clichés had come streaming out of his mouth.

My wife didn't understand me.

We grew apart.

We had nothing in common any more.

I'd heard the same litany from my patients a thousand times.

All of a sudden, I thought of Pekka's affairs. He'd never admitted anything directly, and I'd never asked him. Yet, I'm convinced he was cheating on me in the early years of our marriage. He would probably still be cheating on me if he weren't so old and chubby, I thought with a sour chuckle. Had my beloved Pekka lured women into his bed with dusty old pick-up lines like these?

I heard my mother's voice in my ears. *You can't trust men.* She was right, at least when it came to my father. And Pekka.

But how had the evening ended? Did we have the good sense to leave the bar by ourselves, or had the bouncers thrown us out?

Yes, I'd been there too. I didn't care to think about it, but the image appeared in my mind against my will. On Friday evening, I'd decided to celebrate the weekend by relaxing with a few glasses of red wine, but one glass had led seamlessly to the next, and the next. Eventually, the bouncer had been forced to carry me out to the taxi rank because I'd refused to go voluntarily.

I returned to the subject of my karaoke evening with Arto. Just then, a tattered image appeared that I was able to grab hold of. I was sitting at the bar, alone. Arto must have disappeared hours earlier. When, and why?

I hadn't the faintest idea.

Ida

At first, I tried to resist my bloodthirsty urges. You know the way people are encouraged to think compassionately about junkies and down-and-outs? They're human beings too, just like you and me. They're someone's children. They have parents, maybe siblings too, other relatives, friends. Somebody loves them or at least used to love them. If they were to die, someone would miss them.

I always tried to find a level of humanity in my victims, something, anything I could identify with. If either of us cut our finger, it would hurt. We would both be startled if we heard a sudden loud bang. We both felt an array of emotions.

I tried my hardest, but I couldn't fully grasp these thought exercises. They left me cold. Even the Bastard had been a child once upon a time, but that wasn't a good enough reason not to loathe him.

I don't know where I found the willpower to make sure my thoughts remained thoughts for so long, to stop myself acting upon them.

This latent phase lasted weeks, maybe even months.

I started writing my fantasies down. One after another, notebooks filled up with descriptions of different methods of killing people. I'm glad I saved those notebooks, as I've turned to them for tips on more than a few occasions.

I wasn't worried about anybody finding these notebooks and having me committed. I could say I was just writing a thriller.

After all, Agatha Christie was left in peace to kill hundreds of people—in her novels.

Crime magazines became my favourite reading material, but I soon got bored of them too. Don't people have the slightest imagination? Nothing but knives and shotguns. Yawn! Banality like this gives murderers a bad reputation.

I felt like writing to prisoners serving a life sentence and sending them new ideas. Back then, I was still trying to convince myself I could keep everything in the realm of fantasy and resist escalating to concrete action. Subconsciously, I somehow knew it wouldn't work because I kept my visions to myself.

I came up with different ways to kill a person, each more sadistic than the next. But these fantasies didn't give me the slightest pleasure. They just seemed to flood my mind, so it felt natural to write them down.

Actually, I shouldn't call them fantasies; they were more like apparitions. These apparitions could appear out of nowhere, while I was doing my groceries, for instance. Sometimes I would see a bloody axe; other times an image of myself battering a corporate suit over the head with a hammer.

Often, all I would see was blood.

Pools of blood on the kitchen floor, red droplets along the aisle at the supermarket, blood spatter across a running track—blood, blood, blood.

But, as I've already mentioned, you could say my trademark is a certain... clinical approach. I never got carried away by these blood-filled apparitions. If I decided to act them out, I'd do it without causing any unnecessary bloodshed.

I fantasized about murders, but it didn't take long until I realized that mind games like this no longer satiated me. I'd have to get down to business; take out the hammers, the saws and scissors.

Why are you still so shocked at my fantasies? You watch horror films too, don't you? Has it never occurred to you that someone actually had to write those scripts?

Someone who wants to watch women being tortured and murdered in the most grotesque ways possible.

Over and over again.

Clarissa

Once I'd recovered from my conversation with Arto, I went out onto the patio, still hungover, and had a cigarette, though I was supposed to have given up smoking. How many times in my life had I stubbed out a cigarette for what I told myself would be the last time, only to light up again a few hours later?

I squashed the stub against the patio railing like a cockroach.

It was sleeting so heavily that I could barely make out our hawthorn hedgerow, let alone the neighbours' house opposite. I hurried inside out of the wet. I felt restless. I decided to wait until there was a pause in the snowfall, then soothe myself with a spot of retail therapy.

According to the weather forecast, this would only be a short flurry. After an hour's wait, I noticed that the forecast was accurate. The sleet had turned into tiny snowflakes that melted as soon as they touched the ground. I pulled on my outdoor clothes, grabbed my handbag and set off to the tram stop.

I stood at the stop by myself, wondering how the weather could change so much in such a short space of time, much like our moods. From grief to rage, rage to shame, shame to guilt. The white gleam of the snowflakes made me think of innocence, but above all of how easily innocence can be corrupted.

Riku's face flickered in my mind, as pale as when I'd seen it for the last time. A solitary drop of blood was trickling down his right cheek.

With some determination, I locked the image away again and concentrated on watching the snowflakes dance through the air.

The tram was almost full. Just as I managed to find a seat by the window towards the back of the carriage, a man and a woman on the back seat, clearly junkies, lunged forwards to snatch something from the floor. I turned to see what they'd found, but they were standing with their backs to me like a wall.

Just then, the woman bellowed to the man so loudly that the whole carriage heard them:

'There's one left!'

'What is it?' the man replied, every bit as excitedly.

'Temazepam!'

I slipped my hand into the pocket of my mink coat. The blister pack of temazepam must have fallen out of my pocket when I took out my travel card. I only used sedatives sporadically, only when I was under considerable stress at work, because I didn't want to become addicted to them. It's so easy to get hooked, and it's a tough habit to kick. There was only one pill left in the pack of ten, but I'd been using that same pack for almost a year. I'd have to ask Harri to renew my prescription.

The junkies hopped off the tram at the next stop. I watched them go and thought about the woman's fate. How had her life gone so awry? When had the idea of snatching someone else's pills from the floor of the tram gone from being completely alien and unpleasant, as it is for most people, to something perfectly normal? Had things started spiralling out of control as a teenager? Had her childhood defined the rest of her life?

I gave a sudden start, as though I'd fallen asleep on the seat and someone had nudged me awake. Could that man have been Riku's father? No, he was in his thirties; Riku's father would have been older. I hoped his father was dead already, and his junkie mother too.

It would serve them right.

The tram came to a halt outside Lasipalatsi. I stepped off and began striding towards the Kamppi shopping mall. My thoughts returned to Ida.

I still didn't have a proper understanding of why she had sought out therapy in the first place. I'm not in the habit of steering my patients in any particular direction. I want them to tell me their story in their own words. But was Ida up to it?

In a stalemate like this, I would often refer my patients to a colleague who I knew was looking for clients. This is normal practice in our field. My colleagues had sent me clients too; people who they thought might respond better to my approach.

But I couldn't do that this time.

In her moment of need, Ida had turned to me specifically.

I had to take responsibility for her life.

And her death.

Arto

Clarissa bluntly ended our call, leaving me to tend to my hangover. As I wallowed in self-pity, the same thought kept popping back into my mind: I had only one reason left to live.

A few years ago, I used to enjoy watching my alcoholic friends' lives spiralling out of control. I managed to convince myself that if someone else had an even bigger alcohol problem than I did, there was nothing to worry about. In the past, Clarissa's behaviour would have been evidence enough to tell myself that I was fine. If someone like her could knock back the booze in the middle of the week and still work in a position of considerable responsibility, there was no need for me to stress about my own consumption.

These days, however, I realized I had to face facts. I was an alcoholic, and it was more than likely I would drink myself into an early grave.

I picked up the photograph album on my bedside table. It was filled with pictures I'd taken on the park bench, pictures of her standing at the window cradling her mug of tea. The shots were all a bit crooked. I couldn't take them any closer without her noticing.

It was hard to take decent photographs through the window. Her facial features were blurred. All the pictures showed was an indistinct figure, like a ghost. Besides, that's what she looked like: nothing but a gust of air, as though someone had tried to rub her out, leaving only the smudged borders visible.

I shuddered at the thought that we had once been in the same room together, and I knew such an opportunity would never come again. Now I was only able to look at her from afar. But I couldn't have kept her prisoner! After a while, I had to let her go.

Did she know I'd been following her all these years, hovering behind her like a shadow?

It was as though my presence could protect her from all evil, though the only person she needed protection from was me.

Clarissa

The following week was spent waiting. I sat in my office, but I wasn't really there. It's a wonder none of my patients pointed out that I seemed distracted. Maybe I had such a strong sense of routine that I was able to keep the show on the road though my mind was elsewhere.

My clients laid out their problems before me, but I couldn't bring myself to concentrate on them properly. My thoughts were all over the place. I tried to follow my patients' words, but it was futile.

Without wanting to blow my own trumpet, I want to say for the record that I was very good at my job.

Of course, I can't talk about my clients in a way that might reveal their identities. But I had cured dozens of anorexia patients, bulimia patients, alcoholics, neurotics. I'd helped schizophrenics and people with bipolar disorder. I'd supported women going through a divorce, people suffering from harassment in the workplace, rape victims.

And I still blame myself. I should have succeeded.

Though the task was insurmountable.

I couldn't have guessed what kind of Pandora's box I'd opened when I started confessing everything to you. Yes, a confession. That's what I want to call this.

I'd always hated patients who, in the name of honesty, confessed to their partners about being unfaithful, regaling them with all the sordid details. Where, when, who with and in which positions. To my mind, these confessions had nothing to do with remorse or honesty. The unfaithful party wanted to shift the guilt onto their partner's shoulders and wash their hands of the whole affair. The most sadistic among them even enjoyed the suffering that such confessions caused their partners and took undue satisfaction in this sudden bout of openness: I might have betrayed you, but at least I was upfront about it.

I found this attitude deeply unpleasant. Yet now I find myself behaving in exactly the same way. I'm handing all my guilt over to you, as if that will undo all my mistakes.

But don't be too concerned! Opening up hasn't eased my conscience. On the contrary, it feels like I'm tearing open barely healed wounds.

I can sense your accusatory glances, feel your scorn washing over me, though I'll never meet you. You would never get yourself tangled up in a situation like this.

Would you?

Do you remember when I took out my notebook to remind myself what happened at our first session? I shouldn't have done that. Since then, I've been reading through my notes over and over again.

I've been leafing through the dog-eared pages and scribbling questions in the margins. Once I run out of space, I cover the pages with Post-it notes and continue taking notes. I've underlined every other word. Yet every time I pick up my notebook, I desperately hope to find something new in there.

What am I looking for exactly? A key to open up this mystery, perhaps. No, I swore I would be honest. A detail, a sign, anything at all that might prove my innocence.

I fantasize that one day an extra sheet of paper might fall out of my notebook and float to the floor like autumn's last maple leaf. On that sheet of paper, there is something I'd forgotten ever writing. The missing piece that makes the puzzle look completely different.

I know, you probably feel like laughing.

Well, I feel like crying. How futile it is to search for the Truth with a capital T! Especially because I know that a record a therapist writes about a patient cannot be considered a definitive document telling the exhaustive truth about a patient's life. Quite the opposite, these records in fact represent two layers of interpretation; an interpretation of an interpretation. First the patient gives the therapist a personal account of her life. What does she want to reveal? What does she want to hide? And what doesn't she even remember? After this, the therapist presents another interpretation, and this is what we call a record. What does the therapist consider worthy of writing down? Does the therapist understand what the patient means? Does the therapist even want to understand? Or does she deliberately misunderstand? Because, as in all interpersonal relationships, the relationship between patient and therapist is primarily an emotional one. A therapist certainly doesn't always have to like her patients, though generally, she is quite adept at hiding any disapproval she might feel towards them. But all that disgust, that rage and aggression, flows into the written records unimpeded, and thus the impression of the patient that we are left with can be a very distorted one.

My duty of confidentiality will bind me to the day I die, but let me just say that there is barely a single celebutante in Finland who would have survived without my help.

You'll appreciate, my fall was dramatic. I'd got as far as anyone in my profession can in Finland. If I were in the United States, I would have had my own TV show like Dr Phil. But now: nothing.

In fact, it was my very success that sealed my fate. Show me anyone who wouldn't be proud of having the prime minister as a patient (for obvious reasons, I can't tell you which one). But I became arrogant, careless. And now here we are. *Sic transit gloria mundi.*

I know the answer, but I won't stop looking for it.

In the past, my life's purpose was to make an NHL ice-hockey star understand that his wife might need a little more than just a new kitchen. There is no purpose to my life any more.

Now I have an obsession: to get to the bottom of this matter, right down to the last detail.

I hadn't met Ida many times when I started to have an inkling of what I'd got myself mixed up in. Occasionally, I even wondered whether I was up to the task. I rejected the thought, as ludicrous as it was. Me, bitten off more than I could chew? But little by little, my doubts started to grow. What if I wasn't up to it after all? Such a thought didn't bear thinking about. The consequences would have been catastrophic. For me, for Ida, for everyone.

I tried to erase any doubt from my mind. I was overreacting.

Now, of course, we know quite how justified my fears really were.

At some point, it started to become clear that I was no longer in control of matters. I was desperately trying to extinguish fires here, there and everywhere. I should have asked for help. A short stay in hospital might have calmed the situation. I could have asked Harri for advice.

There's no question that I would have received the help I needed, but then I would have lost her for good.

I didn't want anyone to steal her from me. I clung on to her until the very last, heedless of the repercussions. Eventually, all I could do was watch as she tumbled down the slippery slope into the ravine she had dug for herself—and pulled me down with her.

Disastrous scenarios, one more dreadful than the next, were spinning through my mind. What if I never saw her again? What if she were to call me, tell me she was planning to commit suicide, then hang up before I could do anything to stop her? What if I opened *Helsinki Today* in the morning and read about her death in the obituaries section?

What if I received a letter containing her suicide note?

Ida

Of course, I was worried she might use the Beck test to have me locked up. The mere fact that I'd told her I was planning my own suicide would be enough to call the men in white coats. Having said that, funding for public health services had been cut back to the bare minimum. Maybe people didn't get put in a padded cell any more until they'd literally tried to top themselves. Besides, now I knew my therapist well enough to know she wouldn't send me to a mental facility.

I'm an excellent judge of character. When you kill people, you learn about the human condition in a unique way, far better than in even the closest relationship.

When they beg for mercy, people go through the full gamut of human emotions from horror to rage, grief and, eventually, humility. I hadn't met my therapist many times yet, but mentally I'd already created a detailed psychological profile for her.

She'd experienced a terrible loss, one that meant she carried a deep sense of guilt.

I didn't know quite what she'd lost, but it was obvious she hadn't recovered from the experience. Had she been in love with someone and then been rejected?

Or had her lover died?

The loss had torn a human-sized hole in her heart, a hole that she was trying to fill in any way she could. She was trying to compensate for her loss by gobbling up her patients. It was as though she was motivated by a narcissistic desire to signal her own virtue to the whole world. On the other hand, her overbearing motherly dedication to her patients seemed genuine enough.

I knew I could rely on the fact that she would never agree to give me up. She would be prepared to risk my life just to keep me all to herself.

That's right, she would rather I killed myself than allow anyone else to take over my treatment.

But there was one problem with this dynamic that I didn't understand until much later. How could I have been so stupid?

By not transferring me to a care facility, my therapist was guilty of serious professional malpractice. If I were ever held criminally responsible for my actions, her statement wouldn't carry any weight as there's no way she would be considered a reliable authority. Would she even be allowed to testify in court? This was such a serious dereliction of duty that she might even lose her licence.

If I'd thought of this sooner, I would have insisted that she have me sectioned.

But the thing I'm most angry about is that I would only have been left to languish in the psychiatric ward for a day or two at most. These days, the system doesn't want patients to become institutionalized; instead, they're sent home as quickly as possible.

I've mulled this over again and again and cursed my therapist to the darkest corners of hell. It was because of her naivety, her martyr complex, that everything went wrong. Her meekness and piousness make me sick. Who does she think she is? Mother fucking Teresa?

Do you want to hear a good joke?

What if she had it all planned out?

What if the real reason I missed out on the psych ward wasn't because she didn't want anyone else to treat me? What if that was part of the plan all along, and she'd been masterminding the whole thing right from the start?

Back then I didn't want to believe it, but now I have to.

Arto

Clarissa and I were sitting opposite each other in the Coffee Bean again, Marja's ghost hanging over our table. In seriousness, though, Marja's spirit had never visited me from beyond the grave. I sometimes wondered whether I would welcome her with open arms, though she was nothing but a spectre. Probably.

I was so lonely that I missed the woman I'd hated while she was alive.

I tried to forget about Marja, to leave her on the other side, as it were, and turned to Clarissa.

'What did your husband say? Can you tell me something about your marriage?'

'Pekka agreed, begrudgingly, though he told me not to make any scandalous revelations.'

Pekka's reluctance didn't surprise me.

'I've been giving the title a little thought. How does this sound: *My husband helped me kick the bottle?*'

What the hell? Clarissa was anything but sober.

I couldn't wait to hear more about her self-deception.

'Sounds intriguing! Tell me more.'

Clarissa launched into a monologue that wandered all over the place without ever getting to the point. She seemed particularly pleased with herself when talking about her own appearance and wardrobe.

'An expert would notice my recovery from my clothes. Can you imagine—I used to wear blue! It's obvious blue doesn't suit me in the least!'

There could only be one explanation for such a disjointed narrative: she was drunk again. On a weekday—in the middle of the afternoon.

'I was so blocked inside that my malaise was seeping into my clothes. Blue and denim—the very thought!'

What did any of this have to do with her drinking problem, her recovery and her husband's help?

'If we think in terms of colour analysis, I'm summer, so that means shades of pink suit me best, especially fuchsia...'

Clarissa seemed to believe in colour analysis just as unquestioningly as she did in psychoanalysis.

'I was in a very dark place at the time. I'll be honest with you, I used to drink like a fish.'

If you ask me, the present tense would have been more appropriate.

'I had an unhappy childhood, but Pekka's love was unconditional, and over time I managed to get sober.'

This interview would save my skin, if I could just put Clarissa's flow of consciousness together into a story with a beginning, a middle and an end, preferably in that order.

Irmeli would squeal with excitement when she heard I was the first reporter in the country to get Clarissa to open up about her private life in the press.

It didn't matter that the interview was bullshit from start to finish; that didn't bother me. But the investigative journalist in me didn't want to let Clarissa off the hook just yet; he wanted to watch her squirm a little longer.

'How long have you been sober?'

'Over twenty years now, the whole time I've been married.'

'So, what was all that about last time we met? I wouldn't call that very sober.'

Clarissa's face was always covered in a thick layer of slap, but despite her foundation you could tell she was blushing.

'Arto, you of all people should know that being sober is like a dance: two steps forwards, one step back. There's no point crying over little setbacks like that!'

If only I could think of my own failures with as much levity, instead of punishing myself even years later.

I imagined myself sitting in my regular spot on the park bench. I saw her standing by the window and looking me in the eyes. Her eyes were burning with accusations.

I deserved that gaze, that contempt.

I was guilty of everything for which she demanded I atone.

Clarissa

I'm going to kill myself. It's inevitable. You can't do anything to stop me. I'd been having another nightmare about Ida committing suicide. This time, she'd shot herself. I'd tried to wrench the pistol from her hand. She and I ended up wrestling on the office floor. As I managed to prise the weapon from her right hand, she grabbed it with her left. I had just enough time to glance at the gun before Ida pressed the barrel against her temple and pulled the trigger.

Her eyes stared at me, wide open, as her body began to cool.

I'd woken up in a cold sweat. The shot was still ringing in my ears as I sat down at the kitchen table and reluctantly tried to swallow my morning porridge. The dream had taken away my appetite.

I was plagued by the suspicion that Ida didn't trust me enough for us to get the hard work of therapy properly underway. For this reason, I was keen to know how honestly she had answered the questions in the Beck inventory.

And above all: if she was lying, was she trying to fool me or herself?

Before the test, I'd managed to convince myself that my mind was prone to catastrophizing about Ida's theoretical suicide. After seeing the test results, I had to face the truth. I knew she could commit suicide at any moment.

It was down to me now. I had to act fast.

Every conversation we had might be our last.

After my morning routine, I went to the office to await Ida's arrival. She was my first client of the day.

The doorbell rang, and I walked to the door to open it. We filed back to the office.

'How have you been?' I asked, but immediately regretted it. We both knew Ida's well-being was at rock bottom.

She didn't respond, she just furrowed her brow as though she hadn't understood the question and didn't care to comprehend it properly. I noticed she kept looking up at the window.

I decided to forget the small talk and get straight down to business.

'You've decided to commit suicide,' I said, my voice gravely serious, and waited to see her reaction. My question made her look away from the window—the heavy snowfall lashing against the outside of the windowpane, the birch branches bent in the wind—and turn to face me.

'Yes. I've always known I would die by my own hand. I don't have the energy to live long enough to die of natural causes.'

She told me she'd been planning her own suicide for years. I was sure she must have attempted it, perhaps even a few times. Statistics suggest that failed suicide attempts outnumber successful ones by ten to one.

Exhaustion engulfed my mind. Yet another suicide to prevent.

Why hadn't I trained to be a florist or a pastry chef? In their line of work, they see nothing but beauty, flowers and cakes; I see only black.

I noticed that I too was staring up at the window. I watched the individual snowflakes, melting as they landed, turning to water and trickling down the windowpane. I forced myself to look at Ida and continued interrogating her.

'Have you ever tried to kill yourself?'

Ida scoffed as though I'd asked the bleeding obvious. She started scanning around for something else to stare at.

'Three times. Next time I'll do it right, that's for sure,' she replied. Her voice didn't convey any emotion as such; it sounded hollow, abandoned. She might as well have been reciting a shopping list.

The thought came to me with such force that I almost said it out loud: I can't take this any more. But I must carry on.

'Do you have a plan? How are you going to do it?'

My question sounded bleak, but it was extremely important that I ask it. Of course, it's always serious if someone has destructive impulses like this. But if a patient has already drawn up a plan of how she intends to kill herself, this could be the last opportunity to save her.

And who else would save Ida if not me?

What if I couldn't cope with it any more?

Ida responded right away. Yes, she had a plan. She told me she'd tried to kill herself a different way each time. This time, she had another method in mind. She proceeded to give me a very detailed account of her plan. In fact, she seemed thrilled at being able to tell someone about it.

I won't divulge the details here. Suicidal ideation is a social contagion. Whenever the media reports on a suicide and reveals the manner in which the victim died, a whole group of people decide to kill themselves in exactly the same way.

I was in a hell of a hurry.

I had to save her life.

I. Cannot. Cope. Any. More.

My only option was to try to play for time until I could decide what to do. I would have to improvise. I came up with a wild idea. God help me if my colleagues ever found out about it!

'You came to see me because you wanted help. If you kill yourself, I can't help you. And we can't solve your problems after only a handful of sessions. Shall we agree that you won't kill yourself for the next six months? If I haven't been able to help you by then, our agreement will lapse. Meanwhile, I will do everything I can to help you get better.'

Ida seemed so subsumed in her own world that I wondered whether she'd heard me at all. I was about to repeat my suggestion when she looked up at me and whispered, her voice barely audible:

'Deal.'

I had six months.

The sense of relief was indescribable.

Ida

I'd got her. She was stuck with me for the next six months.

I'd been googling more information about my Get Out of Jail Free card. If I'd understood right, six months would be a long enough course of treatment for my therapist to draw up a professional statement about my mental state that would stand up in court. This time I didn't need to fake a smile when we shook hands on her agreement.

Despite my jubilation, there was one thing I was still unclear about. My therapist seemed a little jittery. As if my fate had really touched her. As if she really did care about what happened to me, about whether I lived or died. People with mental-health conditions die every day. She couldn't cry a river for all of us!

Still, her concern moved me. Was this what it felt like when someone genuinely cared about you? I felt a warmth inside but quickly pushed the sensation away.

You must trust nobody. Nobody at all.

I'd never told my parents about the cage or the Bastard because they were always so distant. As if at any moment they could have floated away and left me high and dry.

Sometimes they chivvied me out into the common garden to play, but then they never called me in again, as though they hoped that one day they would shoo me away so effectively that I'd never return.

My parents never showed me any physical affection either, if we don't count the occasional quick hug. Even this they did sparingly, as if simply to fulfil their parental duties. The only regular display of affection that I remember from my childhood was my father's habit of patting me on the head, then carefully wiping his hand on his trousers as though he'd just stroked a wet dog.

I didn't want to reminisce about my childhood, so I thought about my therapist's voice instead. It was exaggeratedly calm, almost forcibly controlled.

'Can we make an agreement in writing too?' she asked, leaning eagerly towards her pen and paper.

If there was any truth in the old adage that the messier the desk the more confused the mind, then there was nothing at all going on in my therapist's mind. There was never anything on her desk except a notebook, a ballpoint pen and a pencil. By 'agreement', she presumably meant some kind of official document, and she snatched up her ballpoint pen.

She spent a moment carefully drafting the text, then handed it to me. It was only as I read her draft that I fully appreciated how well this agreement would serve my purposes. My therapist wouldn't be able to wriggle out of it at the first sign of trouble. If she tried to break off my treatment, I could appeal to the document she had drawn up. I assumed even therapists must be overseen by some kind of official body that I could use to threaten her if need be. I remembered reading that complaints about therapists can be addressed to the national watchdog. I'd have to double-check the matter.

'At our next session, I want you to write a suicide note.'

A suicide note? What the hell...? Had she lost her mind?

I was about to ask what on earth she meant when the next patient rang the doorbell. We'd spent the whole session drawing up our agreement, and the time had flown by.

'I hope you'll stick to our agreement,' she said to round off the session. I was tickled at the thought that she didn't have the slightest idea what kind of document she'd just put her name to.

She was caught in the snare.

It was up to me whether to let her go or not.

Of course, you already know I had no reason to celebrate.

Clarissa

I stood at my office window, waiting for Ida to take off her slippers, put on her shoes and coat and step out of the front door.

It was still snowing.

Our neighbours' dog Rekku had managed to escape from their garden again and was relieving himself against our redcurrant bushes. I shook my head disapprovingly.

Ida finally came into view. We had only met a handful of times, but now I felt as though I knew her better. She walked with her shoulders hunched, her whole posture dejected. Had I promised her too much? Would I be able to take her apart and put her together again so that the pieces all went back in the right places?

She didn't have a raincoat or an umbrella. She tugged up her hood and her head disappeared, like a tortoise retreating into the safety of its shell. Then she turned and walked off towards the bus stop. Suddenly, Rekku bolted after her, his tail wagging behind him. The dog startled Ida, and she ran a few steps. Rekku stretched out his muzzle towards her, lost interest and returned to our currant bushes.

I turned and continued watching her. She was standing at the bus stop, shaking the snow from her coat. She looked anxious.

One of the professional hazards of being a therapist is the feeling of omnipotence. We think we can succeed at even the most impossible tasks. We save patients, we heal them, whatever their problems.

Giving up is never an option. Even with my most complex patients, I'd always gone the extra mile. Treating people who have already tried to kill themselves is the most challenging of all. Some will try again—and again and again, until they succeed. This had happened to a number of my patients too.

How do you get over a thing like that? All you can do is try to kid yourself. You have to make yourself believe that you are in no way responsible for their death.

An admission of guilt would have meant I might as well quit my profession. If it can happen once, it can happen again.

It had happened to me three times. And still I carried on, lying to myself all the while. Here are a few examples of the kinds of arguments I used to fool myself.

You must understand, I'm not alone. All therapists have their own suicide cases. It's unavoidable. Our patients are mentally ill or, at the very least, they're going through some kind of crisis. What was the alternative? That they didn't get any help at all and killed themselves even sooner?

Don't the lives of the dozens of people I have saved over the years weigh more than those three deaths?

Besides, none of the relatives of my suicide patients has ever blamed me for what happened. Two of them even asked me to attend the funeral.

This wasn't my fault. I could carry on taking responsibility for people's lives.

Naturally, I didn't say any of this to the grieving families. I didn't give them any recourse to doubt me or blame me for anything. I made it clear to them that the deceased would have reached this decision sooner or later. Nobody could have prevented it.

For a therapist, a patient's suicide is a catastrophic failure. Nobody talks about it, but it's an experience we all share in this profession.

Sometimes, when our group of colleagues got together, we would have one glass of wine too many. At times like this, the dead would sit at the table with us. Just imagine all the explanations! *Her father was a real monster. His wife's behaviour emasculated him. She wouldn't take her medication. He had no motivation to get better.*

We therapists weren't responsible for anything. So why did we bear such a terrible sense of guilt?

Then along came Ida. This was my chance to make amends for everything that had happened. I was afraid she might follow in the footsteps of those three dead patients. The very thought caused me constant anguish. I was only at peace when Ida was sitting safely on the couch opposite me and I could keep an eye on her throughout our session. At all other times, I lived in fear. I wondered what she was up to whenever she wasn't with me.

Perhaps she was already dead…

Nights were worse than days. Nightmares came one after the other.

I came home from work and switched on the lights. She was dangling from a noose attached to the ceiling.

I went into the bathroom, and she was lying in the bathtub, her wrists slit open.

I found her in the bedroom, cold, an empty bottle of pills on the floor beside her.

I stood on the platform of the underground station while the police lifted her battered body from the tracks and placed her in my arms. My legs buckled, I dropped to my knees, and my screams echoed along the stone tunnels.

Pekka

The next time I had the occasion to pull the sketches from under Clarissa's couch, I was in for a surprise. This time there were more of them.

I sat down on the couch and started looking through them in bewilderment. I asked myself two questions: what were these drawings about and why had a patient brought them to Clarissa?

I felt the same as I sometimes did in the mornings, when I tried to remember the dreams I'd just had. It was as though the dream was just out of reach, I could almost touch it with my fingertips but never quite grab hold of it.

Again I had an unpleasant sensation, as though someone was drawing their nails along the pit of my stomach.

There was something familiar about the drawings, but I couldn't for the life of me make out what. I was so frustrated that I almost felt compelled to throw the papers into the living-room fireplace and set the whole pile ablaze.

What the hell did I have to do with these sketches?

I had already examined two of them the first time. I decided to look at them again. The first one was a true example of modern art. All I could see were smudges, streaks of charcoal that didn't create any tangible forms or shapes, lines that had no meaning at all. A scrawl from start to finish. The second drawing showed the cruel man in the suit; again, his sadistic smile made me flinch. He looked familiar. But why?

Where had I seen him before?

All of a sudden, I had the terrible sense that someone was watching me.

Before taking out the drawings, I had again pulled the curtains across the office windows. I took two long steps towards the window and opened the curtains.

Outside it was already dark. The garden was shrouded in shadows.

A figure scuttled across the lawn.

A squirrel turned, then frantically began climbing up the trunk of a pine tree, all the way to the top.

I scoffed at my own paranoia and returned to the drawings.

Next in line were the drawings that had appeared under the couch since the last time I looked and which I now saw for the first time. These new works used the same motifs as before. If I understood them right, they appeared to show some kind of cellar. The space was empty, save for a small bathtub and a metal cage in the middle of the room.

The cage was empty. Assuming the drawings were to scale, the cage was so small that there was only room inside it for a small animal, a dog perhaps. It would have been too small to transport cattle. On second thoughts, even keeping a dog in there would have been against animal cruelty laws.

Two pink silken ribbons had been placed along the side of the bathtub, the kind that mothers use to tie little girls' hair in plaits.

Ida

Uolevi Mäkisarja's family were just beginning to recover from the death of their loved one by the time I saw off my next victim.

The disappearance of Ripa Raasteenlahti made the headlines that day. The gaming company Game Off had just announced the release of their first ever game designed specifically for women, so the name of the company's CEO was on everybody's lips.

Raasteenlahti stared sassily at me from a newspaper stand at my local corner shop, but in his last moments he'd whimpered like a baby.

'CEO Ripa Raasteenlahti has disappeared' ran the headline in one of the tabloids.

Disappeared. Not murdered. That meant nobody was hunting for his murderer.

Yet.

My fingers instinctively crept up to my neck. I brushed the slender golden chain hanging under my shirt. A simple chain without a pendant.

The clasp was so small that I'd had to use all the dexterity in my fingers to open it and remove the chain from Raasteenlahti's sweaty, deceased neck.

I bought a packet of cigarettes at the shop and hurried home. I was afraid Raasteenlahti might start shouting out from the head-lines that it was me who had killed him. I tried to forget about him and turned my thoughts to my therapist's other patients instead.

What would it feel like to tell my therapist about my problems, honestly, without hiding anything? To take comfort in her empathy? To believe that my life really could change, that my problems were only temporary, that life wasn't just a deep well, its walls so slimy and covered in moss that it was useless trying to clamber out of it?

Envy gripped me so profoundly that it felt physically painful.

I'd realized a long time ago that comparing myself to other people was pointless. It was like comparing broken shards of porcelain to a pristine china cup. But sometimes everything felt so damn unfair. Other people were moving on, but my life had come to an end when I was ten years old. What metaphor would be suitable for that? Was I just a shadow? No, I couldn't find the words to describe the emptiness I felt inside.

In a way, I'd already accepted the matter. That's just the way it was. But sometimes everything felt completely insurmountable. That, and the fact that I couldn't do anything about it. Nobody had ever asked me whether I wanted to be locked in a cage.

Why did it have to happen to me? Can fate really be that sadistic?

Then I started second-guessing myself, though deep down I knew it would only make me feel worse.

How far back would I have to rewind my life until it wasn't too late? What if I hadn't gone to the fairground that day? What if I'd had a cold and spent the whole day in bed? What if my parents had known I'd gone there alone and not with my friend Ella, like I'd told them? Would they have forbidden me from going? And what if the Bastard had offered me some other sweets at the fairground gates instead of my favourite liquorice candy, Turkish peppers? Would I have been able to resist the temptation?

Then there was the most awful question of all: what if the Bastard had chosen someone else, another victim?

I'd have been able to live a normal life. The Bastard would have destroyed some other poor kid's innocence.

And I would never have heard anything about it.

HELSINKI TODAY

COMPANY CEO DISAPPEARS IN HELSINKI

Ripa Raasteenlahti, CEO of the gaming company Game Off, disappeared from his home in Hakaniemi, Helsinki, on Sunday morning. Raasteenlahti was reported missing by his daughter. The last confirmed sighting of him was on Saturday evening.

42-year-old Raasteenlahti is 5'10" tall and heavy-set. He has green eyes, naturally curly blonde hair and a beard. At the time of his last sighting, he was wearing a brown suit and a black tie.

Members of the public are encouraged to report any sightings of Raasteenlahti to the Helsinki Police by phone or email.

Pekka

When did innocent curiosity turn to a corrosive, all-consuming obsession? When did I lose control? When did I become a slave to my own obsessions? Certainly, one could say, by the time I felt the need to dash into Clarissa's office to examine the drawings every time she left the house.

And as if the drawings didn't present me with enough of a mystery, I found myself pondering the nature of the therapeutic relationship between Clarissa and the Princess. Their sessions had been going on for some time now, but the Princess's charm still didn't appear to have worn off. Things had never escalated this much with any of the previous princesses. Clarissa was drifting further and further away from me.

During the daytime she avoided me as best she could. Her office door was always closed, except when she was out or away somewhere on business. Sometimes I felt as though I saw more of her patients than I did of her.

Clarissa spent her nights on the couch in her office too. My company was no longer good enough for her.

Of course, I was offended, but I decided to keep it to myself. My pride wouldn't allow me to let her know quite how much it hurt me to be left out in the cold like this.

I decided to behave as if nothing had happened. My tactic was to grind the enemy down, as it were. If I didn't say or do anything,

I thought, things would get better of their own accord. Clarissa was a grown woman, responsible for her own actions.

I couldn't protect her from herself.

Later on, I realized she had no intention of protecting our relationship. The Princess was more important to her than our marriage.

Clarissa

A solitary candle flickered at the graveside. The tea light had been placed on the headstone beside a small plastic angel. The angel was leaning on its left elbow, just like the one in Raphael's painting. Someone had removed the foil wrapping from around the candle. Wax had dribbled down the headstone and stained the white, moss-covered marble. The heat from the candle had melted half of the angel's face. Its expression was set in a grotesque smirk.

The previous night, it had snowed. The ribbons around the wreaths were so wet from the snowfall that the ink had smudged, and it was hard to decipher the words of their messages.

I picked up one of the ribbons and tried to make out the poem written on it. 'There is only longing, only yearning.' I let go of the ribbon and it fell back to the grave, as lifeless as the body buried underground.

Neither of us recognized the name of the deceased.

I turned and stepped back to the path through the cemetery, trying to avoid the muddy puddles. The heel of my suede boot slipped into the mud, making me stagger. These Guccis weren't exactly the most practical shoes ever made. I almost fell over. Harri grabbed me just in time and helped me over the puddle like a true gentleman.

'It's the next one,' he said, took a paper tissue out of his pocket and pointed to the next headstone, though I knew perfectly well where the grave was. Over the years, we had visited it together countless times.

Kaarina.

Harri's first suicide.

It had all happened at the beginning of Harri's career. A 36-year-old woman whose mood swings ranged from euphoric mania to the depths of despair.

These days, Kaarina's diagnosis would have been blindingly obvious: bipolar disorder, or what we used to call manic depression. The symptoms always follow the same pattern: first the patient is manic, on overdrive. Some shop so frantically that they lose their credit rating, while others drink so much alcohol that they almost kill themselves.

In Kaarina's case, the condition manifested itself in heightened and reckless sexual behaviour. During her manic phases, she forgot all about her husband and had sex with a string of random acquaintances.

The manic phases were always followed by bouts of depression. Kaarina regretted her behaviour and felt a profound sense of guilt. Her husband was always prepared to forgive her, but Kaarina couldn't forgive herself.

Bipolar disorder can be managed with the right medication. The most common drug prescribed is Priadel. Its active ingredient is lithium, which helps to level out the extremities of the patient's mood swings. The euphoria doesn't escalate to full mania, and the downers that follow aren't quite as devastating. If they stick to their medication, most patients can live a perfectly normal life.

But in the 1970s, Harri was at a loss.

And this was the result.

We stopped at Kaarina's grave. It was bare, no candles, no flowers, no shrubs. Everyone had forgotten about Kaarina, everyone except Harri. He would never forget her.

Harri took a bright red rose from his bunch of flowers, crouched down and placed it on the grave.

We knew Malmi cemetery like the backs of our hands. Every year at Christmas and All Saints' Day, we visited the graves of our suicide patients. I'd asked Harri to visit them with me again, though it was only a few months since Christmas.

My mind had been consumed with morbid thoughts, and I thought a walk round the cemetery might bring me some peace.

We left Kaarina behind and made our way towards Pirjo's grave.

Pirjo was the second of my patients to commit suicide.

With hindsight, I'd come up with a posthumous diagnosis for my two other suicide cases, but Pirjo was still a mystery to me.

I thought I would never understand what had happened to her.

I took a white rose from Harri's bouquet and placed it on Pirjo's grave. Ten years had passed since her death. I stood at her grave for a moment of reflection, as if waiting for Pirjo to whisper her final secret to me.

But she remained silent.

We walked on. I noticed that Harri was limping on his right leg again. He had been suffering from hip pain for a while now. He was on a waiting list for a hip operation, but he'd stoically agreed to accompany me on this walk all the same.

We walked along the moss-covered pathway to my final grave.

I thought about Riku's suicide every day. He was only 15 years old when he died.

Someone had left some heather planted in an ugly red-plastic flowerpot at his grave. I've always hated the artificiality of blue flowers on heather bushes. You can tell just by looking at them that they're actually white and have been dyed blue. At the graveside, the flowers looked all the more tasteless.

I felt the urge to throw the flowerpot in the bin but thought I'd better not do it in front of Harri.

Instead, I selected a long-stemmed calla lily from the bouquet and placed it next to the heather.

After a minute's silence, we continued on our way.

Ann-Marie was Harri's last suicide.

'I'll never get over her death,' he said, placing a white rose on the grave.

For the last five years, Harri had been beating himself up for retiring and not seeing Ann-Marie's treatment through to its conclusion. In my opinion, he had overseen her treatment very professionally. He had arranged for her to become a patient of his distinguished colleague Leo Maastola.

It turned out that Ann-Marie only visited Leo once before giving up altogether. Harri received news of Ann-Marie's suicide halfway through his retirement party. I'll never forget the moment when the doctor called Harri from the hospital to break the terrible news. His face went pale, and he had to steady himself against the wall just to remain on his feet. A suicide note addressed to Harri had been found in Ann-Marie's pocket. She had no friends or relatives.

After her death, Harri had had to undertake a course of trauma therapy himself. At the funeral, there was an open casket, allowing the attendees to see her face one last time. Harri couldn't cope with what he saw. The sight plagued him long thereafter. Eventually, every woman who walked past him in the street looked like Ann-Marie.

I tried to encourage him to get help, but at first he refused, saying that because of his professional background he ought to be able to cope by himself and that it would be ridiculous to seek help.

He only agreed to see a professional when one day he opened his chest freezer at home and saw Ann-Marie's naked body inside, covered in a thin layer of frost.

We were still standing at her grave. Seeing Harri this helpless always left me feeling distressed. I was always the one who turned to him in a crisis, and I didn't want our roles to switch all of a sudden. In public, I was supposed to be strong. The only people who were allowed to see the other side of me were Pekka and Harri.

I was still perplexed by the blue heather. How could anyone close to Riku have such bad taste as to leave such ugly flowers at his grave?

I was incensed. And I knew why. If there was one thing I'd learnt as a therapist, it was to analyse not only other people's emotions but my own too. To the point of absurdity.

I would rather subliminally rant and rave at Riku's family than at myself.

Why hadn't I been able to save Riku?

Harri winced with pain again and gripped his right hip. Knowing him as I did, I was sure he would walk right round the cemetery, even if it was the last thing he did, so I decided to put him out of his misery and pretended I was the one with the problem.

'Harri, would you mind awfully if we called it a day? I've got a terrible migraine coming on.'

He seemed relieved. 'Of course not. Let's go.'

We walked towards the car park next to the small chapel, where we usually parked. We hugged each other goodbye and got into our respective cars. Harri started the engine and drove off.

I waited until he was out of sight, then got out of my car and walked briskly back to the cemetery gates. Harri probably had no idea that I was in the habit of coming back to the cemetery as soon as our walks ended.

I needed to speak to the dead by myself.

Pekka

Dreams had never meant anything to me. When I woke up, I didn't try to remember what kind of dream I'd been having. In fact, I hardly remembered dreaming at all.

This was one of the many paradoxes of our marriage. Clarissa greatly enjoyed analysing her patients' dreams. It was risible! The idea that dreams tell us something about the person having them. And as for Freud's dream symbolism. A candle represented a phallus. Christ! The hallucinations of a coke addict, nothing more. You'd think my wife already had her work cut out analysing the things people did while they were awake.

I was always worried that Clarissa would start asking me about my dreams. What kind of dreams did I have and what did I think they meant?

The very thought irritated me, because I believe that spouses don't need to know everything there is to know about each other.

There were sides to my personality that I would never reveal to Clarissa.

That was the secret of our long marriage.

To me, dreams were too personal to share with others. I would have been embarrassed to tell my wife about my nightmares. At the start of our relationship, I thought I'd better lie and tell her I simply didn't have any dreams. Then I remembered hearing somewhere that only psychopaths don't have dreams. So, in preparation for

Clarissa's questions, I invented a dream that would give as normal an impression of me as it was possible to give. I can't remember what my made-up dream was about, but I think it had something to do with sex. In actual fact, I don't think I've ever dreamt about sex, not even as a teenager.

After we got married, I no longer saw the point in coming up with dreams that might be to Clarissa's liking, though I still didn't want to tell her about my real dreams.

Luckily, she never asked.

Maybe she didn't have the guts. Without any warning, I might have recounted the kind of dream that would reveal to an experienced professional like her that her beloved husband was a raving lunatic.

I wasn't in the habit of paying my dreams the least attention. Even the most gruesome nightmares faded from my mind as I was going about my morning routine, shaving and brushing my teeth. So it felt all the stranger when the drawings started appearing in my dreams.

Or rather, my dreams felt so real that they started to seem like hallucinations.

I had the same dream night after night, only the details changed. I was standing in a mouldy cellar next to the now familiar man in the suit. His face was covered in soot, as though it too had been sketched in charcoal. The man never said anything but behaved as though I didn't exist.

When I woke in the morning, the nightmare still hung around me. And just when I thought I had shaken it from my mind, it flooded back into my subconscious.

Sometimes I was doing a mundane chore, vacuuming or washing the dishes, when the stale smell of the cellar suddenly wafted into the room. Sometimes it felt as though the ceiling in the room had lowered and was now as low as that in the cellar, and I instinctively hunched my shoulders to protect my head.

I was suffering from delusions.

That's right, my symptoms were psychotic.

I sensed things that weren't there.

And yet, while I was experiencing them my delusions seemed real, though I wished they weren't.

At some point, I even wondered whether I should ask Clarissa for help. But as I'm sure you can imagine, there was no way I could tell her about my dreams. If I did, I would reveal that I'd been snooping around her office and had discovered the drawings.

These nightmares soon plagued me every night. One night, the images were so gruesome that they woke me up. I'd been dreaming that I was standing in the cellar next to the man in the suit. I wasn't an adult yet; I was a little boy, my ten-year-old self. Suddenly, the man in the suit noticed me for the first time. He walked out from the corner of the room and stood in front of me, looking me right in the eyes. Then he leant down, picked up a shard of mirrored glass the shape of a knife from the cellar floor and thrust it into my chest, right into my heart.

I sat up on the edge of the bed and pressed my left hand against my heart. It was beating frantically, as though it were sending a distress signal in Morse code. I was consumed by an inexplicable sense that something terrible was going to happen.

I berated myself for having such a ludicrous idea and tried to forget about it, but I still felt restless. I couldn't get the man in the suit and his cruel smirk from my mind. I almost felt the urge to look under the bed and check he hadn't followed me from the dream world into the real world, that he wasn't lurking just out of sight.

I pushed this silly notion aside but didn't yet dare lie down in bed and try to fall asleep again.

I decided to have a beer and then go back to bed. Half-asleep, I shuffled into the kitchen and switched on the lights. I opened the fridge and took out a bottle. I knocked it back so quickly that it gave me hiccups.

I still felt restless. The beer had done nothing to relax me. I decided to go into the garden for some fresh air. I stepped out into the mild winter's night. I wasn't alone on the patio: Her Highness was sitting in a dark corner. She cast a long shadow across the patio, more like a lion than a cat.

I noticed that Her Highness was playing with something. She saw me, then proudly brought me her prey. She dropped the shrew at my feet, a gash running the length of its stomach, leaving its guts hanging out. I kicked the corpse from the patio onto the lawn, leaving a thin trail of blood across the white-painted floor.

Her Highness slunk away from me, before my next kick could strike her.

I sat down on the step to wait for my hiccups to pass. The silence and tranquillity of the night finally calmed me down.

When I turned, the shock made me drop the house keys. They slipped through the gap between the planks and fell under the patio, where I kept the lawnmower and other gardening tools. I had to grab the edge of the door for support, as my legs trembled wildly with fear.

A carefully drawn piece of graffiti had appeared on our front door. It showed the man in the suit.

I stared at the image in shock. Who had painted it there? When? And why?

I froze on the spot and stood staring at the image.

I don't know how long I stood there. I tried to come up with a rational explanation for the picture, but it was impossible. It felt as though my whole life was collapsing around me and all I could do was watch helplessly.

Suddenly, my fear turned to anger. I would find out who had done that graffiti! Rage bubbled within me, uncontrollably, and I instinctively clenched both my hands. Except I couldn't, as in one hand, I was holding a can of spray paint.

I had painted the image on our door myself.

I had no recollection of it whatsoever.

Clarissa

I'd already walked back into Malmi cemetery when I decided to try and communicate with Riku in another way. Riku had killed himself two months earlier by jumping in front of the metro at the Central Railway Station. I hadn't been able to go there since it happened.

I don't know where I suddenly got the impulse to visit the site of the tragedy. Maybe it was high time I confronted the ghosts of the past.

By a miracle, I managed to find an empty parking space in the station car park. I parked my car and began walking towards the station's main entrance.

Was this such a good idea after all?

I decided to steel my nerves and go through with it. Maybe I would finally be able to put my distressing emotions behind me if I could face them head-on.

I walked to the station door and stopped, hesitating. But I wasn't allowed the opportunity to back out, as a young boy on a skateboard politely opened the door for me, lost his balance, wobbled, then grabbed onto my backside so as not to fall over, fell over anyway and in doing so, accidentally shoved me into the station's entrance hall. I decided to think of our comical encounter as a good omen.

There was no backing out now, and I walked towards the escalators leading down to the underground station.

The station was thronging with people. All I could see were the children.

A little girl with blonde hair, maybe five or six years old, cute as a button, staring fixedly at her mobile phone. Her shrill giggles brought a smile to my face.

A bald baby, screaming at the top of its lungs, the poor mother desperately trying to calm it down by sticking a dummy in its mouth.

A teenage girl wearing an undersized top and a pair of tight jeans and sucking on a red lollipop, her smiling eyes framed by a pair of red heart-shaped sunglasses. She saw me looking at her and winked at me. I was taken aback and looked away in a fluster.

Not having children of my own is my life's greatest tragedy. I wanted to have kids, but it wasn't possible. That sorrow never went away. How can we miss something we've never had? And yet, from time to time I think how much luckier I am than people with children.

I'll never have to worry about my own children.

I appreciate why my colleagues are so overly protective towards their own offspring. If you spend all day treating victims of paedophilia, before long you won't allow your child out to play with the kids next door. If you spend more time dealing with the abnormal than the normal, eventually the abnormal *becomes* normal. My children wouldn't have been able to live their lives properly, because I would have tried to protect them from all possible dangers—both real and imaginary.

I felt bitterness clenching around my throat, and for a moment I could hardly breathe. Why hadn't I been blessed with children? I would have been the perfect mother.

Just then, a thought pushed its way into my mind, a thought I'd been trying to suppress ever since Riku's death.

Riku's parents killed him.

They were incapable of parenting.

If I had been his mother, I would have been able to save him.

I stepped onto the escalator and instantly felt dizzy. I remembered the last time I'd stood on it, I'd felt so faint I had to sit down and the ingrained dirt on the step had stained the hem of my Escada trench coat. That time I'd been coming in the opposite direction, up out of underground and back into the entrance hall.

As the escalator jolted downwards, I tried to concentrate on the posters on the wall opposite. Happy, beautiful people smiled at me from the posters, people who never had any problems. All that mattered to them was drinking their chaga mushroom tea, eating protein bars or being able to take out a payday loan that would keep them in debt for the rest of their lives.

They weren't on their way to the site of their beloved son's death. Like me.

No, I had to remind myself. It wasn't my son who had died; it was my patient.

I remember reading somewhere that the underground stop at the Central Railway Station is the busiest in Helsinki with around 53,000 passengers passing through it each day. I almost felt like calling the National Office of Statistics and asking whether there was any record of how many of those 53,000 daily passengers had committed suicide at the station.

People impatiently tried to shove their way past me on the escalator. Some ran down to the platform and wouldn't have cared if they'd knocked me over on the way. I stood until I reached the platform, though my legs were quivering.

Finally, I reached the bottom. I hadn't noticed I'd been gripping the railing on my right-hand side. My knuckles were white, and I saw to my annoyance that the pink artificial nail on my thumb had almost come loose. I carefully tried to remove the nail and put it somewhere safe, but it fell down into the gap between the escalator and the railing.

Perhaps this misfortune was the omen, and not the fact that a skateboarder had bundled me through the station doors. Maybe I shouldn't have come here after all. Couldn't I just let sleeping dogs lie? The problem was, Riku's death would not leave me in peace.

I stepped onto the platform, my legs still trembling. Standing on the escalator, I hadn't paid any attention to the other people around me. Now my eyes were drawn to a tall teenage boy.

I gasped in shock.

He was the spitting image of Riku.

The boy had a blue Mohican, combed back behind his right ear. Dangling from the ear was an earring shaped like a skull. His face was covered in gaudy make-up: bright pink lipstick and black eyeliner like a little girl who had secretly opened her mother's make-up bag. I guessed he must be around the same age Riku was when he died.

The boy saw me staring at him; he turned and kicked an empty drink carton that a child had left on the platform. Juice splashed over his pink combat boots. He left the carton where it was and walked to the other end of the platform, as far away from me as possible.

I forced myself to look at the tracks and to leave the boy alone.

This wasn't Riku. Riku was dead.

The train appeared out of the tunnel and stopped in front of me. A crush of passengers pushed their way out onto the platform. The boy who looked like Riku was joined by a girl of the same age. She knocked into me as she walked past. I staggered and almost stumbled against the carriage. If the train hadn't stopped at the station, I could have fallen onto the tracks.

Riku.

My son.

No, he was not my son.

When Riku had died, the police had difficulty tracking down his parents to tell them what had happened. Presumably they were at home shooting up and hadn't answered the phone.

I would never be able to face his parents.

I wouldn't have been able to hold back my rage. I would have blamed them for Riku's death.

Arto

I'd been typing up a new version of Clarissa's interview until the early hours. Eventually it was ready, and I sent it to Irmeli first thing in the morning. Soon afterwards, my phone rang.

'Arto, you're a genius! What kind of truth serum did you give her?'

I smiled to myself contentedly. The interview was damn good, even if I did say so myself.

'I've got an idea. Why don't you ask Clarissa to show the readers the contents of her wardrobe? We could add a couple of pages after the main interview under the title *A Psychoanalyst's Colour Analysis.*'

'I'll call her right away and see if she's up for it.'

Clarissa seemed only too aware of her own powers of attraction, and it wouldn't have surprised me if she'd agreed to model the clothes herself. The proverb that beauty sabotaged common sense didn't apply to her. When I married Marja, I'd imagined I was specifically marrying beauty. How bitterly wrong I was!

I was keen to get the interview finished so I could put Clarissa behind me.

The more I'd got to know her, the greater the dislike I felt towards her. It was hard to imagine how she could ever resolve her patients' problems—she hadn't even been able to get her own drinking under control.

But to be honest, there were other reasons why I'd found Clarissa's company so repellent. When she lectured me about the link between sexual abuse and eating disorders, I found it so distressing that my brow broke out in beads of sweat. I squirmed in my chair, wondering how I might subtly change the subject. I'd been trying not to listen to her and to focus instead on the conversation of the women drinking coffee at the next table.

I was afraid Clarissa could read my expressions and gestures, that she could tell what I was thinking. She would have shuddered with disgust if she'd discovered the truth about me.

My muscles had been so tensed with guilt that it wasn't long before a migraine informed me of its imminent arrival.

Clarissa

I suppose you're wondering why I asked Ida to write a suicide note. There's a perfectly rational explanation for it. I'd devised a method that I thought would help save the lives of patients who were contemplating suicide.

I admit this method is a bit unconventional, but it works. I'd been using it for years, and the results spoke for themselves.

The method works like this: the patient writes a suicide note during one of our sessions, then reads it aloud. After this, the patient burns the note in a tin bucket, which the therapist keeps in the office for this very purpose. Then they discuss the patient's feelings about writing, reading and burning the note.

I wasn't able to create laboratory conditions that would allow the patient to actually attempt suicide but still survive. Using this method, however, the patient was provided with a safe space in which to experience what it felt like to go through one of the central phases of committing suicide: writing a note.

My idea is that if patients write as authentic a note as possible, they can experience the same emotions as if they were writing one for real. Writing the note is cathartic. And if the patient has the opportunity to process the emotions aroused by writing the note with the therapist, the impact is all the more liberating.

The final touch—destroying the note by fire—might sound a little theatrical. But there is a very powerful symbolism associated with the act of immolation: it isn't just the note that is incinerated but the patient's suicidal feelings too.

The next time Ida arrived at my office, I was waiting for her with paper and pen.

'Do you remember what we were supposed to do today?'

Ida nodded impatiently.

She folded her coat and placed it on the couch, sat down and took the pen and notebook from my hand.

'I want you to write a suicide note. Let's start by thinking who you want to address this to. Take your time. Who might it be? Your parents?'

'I wouldn't exactly address it to you, would I?'

Ida had made up her mind. I encouraged her to make the note as authentic as possible.

'It should feel genuine, as real as it can possibly be. Write down everything you want to say in your suicide note. Don't hold back or try to sugar-coat things. Be as honest as you can. Real thoughts, real emotions. The more honest your approach, the more this exercise will help you.'

Ida seemed to take it seriously. She looked up at the window. From her glassy eyes I could tell she wasn't looking out into the garden but was immersed in her own mental landscape, where she could delve into all the pain and distress that had shaken her mind so terribly that she couldn't find a way out.

After looking deep into her soul for a moment, Ida hunched her shoulders and wrote a few words on the paper, then returned her attention to the window until she worked out what to say next, then picked up her pen again.

This was the most crucial phase of the process. I left her in peace and took from my handbag an article that Harri had written and that he was planning to publish in the next issue of *Psychology*

Matters, a journal that he still contributed to though he had already officially retired. Over the years, I too had published a few articles on my specialist fields in the journal. Harri and I had a habit of reading each other's articles and commenting upon them before publication.

I took a red pen from my bag and began concentrating on the article.

It examined the role of lying in interactions between patient and therapist. The subject was fascinating, and I felt annoyed that I hadn't thought to write about it myself.

After all, I have plenty of experience to draw upon.

Sometimes it felt as though the air in my office was thick with falsehoods.

In his article, Harri used the example of patient X (whom, after a few lines, I recognized as a woman called Aila), whom he had treated in the 1970s. The article was so personal that I couldn't help but admire Harri's courage.

Aila lied so skilfully that to this day Harri still didn't know what was true and what was false. Was Aila married? Did she have any children? What was her profession? And why did she have to lie about everything?

I was so absorbed in the troubled relationship between Harri and Aila that at first I didn't pay any attention to a little cough in the room. It was only the second cough that made me look up from the article.

'Are you ready?'

Ida nodded.

'Are you sure?'

Again, she nodded.

'Excellent. I'd like you to read it aloud to me.'

Ida looked taken aback.

'Then I hope we can talk about it and the feelings that writing it aroused within you.'

Ida gave a deep sigh of resignation and began reading her note in a monotone, as though she was reading the newspaper.

'I am dead. I had no other choice. I couldn't cope with living any more. Sorry. I forgive you for everything. All the best. Ida.'

Ida had completed the task very well indeed; the note was credible, genuine, just the way it should be.

'Your note touched me profoundly. Such strong words, such powerful emotions. What did it feel like to write it?'

'A relief. I've written it in my head plenty of times. Putting the words on paper felt liberating.'

'Let's look at it in detail. Can you give me the note so we can examine it one line at a time?'

Ida reluctantly handed me the sheet of paper, as though the words she had written belonged to her alone and she didn't want me to read them out loud.

'You write, *I had no other choice*. I want to stress that we always have choices. Always!'

'But nobody commits suicide if they've got other options,' she argued.

'Right now, we're not saying that *nobody* would do so. We're talking about you and what you would do.'

Ida said nothing. I didn't push her. My words would doubtless remain simmering in her subconscious.

'Then you write, *I couldn't cope with living any more*. You're tired of living. Well, here I can give some very concrete advice. In future, we can think about different survival methods, ways to help you cope with the traumas of the past and to stop you worrying about the future.'

She nodded cautiously, as though some part of her, hidden deep inside her, wanted to believe my words.

'You don't need this note. I promise you, you're never going to leave it for anyone. That's why we're going to burn it right here and now.'

Ida looked panicked. She tried to snatch the note from my hand but succeeded only in scratching me along the crook of my arm with her fingernail. I winced with pain.

'Calm down. I know what I'm doing.'

I opened the left-hand cupboard under my desk and took out a thick black envelope. I folded the note in half and slipped it into the envelope. Then I licked the glue and sealed it.

Ida watched me, stern-faced.

Next, I took five sturdy candles from the cupboard, one at a time, then a lighter.

Ida could hardly believe her eyes. Without saying a word, she stared alternately at me and the candles.

'You're going to light these candles. Place them around the room. The idea is to make the atmosphere in the office as solemn as a cemetery. Calm and peaceful.'

For a moment, I thought she would refuse, but she picked up the first candle, placed it on the windowsill and lit it.

I stood up and switched off all the lights.

Once Ida had positioned the candles and lit them all, I took a small tin bucket from the cupboard, the same size as the ones that children use to build sandcastles on the beach. I rolled up the rug and moved it to one side. Then I placed the bucket in the middle of the room and walked over to the window to close the curtains.

'I'm going to throw the note into the bucket now. Then I want you to set it alight.'

For a moment, Ida stared at the envelope in disbelief. I was worried she might try to snatch it again and stuff it into her pocket.

She crouched down over the bucket and set the note on fire. The flames cast dancing shadows across her pallid face.

Suddenly, I saw Riku standing beside the bucket.

I'd used this method to try and save him too.

He had burnt his own suicide note, but instead of taking strength from the ritual, it had only exacerbated his destructive tendencies.

I tried to save Riku, but I pushed him over the edge instead.

What if the same thing happened to Ida?

I couldn't bear the thought of yet another grave, another flower to pick from Harri's bouquets.

Ida

I looked on helplessly as this invaluable piece of evidence burned in the metallic bin in my therapist's surgery. My suicide note could have been used in court to prove that, at the time of the murders, I didn't fully appreciate the wrongfulness of my actions and might even be found not guilty. The note proved that I was so depressed I'd resolved to commit suicide, so I was incapable of killing anybody but myself.

But what if the judge latched on to the fact that I'd only written the note at my therapist's suggestion and that the act of writing it was simply my therapist's way of preventing my suicide? What then? My therapist wouldn't have asked me to write it unless she truly believed I was in danger of taking my life.

I felt the urge to snatch the burning note from the bin and try to save what was left of it. Rage flared up inside me. I imagined grabbing my therapist by the wrist and thrusting her hand into the flames. She would shriek with pain, but I'd only release my grip on her wrist once her skin started bubbling and blood began to trickle from her palm.

Arto

Clarissa would entertain our readers by agreeing to show us the hidden treasures of her private wardrobe. I asked our fashion editor to send me the finished piece so I could forward it to Clarissa in the same email as the interview.

I was convinced that the longer she had to wait for the interview, the more likely it was she would change her mind and decide she didn't want it to be published; after all, her alcoholism was something of a delicate subject.

To my astonishment, she didn't ask for any corrections to the article. She seemed to have resolved herself to the reality that soon the whole country would read that she was once an alcoholic— albeit, in her own words, a reformed one.

Amusingly, the only alterations she suggested were to do with the fashion supplement: *The hat in that photograph isn't pink, it's rosé. I didn't buy that dress in Paris, but in Milan. I own four Hermès handbags, not three.*

Having said that, the visual aspects of the article didn't please her at all. Apparently, she'd called Eero Räystäs, the photographer at *Helsinki Today*, and bawled him out down the phone. She thought the photos didn't do her justice, said they made her look pale and tired. Eero later told me that Clarissa had arrived for the photoshoot with such a terrible hangover that she looked like a flounder washed up on the shore.

Luckily, Eero wasn't an easy man to upset. An experienced photographer, he'd seen his fair share of celebrity meltdowns and had a good sense of humour about it. He knew his way around image-processing software. After some extensive retouching, Clarissa was purring with satisfaction and apologized for her earlier outburst.

It seemed Clarissa's modus operandi was the same as mine: screw up, apologize, screw up, apologize, screw up, apologize, and so on, until the other person runs out of patience and cuts all ties.

Clarissa

Ida was locked, and I couldn't find the right key. Our progress had been so sluggish that I was beginning to feel desperate. I didn't usually have to deal with such acute suicidal impulses. The brutal truth of the matter was that people who have already resolved to commit suicide don't usually bother to seek professional help. I could almost hear the clock ticking, time slipping away.

I often use dream analysis as a tool in my work. Don't get me wrong: I'm not all that interested in interpreting my patients' dreams per se; rather I want to hear them interpret their dreams by themselves. The patients' interpretations reveal far more about their subconscious than if I were to go through them with Freud's *The Interpretation of Dreams*.

Luckily, I managed to get Ida to pick up the idea—albeit with more than a little coaxing and cajoling on my part. And as for the results!

I wasn't expecting us to get on to such important topics at the very first attempt. Normally, it takes a few sessions before the patient has the courage to analyse the dream at the root of all their psychological problems.

We started with the dream that Ida had had the previous night.

The beginning was tentative. I had to prod her a little.

'Don't be shy! Tell me everything you remember! This isn't a test. If you forget something, it doesn't matter. I'm here to support you.'

'I'm sitting alone in a white room. Everything in the room is white: the furniture, the walls, the ceiling, the curtains. The sun is shining in through the window so brightly that I have to shade my eyes with my hand. I'm wearing a white velvet dress. I had a dress just like this when I was a child.'

Ida had closed her eyes. They were twitching behind her eyelids as though she had slipped into the REM phase and was talking in her sleep.

'You had a dress like this as a child, you say?'

'Yes, a white dress, made of velvet and lace, with puffy sleeves.'

For a moment, she was silent.

'I just thought of something weird.'

'What?' I held my breath in anticipation. Had we reached one of the central themes this quickly?

'I'd forgotten I had that dress as a child. But when I woke up this morning, I remembered that it was exactly the same dress I was wearing when...'

The sentence was left unfinished.

I waited patiently, but Ida didn't continue, then she opened her eyes, turned and gazed out of the window. Grey clouds were gliding across the sky. It was about to rain.

I was right all along. There was a reason for Ida's reluctance to talk. The dream had revealed something to her, something hidden so deep that she didn't have the strength to process it. I had to gently nudge her onwards.

'Let's go back to that room. It was completely white. And you were sitting in the middle, all alone. What happened next?'

I hoped Ida would have the courage to grab hold of something we can only reach in the realm of dreams.

'I felt tired. It wasn't the usual tiredness. I felt as though I'd been drugged. I tried to keep my eyes open, but they kept drooping

193

shut. It felt as though I'd been in that white room forever and would never see the outside world,' she whispered, so quietly that I struggled to hear her.

It seemed that Ida had sunk deep into her own dream world. It was only her fingers that showed that she was still in the here and now: she was scratching the cuticle of her left pinkie again. It was already ragged as an old pine tree, its bark scratched off by a bear looking for larvae.

'Time seemed to have stopped. You were alone in the room. What happened next?' I asked.

'Suddenly, something black started dripping from the ceiling. Ink, maybe, or oil. It dripped onto my hair, my face, my lap. It trickled down my cheeks. I tried to wipe it away, but I only ended up smearing it with my hand. I felt dirty.'

I finally started to make out her dream. White, innocent. Black, tarnished. Stark contrasts, potent symbolism.

'Then I noticed that a mirror had appeared on the wall.'

'A mirror?'

'Yes. I stood up and walked over to the mirror to look at myself. My hands and face were smudged and black. I tried to wipe my hands on my dress, but the ink wouldn't come off. My dress was still gleaming and white.'

'Then what?'

'Then I woke up.'

We sat in silence for a moment. I let Ida catch her breath. Interpreting such an ominous dream required immense concentration. And space.

I mustn't steer her interpretation; I needed to give her the space to draw her own conclusions. And so, I decided to ask the most neutral question possible under the circumstances.

'What do you think this dream means?'

'It's about the day when… everything happened… and everything changed… and I wasn't me any more… I was locked up there and someone else came out… and…'

I didn't understand a word.

The alarm clock rang. My next patient would be here in five minutes.

The office door closed behind Ida with what sounded like an exhausted sigh. I pressed my hands against my face, which was tacky with sweat, and cursed.

We were so close to a breakthrough.

Ida

The interpretation of dreams! For Christ's sake! As if my therapist was some kind of neurotic Dr Hatter who first gaslit the Moomins then decided they were all a few sandwiches short of a picnic.

What next? Before long she'd probably want to record all our sessions on her phone and trawl through my every utterance for Freudian slips. Give me a break!

I wouldn't have been surprised if, even after such a short acquaintance, my therapist was ready to throw in the towel. If I were in her position, I would have given up right away; after all, I was a hopeless case. But I'd underestimated her, and now she surprised me with yet another trick: analysing my dreams.

That old chestnut, I thought. Well, you asked for it. Now I can let my imagination go to town!

My therapist had a smug expression on her face, as though she had invented the interpretation of dreams herself, and, instead of me, the room was filled with an adulating audience to whom she had been asked to present her achievements and who rewarded her with volleys of applause.

I closed my eyes and pretended to concentrate on remembering my dreams. My mind was a blank. I couldn't think of anything. For the first time in this course of therapy, I could lie to my heart's content, but my imagination was suddenly frozen.

My therapist was getting agitated. She started tapping her heels against the floor and frantically twiddling a bright orange rubber band in her fingers.

'Last night's dream. That wasn't so long ago. Surely you remember something?' she scoffed irritably.

Did that moron really think I was going to reveal my bloody nocturnal fantasies, the blind violence that I saw every time I closed my eyes? The limbs twisted into unnatural positions, the decomposing corpses, the broken bones?

The blood? All that blood?

She pulled and pulled at the rubber band. I could see it was almost stretched to the limit, but I was still startled at the loud crack it made as it snapped in two.

I tried to come up with something. Something full of profound symbolism.

A labyrinth?

A tunnel?

A horse?

Nothing.

I started gingerly.

'I was walking along the street, alone. Everything around me is deserted. You know that feeling when, in a dream, everything looks normal but there's one detail that's out of place?'

My therapist nodded eagerly, as though I'd just made a revolutionary contribution to the field of dream analysis.

'My dream was just like that. Everything was just like it was in reality, only the name of the street I was walking along had changed. I was walking along... what was the name again? The one named after the old guy. Well, all streets, squares and plazas are named after old guys, but I mean the one who collected folk poetry.'

'Elias Lönnrot.'

'That's the one! So, I was walking along Lönnrotinkatu, but the name had been changed to Snellmaninkatu.'

My therapist looked so dissatisfied I could only conclude that my made-up dream hadn't pleased her.

I had to admit it sounded deadly boring to me too. As far as I was concerned, talking about your dreams was a bit like talking about the ins and outs of your digestive tract: nobody was remotely interested.

What could I come up with next?

I had a brilliant idea. Why bother trying to come up with something original, when the movies were full of ludicrous dream sequences positively choking on their own clumsy symbolism? How did that dream sequence go in the cheap horror film I'd seen on TV last night?

'I was sitting in a white room, alone...' I began, trying to remember the beginning of the film.

The therapist could barely sit still. Smoke rose from her pen as she scribbled down the details of this second-rate 1950s horror film. She nodded along to my story as if she'd had exactly the same dream, and her nods only confirmed that I'd remembered everything correctly.

How was it possible that my therapist just sucked up all this bullshit? Hadn't she seen a single horror film in her life? Weren't the clichés I was describing far too implausible? Apparently not. She nodded excitedly and wrote everything down in her notebook.

I felt the urge to add another hollow symbol from a different film but decided to save this for our next session. Then I would tell her I dreamt that Jack Torrance came crashing through my door with an axe, that Freddy Krueger lived next door, or that I was being stalked by Michael Myers.

It's a wonder I didn't burst out laughing.

Luckily, I was saved by the alarm clock and dashed straight out into the yard for a good giggle.

Who would have imagined going to therapy could be this much fun?

But I'm not laughing now. Not by a long shot.

Part Three

ROBERT HARE'S PCL-R TEST

Clarissa

I wasn't invited to Riku's funeral. I saw the announcement of his death in *Helsinki Today*.

Instead of a cross or a dove, his parents had chosen a photograph of Riku to accompany the announcement. I'd never seen a photograph used in an announcement like that, and I've never seen one since.

And what kind of photograph had his parents chosen? It must have been the worst portrait ever taken of him.

The photo looked like it had been taken two or three years before his death, so he must have been around twelve years old. He was standing in front an oddly decorated Christmas tree and looked ever so slightly lost. The branches of the Christmas tree had been adorned with strips of toilet paper with something green smeared on them; it looked like toothpaste. The foremost branches were pushing their way past Riku and covering almost half his face. He didn't yet have his Mohican in this picture; instead his head was shaved completely bald. His forced smirk looked more like a grimace.

The photograph was so large that there was only enough space in the announcement for Riku's dates of birth and death, his grieving relatives—it just said 'Mother and Father'; it didn't give their names—and information about the funeral. No poetry, no verse from the Bible. The funeral was to take place at the chapel on the eastern side of Malmi cemetery the following Sunday. I would be able to attend.

The weather forecast for the day of the funeral predicted heavy snowfall. I prepared for the weather by putting a see-through, waterproof poncho over my Escada trench coat and took a sturdy wooden-handled umbrella that wouldn't turn inside out in the wind.

When I drove to the cemetery, I started thinking that this would become yet another stop on the walks that Harri and I took around the gravestones. Would Riku's grave be on our existing route or would we have to plan a new one?

I parked in the furthest corner of the car park. During the drive there, snow had started flurrying from the sky. Again, I cursed my own dandyness. Why couldn't I have dressed appropriately for the weather? The poncho and the umbrella were no use whatsoever as I struggled to keep my balance on the icy pathways in four-inch Louboutin heels.

I arrived at the chapel. The door was closed. The funeral had already started. I pressed my ear against the door and strained to hear what was happening. The muffled sound of an out-of-tune hymn came from inside. The bombastic organ almost completely drowned out the singing.

The hymn was 'Blest are the Pure in Heart'. As if Riku was a little child! Maybe his parents had spent so many years in a drug-induced stupor that they hadn't noticed their son wasn't an innocent little boy any more.

The hymn ended abruptly, and I heard movement inside. The service was over, and it was time for everyone to walk to the graveside.

I hurried round the corner out of sight just before the pitifully small group of mourners appeared from the chapel.

The first to step outside were Riku's parents. I recognized them all too well. His mother's face was covered in bruises. She had a black eye, and across her lower lip was a bloody gash that hadn't healed properly. She couldn't have been much over forty, but she already looked as though she'd had enough of life. She stared blankly into the distance, her face grey and expressionless.

Riku's father had already lost most of his teeth. His cheeks were so gaunt that a blackbird could have nested in the dents. Well, a sparrow maybe. His arm was in an improvised sling. He must have injured himself while beating up Riku's mother. The sling was nothing but a dirty rag. It looked familiar: an old Dead Kennedys T-shirt. How could he? That was Riku's favourite T-shirt! He'd shown it to me proudly the first time he visited my office.

What kind of father was this man? His own son hadn't even been buried yet and already he was tearing his clothes to shreds!

All of a sudden, I heard Riku's last words.

'I'm sorry,' he'd shouted as he fell onto the underground tracks.

I'd dropped to my knees on the platform and watched the train come hurtling over him.

Riku's parents were followed by a young priest, nervously fidgeting with her Bible as she stepped out of the chapel.

I watched the little group and only followed them once they were far enough away that none of them would notice me.

When they reached Riku's grave, they stopped.

'Earth to earth, ashes to ashes, dust to dust.'

The priest threw some sand on top of the coffin. Once she had thrown the third shovelful, Riku's father turned, as though he had forgotten all about his son, the grave, his wife and the priest, and headed out towards the car park, half running. Riku's mother dashed after him, without even saying goodbye to the priest. The priest shook her head and began walking back towards the chapel. This would be a great anecdote to tell her colleagues.

I walked up to the grave, sobbing, and dropped a red rose into the earth. One of the thorns pricked my finger. A droplet of blood dripped onto the coffin.

Ida

I guess you've already drawn your own conclusions about me by now, formed your own diagnosis. I'd bet my life I know what you've decided.

I'm a psychopath.

You know what we're like. Cold-blooded predators who don't care about anything or anybody but themselves. Woops—that could apply to all the exes, bosses and colleagues in the world! If online forums are anything to go by, every school and workplace is full of us. Even Tinder.

But there are psychopaths, and then there are psychopaths. There are the ones diagnosed by a work colleague, a friend or a former husband. These are the ones who would never get a proper diagnosis from a psychiatrist. Then there are the rest of us who get a diagnosis from the psychiatrist as soon as we walk through the door.

Again, I've left out some of the details. You've only got yourselves to blame. I warned you to be on your guard.

I was diagnosed at the age of fourteen. Back then, I spent two months in the children's wing of the psychiatric hospital. After my first suicide attempt, I was sectioned and diagnosed with depression. Still, the psychiatrist looking after me wasted no time coming up with a more appropriate diagnosis for me.

So be my guest, you can call me a psychopath all you like.

I won't take offence.

I recently read a report presenting the easiest way to identify a psychopath: just ask. We'll all proudly say, yes.

First off, I was assessed with the PCL-R test developed by Robert Hare, a guru of the psychological profession. I didn't get full points, but I wasn't far off.

Had I tortured animals as a child?

At that question, I felt like arguing the point. What exactly did the word 'torture' mean in this context? Personally, I didn't consider hanging my pet kitten with a shoelace tied to the front door a form of torture. It's a far nicer way to die than drowning, for instance.

The psychiatrist disagreed.

The human brain continues developing until the age of twenty-five, and according to some psychiatric professionals, this developmental phase can last even longer. Psychiatrists tend to avoid identifying diagnoses in teenagers, as their pathology isn't yet set in stone. And they most definitely don't like diagnosing youngsters as psychopaths.

But it seems, in my case, the psychiatrist was willing to make an exception. He thought I was a danger to other people. That being said, I hadn't actually harmed anyone at this point, if we discount my pet kitten and the neighbours' cats. But unfortunately, you can't punish people for crimes they haven't yet committed. You can't even have them sent to the psych ward. And so, the psychiatrist had no option but to release me back into the wild. By way of a goodbye, he said he believed it was only a matter of time before I committed a homicide. If only he could have chosen his lottery numbers with such accuracy—he'd be a millionaire.

I never told my therapist about this diagnosis. After all, she wasn't a psychiatrist, so she couldn't diagnose me herself. But that wouldn't stop her recognizing a psychopath when one sat down on her couch.

So, what do you think? Did she realize I was a psychopath?

I don't think so.

My course of therapy would have stopped there and then. Psychopathy is a chronic disorder of the psyche that can't be cured with therapy any more than with medication. It might be a better idea to lock us up right after our diagnosis, either in prison or in a psychiatric hospital, and throw away the key.

I was a hopeless case. Why would my therapist waste her time on me if she knew it was futile?

I'm convinced that she didn't recognize my psychopathy for the same reason that the police never managed to connect me to my crimes: I was a woman.

People have no idea how much I benefitted from their chauvinistic attitude problem. We female serial killers are such a rare breed that it never occurred to the coppers to suspect a woman of the murders I had committed. Gender stereotypes ruled supreme in their minds: whereas men want to tear the world to pieces out of sheer masculine angst, we women want nothing more than to cherish and nurture it.

It's no wonder I felt like I was invisible.

I'd committed so many murders that it was completely incomprehensible to me that I hadn't been caught yet.

But if any of you out there are still dreaming of life as a professional serial killer, there's one crucial tip I should probably share: never trust your own abilities.

You'll be caught sooner or later, no matter how good you are.

Clarissa

Yet again, I found myself sitting in the dusky kitchen, wide awake, drinking and contemplating Ida's problems. I was convinced her difficulties stemmed from a deep-set childhood trauma. But what kind of trauma? I would have been able to establish this easily enough using hypnotherapy, that is to say, by actually hypnotizing her. Hypnosis is a far quicker method than, say, dream analysis, but I'd stopped using it in my treatment programmes years ago.

I trained as a hypnotherapist soon after graduating. I've always believed that the subconscious reveals more about a person than anything patients might tell me by themselves. There are only two ways into a person's subconscious: dreams and hypnosis. Under hypnosis, patients take off their armour and reveal their secrets to the therapist.

At first, I was very taken with hypnosis. It saved me so much time. Instead of going through the patient's dreams again and again and trying to prise out their various meanings, hypnosis meant I could get to the nub of the problem right away. Usually I managed to work out what was causing the patient's problems after only a few sessions. But it didn't take long before I realized hypnosis has its drawbacks too.

Once, I was treating a young woman suffering from severe depression. Nothing in the patient's history could explain why she was so depressed. She was getting ready to marry the man of her dreams, she had a stimulating, well-paid job, and she was expecting their long-awaited first child. Everything should have been perfect, but it wasn't.

I decided to try hypnosis. If my patient's symptoms were the result of a previous trauma, hypnosis would bring it floating up to the surface. And that's exactly what happened. Hypnosis revealed that the patient had been sexually abused as a child.

However, the hypnosis had an unexpected side effect that had never occurred when I'd used it in the past.

At the time of the trauma, the patient was only eight years old. The child's psyche wasn't able to cope with what had happened and had suppressed the memory into the annals of the subconscious. Once I teased it out through hypnosis, her psyche collapsed. Over the course of the following weeks, the patient sunk into a powerful psychosis, and eventually, I had to have her sectioned against her will in a psychiatric facility.

The moral of the story is this: the patient's psyche had not rejected the trauma without good reason. The psyche has its own reasons for reacting the way it does. We should respect the decisions it makes.

As I scratched the patient's traumatic memory into view bit by bit, the psyche had no defence mechanisms against the damage caused by the initial trauma.

I should say, at least the incident didn't permanently damage the patient's psyche. She responded well to hospital treatment, and before long we were able to continue our therapy sessions together.

After this terrifying experience, I swore I would never poke around in my patients' psyches ever again. I wanted nothing more to do with hypnosis. The incident shocked me so much that nowadays I can't even watch entertainment shows in which a mentalist pretends to hypnotize a studio audience.

This is no laughing matter. In Finland, the hypnotherapy profession isn't at all regulated, which means any old quack can set up a practice without the slightest training. If I, a professional psychologist, could bring about the havoc described above, I dread to think what kind of tragedies unregulated hypnotherapists could cause.

I knew Ida had seen other professionals before me, but she'd been unable to process her trauma. It was sheltered in a protective cocoon deep inside her psyche. The question was: was there any sense in opening up a trauma that had been shut away for so long? Would her psyche be able to cope with it?

Ida

Yet again we spent the entire session on her stupid dream analysis. I really wonder how I managed to control myself and not voice any of my sarcastic thoughts, though it felt as though there was no room in my mind for anything else.

At least my therapist had warned me last time that we were going to continue examining my dreams. This time I didn't need to rack my brains thinking of yarns to spin her.

She'd advised me to write my dreams down. Apparently, the best time to do this was right after waking up, when the dreams are still fresh in your mind. I'd given her a nod by way of a promise, but I hadn't followed her advice. The morning of our session, I prepared by watching *Eraserhead*, a film with no shortage of symbolism. Thank you, David Lynch—the patron saint of us poor souls condemned to a life of therapy!

'I'm in a white room. I'm sitting on a white sofa, alone. Time passes. Everything is just as it was in my previous dream, but this time there's no mirror on the wall,' I said and peered up at my therapist.

'No mirror?'

She looked worried. The missing mirror was clearly a dangerous sign. The first time we tried dream analysis, I'd found it hard to hold back the laughter. Now I was bored to death. Mirror or no mirror—who cares? Well, my therapist apparently cared about it. The nib of her pen scratched across her notebook.

I had difficulty concentrating.

I started scrutinizing my therapist's outfit.

The necklace with her name on it had become caught in her hair. Only the final 'A' was visible. Even the diamond dot on the 'I' was hidden in her thick tangle of curls.

On countless occasions, I'd imagined that necklace hanging round my own neck.

I noticed a thick white cat hair caught in the breast pocket of her blazer. If you'd asked me, I would have said my therapist was a dog person. Cats do their own thing. I could see her smothering her pet with affection, and dogs didn't mind putting up with that kind of thing.

My therapist's appearance was always very carefully curated, as though she'd been cut right out of the pages of a woman's magazine. How was it possible she hadn't noticed the cat hair? I tried to look away, but my eyes kept wandering back to it.

My latest victim—a student by the name of Lassi Laajasrauha—had had a cat. I killed it too, so it wouldn't be abandoned after its owner's death, and slipped its leather collar onto my right wrist. My therapist hadn't noticed this though, as I was wearing a long-sleeved sweatshirt and a woollen jumper on top.

'Then what happened?'

My therapist's question startled me. My attention was still drawn to the cat hair. I felt the urge to stand up and pluck it off her blazer. Well, well, a cat person. I'd never have guessed!

I tried to envisage my therapist sitting in an armchair stroking a white Siamese cat in her lap. No, the idea just wasn't credible.

She was still waiting for my answer.

'The door opened. The hinges gave a terrible shriek. I was so startled that I jumped to my feet.'

She was frantically writing in her notebook. It was time to move on to *Eraserhead*.

'I heard footsteps. A man appeared in front of me, a head of thick fuzzy hair. He was wearing garish red lipstick,' I continued.

Eraserhead was filmed in black and white, so I don't know whether the protagonist, played by Jack Nance, was actually wearing lipstick or not. I doubt it. But he had a hell of a haircut.

'Can you describe the man more closely?'

My therapist was clearly excited about this. Could the man be my father? Were we finally closing in on my Electra complex?

'His hair was so... large that I didn't notice anything else.'

She scoffed in disappointment. If only the man had had my father's face! I was beginning to feel sorry for my poor therapist. I decided to give her a few crumbs of mercy.

'Oh, now I remember! He said something to me! *I took the mirror away.*'

My therapist was visibly happy with this. It was only then that I realized what she was driving at. Not an Electra complex, but the myth of Narcissus. Freud named the concept of narcissism after Narcissus who gazed into the water and fell in love with his own reflection.

'Okay, now let's try to analyse this. What do you think this dream tells us?'

My therapist could barely contain herself. She craned her neck towards me like a swan trying to reach some breadcrumbs.

'I don't know. But I'd like to dream about you. About us.'

My therapist blushed.

HELSINKI TODAY

STUDENT FOUND MURDERED

Twenty-five-year-old student Lassi Laajasrauha was yesterday found dead at his home in a student dormitory in Kivikko, Helsinki. Police suspect Laajasrauha was the victim of a homicide.

'The manner of Laajasrauha's death reveals evidence of foul play,' confirmed Detective Inspector Paula-Liisa Talas from the Helsinki police's violent-crimes unit.

'We believe Laajasrauha and his killer were already acquainted,' Talas revealed.

Clarissa

For the first time, I felt positive about the direction our therapy had taken. I hadn't got through to Ida yet, but now it felt as though contact had at least been established. Finally.

Ida asked if we could go through the dream she'd had the previous night. I decided to allow this. And it was a good thing too, because it revealed something I could never have imagined.

I was so enchanted with Ida's dream that at first I didn't pay any attention to what she was actually telling me about it. I almost gasped out loud as she described the room, now without a mirror, and the man who had taken the mirror away. It was like something straight out of a psychology textbook, a trail of crumbs leading me right into the labyrinth of her subconscious.

Nonetheless, Ida recounted her dream mechanically, as though she hadn't actually dreamt this at all but had instead read it in a book and learnt to recite it by heart. It seemed as though she couldn't engage with the dream on an emotional level.

I might never have found out what all this was about if Pekka hadn't forgotten to switch the television off in the living room. Typical.

After our session, I remained at my desk and wrote up the notes from our meeting. Tears welled at the corners of my eyes, so moved was I at finally being able to help her.

To save her!

Still, despite my elation, I found I couldn't focus on my work; rather, my attention kept latching on to the noise coming from the television. Cursing under my breath, I walked through to the living room.

I grabbed the remote control and was about to press the Off button when I caught a glimpse of the TV. It was a black-and-white film. My eyes fixed on the screen, a purely subconscious reaction. My conscious self had no idea why I couldn't take my eyes from it. The image showed a curious-looking man, a man with an enormous coiffure. The same man that Ida had described to me during the session when she was supposed to be telling me about her dreams.

No wonder her dream sounded like she had learnt it by rote. She'd simply regurgitated the plot of this film!

Shame and anger brought the blood to my cheeks.

I dashed into my office and read through the notes that I'd written up only a moment ago. The tone of these notes was self-satisfied, almost smug. I had succeeded! I was such a good therapist that I deserved a medal!

My first impulse was to tear the notes to shreds. Then I considered the situation from another angle. Ida had succeeded in pulling the wool over my eyes—until now. I stuffed the notes into the folder where I kept all documents pertaining to Ida's treatment. I should keep these notes, because they were a permanent reminder of how easily she had led me astray.

I pushed the folder into my filing cabinet and slammed the drawer shut.

I went out to the patio for a jittery cigarette. I lit up and drew the smoke deep into my lungs. The nicotine calmed me like a mother's warm embrace.

Had this all been a misunderstanding after all?

Why couldn't Ida have genuinely had a nightmare about the man with the enormous haircut? Maybe this was all pure coincidence.

But wasn't it curious that she had dreamt about a man who looked exactly like the man in the film? It most certainly was, but coincidences are coincidences precisely because they are so unlikely.

I felt almost embarrassed—to think I'd been so paranoid!

Now I understood that Ida had never told me anything but the truth.

I had no reason to doubt her honesty.

Arto

I'd already decided not to tell anyone else. Telling Marja had been hard enough at the time, though even then I'd only told her a fraction of the truth. When she made it clear she didn't even want to hear that much, I realized that neither would anybody else.

Marja could barely bring herself to look me in the eye. Even on her deathbed, her expression was accusatory. There she lay in the hospital bed, her eyes burning with rage like two embers, as if it had all been my fault.

In that respect, she was absolutely right.

I remember blurting it all out to Irmeli one day after *Helsinki Today*'s team-building seminar. I cried on my boss's shoulder. Literally.

Irmeli and I were sitting at a table in the far corner of the Quill and Parchment, and I ended up pouring out my sorrows. Every now and then one of our colleagues would turn up at the table, ask to join us or invite us to the dance floor, but Irmeli gently declined, as though she would rather spend all evening listening to my problems instead of partying and having fun.

Disco hits from the 1970s formed the soundtrack to my confession. My colleagues were letting their hair down to the Bee Gees's *Stayin' Alive* in true John Travolta style, while I was scraping the grime off my soul and smearing it over Irmeli. She patiently listened to my slurred speech and nodded sympathetically. At times, my head rested on her shoulder and she gently pushed me away, as if she was afraid I would leave snot stains on her black blazer.

Wouldn't you confide in your boss? Just you try carrying that kind of guilt around, the kind that had been weighing down on my shoulders all these years!

Maybe it was inevitable that there came a time when I just couldn't cope any more. I simply had to share my sins with someone else. Irmeli was the obvious choice; after all, she used to be Marja's best friend.

I was drunk—I suppose you'd expect nothing less—but luckily I had enough common sense not to let Irmeli know the whole truth. Still, it wasn't long before I came to regret my loose tongue. Ever since that night, Irmeli had insinuated that I needed professional help. I thanked my lucky stars that employers couldn't force their employees to take a course of psychoanalysis, otherwise I'd have been lying on a shrink's couch doing free association for the rest of my days.

Since then, I'd been living under a magnifying glass. I knew Irmeli had been watching my every move, my every expression, and interpreting everything in light of my earlier revelations.

She'd never brought it up directly, but reading between the lines, her concern for me was clear.

I'd made her swear she wouldn't tell anybody else about our conversation, but I was afraid that sooner or later she would let something slip to one of our colleagues. I had no idea that my worst fears would come true quite so soon.

I was so exhilarated that Irmeli had praised my interview with Clarissa that I decided to visit Eero the photographer and thank him for his amazing shots, which really lifted the piece to a new level. To say his reaction was frosty would be an understatement.

Eero barely looked at me and made it clear that he had better things to do than listen to my gushing thanks.

It was clear that, since I'd last seen Irmeli, she'd gone and blurted out my secret to Eero. There was no other explanation for his abrupt behaviour.

And if Eero already knew about it, soon everybody else would too.

How did Irmeli imagine I could continue working as a freelance reporter at *Helsinki Today* if all my colleagues knew the truth?

I would be a pariah within the editorial office. Nobody would talk to me, never mind go on an assignment with me. My colleagues would never say anything to me directly; instead they would peer at me, look down their noses at me, just the way Eero had done.

If I couldn't do my job, what did I have left? Would I sit in front of her window day after day until she noticed me and reported me to the police? I'd be given a restraining order and would never be able to go near her again.

My life was like a house of cards, and now I could see the lower floors starting to collapse. There was nothing I could do to affect my fate. My destruction was inescapable. All I could do was wait until the final card came floating down to the table, leaving my life in ruins.

There was only one option left: suicide.

Why hadn't I had the sense to do it earlier?

Pekka

Heart. I had only one word left. Heart.

Again, I'd spent hours in my office sitting in front of the computer, scrolling back and forth through the Excel file I'd made of the drawings. The X3270 terminal emulator was open on my desktop too, as if the very fact that it was switched on meant I was actually doing some work.

I decided to interrupt my procrastination for a moment and watch the news. I walked through to the living room. The room looked like student digs. The oriental rug was crumpled; cigarette ash lay flicked here and there. The sofa was almost buried under half-eaten packets of crisps. Empty pizza boxes were stacked on the coffee table in a wobbly pile that looked like the leaning tower of Pisa. Next to it was another rickety tower; this one made of old copies of *Helsinki Today* and flyers that had come through the door. I stared at the installation in confusion.

I started tidying the chaos.

I crammed the remaining crisps into my mouth and stuffed the empty packets inside one another. The taste of rancid cooking oil made me feel sick, but I couldn't stop stuffing my face. My hands reached for the open packets almost of their own volition. If Clarissa had seen what I was up to, she would probably have told me you can't fill your inner emptiness with food. Yet the nausea caused by the crisps gave me a curious, sick satisfaction. It was comforting that I felt terrible physically as well as mentally.

I continued tidying up, numbed, and started going through the pizza boxes. I picked out the squashed mushrooms and slices of pineapple and stuffed them into my mouth with the same sense of nihilistic self-loathing as I had the crisps.

I picked up the pile of newspapers and advertisements. Underneath was Clarissa's pink notebook.

Clarissa had doodled on the front cover, so I couldn't help but see what she had drawn.

Two initials and, between them, in a show of love—a heart.

One of the initials was 'C' for Clarissa.

But the other one was not 'P' for Pekka.

Arto

I'd heard that people who resolve to commit suicide find a sense of inner peace once they've reached their decision. In the days and weeks leading up to their death, they take comfort in the thought that their pain and suffering will soon be over.

Friends and relatives might misinterpret their renewed good spirits as a sign that they have put the worst behind them and finally started to recover from their depression. This is precisely why suicide always shocks friends and family the most.

I soon noticed there was a lot of truth to this theory. I can barely describe the tranquillity I felt in my soul. I'd spent years wading through a swamp, never managing to scramble back to dry land, only sinking even deeper. But once I reached this decision, I felt an almost supernatural sense of calm.

I planned to sort out my worldly affairs as quickly as possible; then I could be reunited with Marja, whether she was spending eternity in Heavenly bliss or roasting in the fires of Hell.

I assumed the latter would be the right place for both of us.

As an organized person, I decided to draw up a To Do list. I didn't want to leave anything for others to clear up after me. Even the idea that someone else would have to arrange my funeral felt a little uncomfortable. As far as I was concerned, my body could just as well be left to rot at the nearest landfill site where it would feed the seagulls.

As soon as I got home from the paper's offices, I took out a notebook and began writing down a list of bullet points with everything I had to take care of. As I compiled the list, I realized I had already used up quite enough of the planet's finite natural resources. There were only a few things left outstanding, and once I'd dealt with them, I could choose the coffin and lie down.

What a liberating thought it was!

On the other side of the page, I listed the articles I was still working on. A few interviews and a reportage. I'd already transcribed the interviews, and I could leave the reportage for the crime editors at *Helsinki Today*; I hadn't wanted to undertake the investigation into online paedophile rings in the first place.

Next, I drafted a message for one of the local Facebook recycling groups, saying I would bequeath everything I owned to the first person to respond. A few years ago, I'd written an article for the paper about a young man who had got rid of his belongings in the same way before moving to India to live in an ashram. He at least had a state-of-the-art home theatre and lots of other expensive equipment to give away.

Meanwhile, all I owned was some battered old pieces of furniture, a few boxes of books gathering dust in the basement and the odd bin liner full of ragged old clothes that I doubted anyone except the down-and-outs would want.

I sent a request to join the Facebook group and resolved to post my advertisement as soon as my membership was accepted. I imagined this might take a day or so, depending on how active the group's admins were. A day here or there wouldn't affect my plans.

Organizing your own death is surprisingly easy. But there was one thing I would have to prepare for very carefully: I had to say farewell to her. And I didn't want to do it through a window.

I couldn't kill myself until she knew how much I had suffered for her.

I wanted her to share my suffering.

Only then would I find peace beyond the grave.

Clarissa

When it comes to other people's vulnerability, humans can be a heartless bunch. Under their callous gaze, the weak end up feeling even weaker.

There is nothing so terrible in this world that we cannot learn from it. Survivors can fill our glasses with the elixir of their wisdom.

Tear me to pieces and I will grow as a person.

We live in a fast-food culture where traumas are treated with sticking plasters, not stitches. Our mouths, our eyes and ears are stuffed full of pink fluff: crystals, angels and healing light. But there are some problems that not even a unicorn's kiss will resolve.

It's an insufferable thought that there are things in this world that we simply cannot overcome. Especially as these things can happen to any one of us.

Even you.

But there are some things we just cannot survive. It might surprise you to know that, even as a therapist, I too believe this. I of all people ought to have the unshakable belief that therapy can heal any kind of trauma.

But I don't.

We insist that victims recover as quickly as possible. If they bring up the subject of what they have been through, we tell them to *get over it and move on*, to *look to the future* and to *let go of the past*. But things that are normal and everyday for most people are, and will remain, impossible for some victims.

Victims of sexual abuse have had their lives ripped apart, and to suggest otherwise is to trivialize their lived experience. Nonetheless, we tell them they shouldn't be bitter; they should try to think positively about what has happened. As though it was their own negativity that caused their suffering in the first place.

Only good things ever happen to good people.

I've often thought that we tend to think more charitably about the dead than we do the victims of sexual violence; we no longer demand anything of corpses. It's only after several years of therapy that my clients realize they don't have to get over what they have experienced.

It's enough that they're still breathing.

This cruel 'get over it' attitude absolves abusers of their guilt. Their deeds can't be as depraved as people think if their victims actually survive. Even paedophiles have a knack of putting a positive spin on their crimes.

The guiltier you feel, the more you are willing to forgive others. I doubt anyone can live in such a way that they never have anything to regret. And so, we are prepared to forgive the heinous crimes of others in the hope that our own transgressions will one day be forgiven too.

People always show greater understanding for those who have done evil than for those speaking about the evil committed against them.

Ida

The way I think of time, there are only two eras: BB and AB, the time before the Bastard and the time after the Bastard. In the BB era I was a little girl. In the AB era I am nothing. At least, I'm not human.

Mornings are the worst. When I wake up, there's a brief moment when I don't remember what the Bastard did to me. For a few seconds I think everything is just the way it was before. Then reality comes crashing down on my neck, crushing me under its weight. Every single morning since my time in the cage, my subconscious has tricked me into believing I was never there in the first place.

Why can't that feeling last for hours? Even just a few minutes? Probably because my psyche wouldn't be able to cope with the devastation that returning to reality time and again would inevitably cause.

Every morning I have to relearn how to accept the fact that that was then, and this is now. Every single morning, as the terrible facts hurtle back into my mind, I have to fight off the same thought: *I can't cope with this a day longer.*

And it's this very thought that has had my fingers twitching for the tub of pills, the razorblades and the noose.

The main reason for my insomnia is that I can't deal with the thought of what awaits me in the morning. I'm afraid of falling asleep, afraid of the dreams I might have. If I fall asleep, I'll have to wake up again, and the morning will be like all the other mornings before it: reality will punch me right in the face.

I remember the cage and the Bastard, and I realize that nothing will ever be well again.

Not as long as I'm alive.

Clarissa

I'd been waiting for it impatiently, but when it finally happened, I didn't want to hear a word about it.

On countless occasions, I'd tried to convince Ida that she could speak freely to me. I'd heard everything in my line of work, and nothing surprised me any more. Now, finally, it seemed she was ready to open up to me.

Even at our first meeting, I'd read everything there was to read between the lines. It was likely Ida was suffering from post-traumatic stress disorder, and the root cause was obvious.

We therapists read people backwards, as it were. A layman might be taken aback by a friend's rude behaviour. It's only when they learn of the friend's troubled childhood that they fully understand what's going on. Therapists, meanwhile, factor in the patient's trauma right from the outset, though initially we might not know what it stems from. But it's very different to hear something from the horse's mouth than simply to rely on guesswork and supposition.

I couldn't hold back the tears. You'd think that over the course of my long career, I would have hardened a little. And that might have happened, if I'd tried. But I didn't want to become so hardened that I could take hearing absolutely anything. For me, sensitivity was a conscious choice.

Ida looked at me, as if afraid that her woes might crush me under their weight.

'Don't worry. I might be a bit tearful, but I can carry your burden. I'm crying the tears that you should have cried, that your mother and father should have cried.'

A cool analytical approach was key to therapeutic work. I'd learnt to distance myself from my patients' problems by imagining I was just solving a scenario in a textbook. But now I couldn't do it.

Ida only managed to utter a sentence or two at a time.

'I'm here for you. The more you have the courage to tell me, the lighter you will feel.'

I was usually able to convince myself I was pondering theoretical conundrums instead of the very real problems turning people's lives upside down. This way, I avoided being overly emotional.

My office was reserved for my clients' emotions; there was no room for my own. My patients didn't pay in order to prop me up. I had my mentor for that, Harri, the man I could always turn to in tricky situations. But this time my emotions seemed to get the better of me.

Ida continued telling me her story.

'I know you're afraid. But together we are strong.'

As the session went on, she slumped against the couch like a deflated balloon. It was as though her secret had been holding her together, and when she finally revealed it, she no longer had the strength to hold herself upright.

'You will get through this. Say it: *I will get through this.*'

It was my responsibility to make her believe in the future, in life itself.

'You can get better. You don't have to be stuck in the past. This could have happened to anybody.'

I held a brief pause to underline my point, then continued,

'You are not to blame.'

It was obvious that Ida was severely traumatized. Everything about her spoke to the fact that her entire psyche was built on those traumas. Right from the outset, I'd assumed this must be a case of sexual abuse. There were several factors pointing in this direction, most notably the way she spoke about herself.

Ida repeatedly called herself evil. She had internalized the evil she had experienced and now she thought she was to blame, as if she'd caused it all herself and was therefore guilty as charged.

Guilt gnaws at our soul relentlessly, whether with good reason or not.

'Let go of the guilt. You are free.'

Many patients react to other traumas like this, but I've noticed that victims of paedophilia have a particular tendency to blame themselves for what has happened. This is partly because paedophiles commonly shift the blame onto their victims. For instance, they might claim that the child in question seduced them.

Ida sat in front of me, pale.

Everything had been said.

'It's over. It's over. It's over. Say it: *It's over.*'

The alarm clock rang.

Ida stood up right away. We shook hands. In the faint glow of the salt light, her dark-blue eyes looked almost like they were sketched with coal.

'Ida, you will survive this. I promise you.'

She took her coat from the couch, pulled it on, walked into the hallway, opened the front door, and then she was gone.

I sat down in my chair. Unease pushed its way into my consciousness with such force that I couldn't fight it off.

Ida

There she was, sobbing right in front of me. Anyone looking into the room would have thought I was the therapist and she was the patient.

I was getting a bit angry.

Which one of us had the Bastard locked up in a cage?

Exactly.

Did I cry every time I thought about it?

No.

Did I cry when I told her about it?

No.

Did I tell her about it in order to comfort *her*?

No.

I'd had to deal with these experiences my entire life, ever since I was a little girl.

And she couldn't even bring herself to hear about it!

Tears rolled down her carefully made-up face. I tried to convince myself it was to my advantage that my therapist reacted to my experiences so viscerally. It meant she pitied me so much that she would likely do everything in her power to keep me out of jail.

My case had a profound effect on my therapist. In the future, she would probably focus her energy on me exclusively, to the detriment of all her other patients. I would have her full attention.

What if she delved so deep into my case that I ended up getting special treatment? She might give me her private phone number and tell me I could call her if I was having trouble getting to sleep. She would sleep with the phone near her pillow so she could answer my cries for help straight away. Or what if our sessions lasted longer than the traditional forty-five minutes and the wailing of the alarm clock never interrupted us again?

I could hardly believe my luck.

I wasn't prepared for my therapist's hysterical reaction or her floods of tears. It was a tricky situation. Should I start trying to milk her emotions right away or only once she'd calmed down? Should I wait for her to offer me a little extra or try to solicit her phone number now?

From the pocket of her short dress, she pulled a pink cotton handkerchief with something written in intricate embroidery. It looked like a letter 'P' to me, but it could have been a 'C'. Maybe it belonged to her husband. Maybe his name began with a 'P'. I'd assumed my therapist must be married as she wore a showy, and frankly tasteless, blingy diamond ring on her left ring finger. But I'd never bumped into her husband on my visits to the office.

I didn't know how best to calm her down. She looked completely beside herself. And there seemed no end to her inconsolable sobbing.

Of course, I should've known it would be better not to tell anyone about my childhood. There are such terrible things in the world that people can't bear to hear about them. Still, some of us actually have to live through them.

Arto

I decided to go to the Quill and Parchment to plan our final meeting. It needed to be perfect.

I walked up to the bar to knock back the whisky and refine my plan. The door opened behind me and who should stride inside but Irmeli.

'Arto! You're looking well! It's so nice to see the clouds seem to have lifted from you.'

What could I say? At least Irmeli appeared to think I was finally getting back on my feet. I was about to say something in reply when my phone rang.

'Hi, Arto! I just wanted to thank you for the interview. I've had so much positive feedback, you wouldn't believe it!'

Clarissa.

'No need to thank me. Just doing my job.'

My voice sounded forced.

I thought I'd already got rid of her.

'Modesty doesn't suit you. You should take my thanks at face value.'

I hmphed by way of a reply. I didn't need her gratitude.

'People have thanked me for giving sobriety a face. Alcoholism among women is still such a taboo.'

'Yes, I believe it is.'

Despite my answer, I disagreed. Nowadays, the media was awash with people telling stories of how they had overcome their drinking problems, both men and women.

'It was a terrible risk for me. Of course, I was worried about how this might affect my reputation, but it was a risk worth taking!'

Clarissa gave a pious sigh, as though she had just donated her entire fortune to fighting climate change instead of giving a simple interview.

'That's nice to hear.'

It had never occurred to me that the interview would work out in Clarissa's favour. I'd assumed that alcoholism might not be considered such a merit for a therapist, no matter how sober she was. It seemed she managed to turn everything in life to her advantage.

'I'd like to buy you a glass of Pinot to thank you. Shall we say, the Coffee Bean, later this evening?'

Pinot? A reformed alcoholic?

'Thank you for the offer, but there's so much going on at work right now that I'll have to decline.'

'That's a shame! I would have loved to raise a glass with you.'

For a moment, I wondered whether I should change my phone number and keep it unlisted.

'Talk soon!'

Irmeli had been standing next to me throughout the call, pretending to flick through her phone.

'What did Clarissa want?'

How on earth had Irmeli guessed who I was talking to? Did she suddenly have clairvoyant powers?

'She was ecstatic about the interview; apparently she's had lots of positive feedback.'

'That's nice. I'm proud of you, Arto!'

At least Irmeli wouldn't be left with a bitter taste in her mouth, even if this meeting turned out to be our last.

Ida

Do you remember the story about the boy who cried wolf? That's exactly what happened to me.

As a child, I had quite a lively imagination. I learnt to tell the difference between truth and falsehood much later than other kids my age.

I enjoyed being able to dive into an imaginary world where the rules of reality didn't apply. The dinosaurs might have died out, but that didn't stop me and my friend Ella from running around her house dressed as brontosauruses, shrieking at the top of our lungs.

If my parents or my teachers ever told me not to do something, I imagined doing it instead. In my imagination I was able to throw balloons filled with water right at my teachers' faces, leaving them spluttering and gasping for air, or to fill my bedroom walls with drawings of dragons.

But as a little girl, how could I possibly have had an inkling of what my wild imagination would one day cause?

My parents were used to me spending a lot of time in my own world. It's no wonder I didn't tell them about the cage or the Bastard. I was always concocting stories far worse than that: gnomes, leprechauns, giants, sea monsters. But to end up locked in a cage in a dark cellar? Why would they have believed me on that particular occasion?

If I'd told my parents about the Bastard, they would probably have thought this was because I secretly watched horror films though they'd expressly forbidden it. They'd say it was no surprise my imagination kept hurtling off in the wrong direction. They would probably have thought my story was proof that horror films weren't suitable for little children.

But how could they explain the bruises and contusions I'd sustained in the cage?

I was wild, and my parents couldn't rein me in. It wasn't out of the ordinary for me to fall off my bike or trip over some tangled roots in the woods, leaving myself covered in bruises. My parents had seen me in worse condition than that. Once, I fell out of a tree and cracked my front tooth. It hurt so much that I burst into tears, but at the same time I was proud that I'd been brave enough to climb high up into the tree like a monkey in the first place.

Perhaps it's understandable that my parents never suspected anything.

There was one thing that should have caught their attention though. Overnight my behaviour completely changed. Even so, it's hardly surprising that they weren't particularly worried by this metamorphosis. You see, I turned into the perfect daughter. In the past I was selfish and stubborn. Now I tried to please them in any way I could.

I'd never understood why I couldn't make decisions about my own life by myself, or why my parents tried to get me to do things I hated or that didn't interest me in the least. Why did I have to keep my bedroom tidy? My parents didn't live there; I did.

I had a habit of becoming so engrossed in my make-believe world that I would forget to eat when it was dinnertime or to come home on time in the evenings. I never remembered to do my homework, and my teachers were constantly pointing this out to my parents, who had long since had quite enough of my unruliness.

My mother was thrilled to bits when my character changed so dramatically. Whatever she asked of me, I did as I was told.

I tried to convince myself I was a good, well-behaved girl, so the Bastard couldn't have picked me out because I was bad.

It was my own fault for letting him imprison me. Of course, my parents had taught me about men who offer little children sweets then do bad things to them. They told me I should never go with men like that. But I broke the rule: I took the Bastard's sweets and went off with him. How could I ever have told my parents about what happened? They would have been furious that, once again, I hadn't paid their instructions the slightest attention.

Pekka

How can you tell if your partner is cheating on you? Let's google it! Your partner suddenly pays greater attention to their appearance. Check. Your partner seems absent more often. Check. Your partner doesn't have as much sex drive as before. Check. Your partner suddenly has an array of strange new interests. Check. And, above all, your intuition tells you that your partner is cheating on you. Check.

I didn't have any proof; I only had my instincts. And yet, I was absolutely sure. I could feel it in my bones. Clarissa was having an affair.

If I'd found out that Clarissa was cheating on me at the beginning of our marriage, my reaction would have been very different. Back then, it wouldn't have been about her so much as her suitor. Back then, I still thought of my wife as my property. Nobody else had permission to touch her.

I imagined humiliating the suitor by wooing Clarissa back. For me, the most important thing would have been to show this Lothario that I wasn't some pathetic cuckold; I was a real man who knew how to keep his wife in check.

After living together all these years, things were different. Now Clarissa was at the centre of things. Most important was to keep everything as it had been before. If her unfaithfulness led to divorce, the bottom would fall out of my life. What was I without Clarissa?

I was nothing.

As a young man with no life experience, I might have belittled Clarissa's significance and convinced myself I'd get on just fine without her. Now in middle age, it didn't dent my masculinity to face the fact that I was genuinely dependent on her.

We had been together for so long that I had lived with Clarissa longer than I'd ever lived without her. If she were to disappear, my life would be halved.

We were one and the same. Even the Bible said that a man and his wife shall become one flesh.

I needed to restore the status quo.

No matter what the cost.

Arto

I was sitting on the familiar park bench for the last time, looking up as she appeared at the window, turned, walked away, then reappeared. She shuffled back and forth across the five-metre length of her studio, hour upon hour, as if to punish herself for still being alive, mercilessly, trying to shed those final kilos. As though her studio was a prison and she knew she was going to die in there. She was serving a life sentence, measuring her cell one step at a time. Now and again she would stop by the window and absent-mindedly touch her nose stud, a small black pearl.

It wasn't just her studio window that kept us apart but the years of unspoken words between us, words I didn't have the courage to say out loud, though doing so might have saved us. I wanted to stand beneath her window and shout up to her, spill out all the dross I'd been bottling up inside.

There we were, father and daughter.

Me and my beloved daughter Ida, whose life I had watched slowly crumbling to pieces. And I hadn't lifted a finger to help her.

In order to understand our father–daughter relationship, you need to hear the truth about my marriage to Marja.

I first met Marja on an assignment. She had just been crowned Miss Finland, and I was interviewing her for *Helsinki Today*. We started dating, and before long we were married.

I don't understand how Marja and I ever ended up together. We should have separated as soon as we realized we genuinely had nothing in common. But you can guess what we did instead: we had a child. And once we had a child, we were stuck with each other.

Ida became a civilian casualty in our marital warfare.

I mocked Marja at every opportunity. I thought she was a superficial narcissist who didn't have two brain cells to rub together. Marja placidly sucked up the abuse until she eventually lost her temper. And when that happened, she well and truly let me know about it.

On our wedding anniversary ten years ago, she gave me a book as a gift. A book she'd written herself, in secret, alongside the demands of her modelling career. I opened the gift wrapping and expected to see a weighty tome about the Winter War or new conspiracy theories about the Nazis. Instead, I pulled back the wrapping to reveal a novel written by a woman whose name I didn't recognize: Marja Simpukka. Why would Marja give me a novel by someone I'd never heard of?

Research suggests that men don't tend to read books written by women. I was no exception. I wasn't interested in menstruation any more than I was in childcare.

That's right, back then I really was that narrow-minded.

The truth dawned on me when I opened the book and looked at the jacket flap. Posing in a photograph reproduced on the back cover was Marja, my Marja. Marja Simpukka was a nom de plume. She didn't need to say it out loud; the message couldn't have been clearer. She might as well have shown me the finger. Serves you right for thinking I would never amount to anything, you smug tosser!

My self-esteem came crashing down around me. I was the one who was supposed to write the great novel that would revolutionize Finnish literature! I used to torment Marja and Ida by disappearing into my office after work and at the weekends to write and snapped at them if they dared to knock on the door. But I was never able to write anything substantial and instead spent the time playing patience on my computer. The years passed inexorably, and as time went on, I became more and more embittered. I wasn't destined to become the next great literary genius; I would be nothing but a middle-aged loser, jealous of younger talents.

And that wasn't all, not by a long shot!

Marja's novel didn't just become a bestseller; it was lauded by the critics too. My colleagues and the literary critics I admired praised the book with all the superlatives I'd imagined would one day be used to describe my magnum opus.

And it didn't stop there. Critics make mistakes, and tens of thousands of readers don't necessarily know what they're talking about. The worst of it was that I too thought Marja's novel was good. Exceptionally good.

Of course, I had nobody to blame but myself.

Why did I read it?

That's when the real hullabaloo started. The novel's translation rights were sold around the world. Marja was invited to all kinds of cultural events, whisked from one interview and book fair to the next. She was handed everything that should have been mine.

I was the one who had sat in his office year after year, writing a sentence or two only to delete them right away.

Clarissa

A week had passed since my latest session with Ida, but her words would not leave me in peace. I didn't necessarily want to hear everything she had been through in her life.

Thankfully, Harri called me on the Friday and asked me to join him for coffee the following Monday. Apparently, he had some good news. I tried to ask what this was all about, but he refused to tell me. All I could do was spend the weekend in a state of excited anticipation.

I'd suggested we meet in the café at the Ateneum art gallery. Both Harri and I were so protective of our privacy that we had never visited each other's homes. This might sound strange, but actually all the therapists I know who receive patients at home, treat their homes like a fortress and only their own patients are allowed to breach the moat around it. I usually saw a minimum of eight patients per day, so I didn't want the doorbell ringing during my free time as well.

When I arrived at the café, I couldn't see Harri anywhere. I sat at a table in the corner just in case our conversation turned to work matters. My phone beeped: a text message. Harri told me he was just around the corner and asked me to order him a cup of tea and a pastry.

I was just placing the tray on our table when Harri greeted me. His entire demeanour was like a beaming smile. It was easy to believe he had good news.

I'd barely sat down before blurting: 'So, what's happened?'

Harri was even more impatient. He all but interrupted me.

'I'm getting married!'

My jaw must have dropped, because Harri started to laugh.

'Is it so hard to believe?'

It really was.

Having grown up in a religious home, Harri had internalized the Lutheran church's strict teachings about homosexuality as a child. By the time the church's position on the matter began to shift, albeit agonizingly slowly, it was already too late. Harri had sucked up all the disdain that had been shown him over the years. Other people's loathing had turned to self-loathing.

My friend had lived his entire life in the closet. It felt incredible that now, at the age of 74, he was ready to come out—and with a bang. Of course, he and his companion Topi had been together for years, but only a few of his closest friends knew the true nature of their relationship.

All of a sudden, a curious thought popped into my mind: Harri wasn't about to marry a woman, was he? Was this in fact an attempt to make the façade even stronger?

'And who is the lucky…?'

I didn't know how to continue: groom-to-be or bride-to-be?

'Topi, of course,' he replied.

I gave a sigh of relief.

Harri had never introduced me to Topi. In the past, I'd even teased him, asking whether Topi was only an imaginary friend.

'The big day is next summer. Here's your invitation.'

He handed me a thick pink envelope. I slipped it into my handbag.

'I'm happy,' he sighed.

Three things happened all at once. I realized I envied Harri, I felt a pang of resentment, and I was ashamed. How could I begrudge my old friend's happiness? How dare I?

Harri didn't notice my reaction. Instead, he began describing the decorations for the venue: pink, lace, crinoline, balloons, roses...

He had barely finished his tea when he stood up.

'I'm sorry, I'm in a bit of a hurry. I'm getting my morning suit fitted.'

He leant over and kissed me on the cheek.

'See you!' he chimed over his shoulder.

'Congratulations!'

I felt odd. To my shock, I realized I was jealous. Nobody could take my Harri from me.

The thought was ludicrous. Harri and Topi had been together the whole time I'd known him, longer in fact.

And yet, a paralysing apathy consumed me. Then I remembered that I had a mystery to solve, and I might as well solve it here and now instead of waiting until I got home. I fished the invitation out of my handbag and placed it on the table in front of me. The envelope seemed to bulge with its own self-importance. I tried to push the envy and jealousy from my mind by reminding myself that, after all these years of living in secret, Harri deserved all the happiness in the world.

I opened the envelope, tugged the card from inside and opened it.

Printed on the pink card was a photograph of the happy couple. Harri and Topi were sitting on a swing, hand in hand, cheek to cheek.

The mystery had been solved.

Now I had to believe that Topi really did exist.

Ida

Had I really told my therapist everything? About the Bastard, the cellar and everything that happened afterwards? Had I been honest with her?

Everything felt oddly surreal. Our session was only just starting, and memories of the previous session were still rippling through my mind like a dream. I couldn't be certain whether I was imagining it all or whether everything really had happened.

I recalled a metaphor my therapist had used at the beginning of our sessions. A secret was like a bag full of stones. You can lighten your burden by letting someone else carry some of the stones. It didn't seem like that to me. On the contrary, I had a niggling feeling that she'd torn a piece out of me, leaving me incomplete.

I'd lost something I could never get back.

I felt distressed. I wanted to be anywhere but in my therapist's surgery. The window caught my eye. Not again! But yes, the thick bars had reappeared in the window. I could smell the rust as it flaked off the bars and landed on the snake plant, its leaves pointing in all directions, on the windowsill.

The sight was made all the more grotesque by the pair of pink lace curtains fluttering against the bars. The cognitive dissonance was so glaring that I must have been seeing things. One of them had to be an illusion: either the rusty bars or the pink lace curtains.

But both felt equally real.

My therapist was sitting opposite me, anxiously waiting for more revelations. This time she'd come prepared with her own packet of tissues, which she was already twiddling in her fingers, as though she was sitting in the cinema waiting for a romantic tearjerker to start.

Was I nothing but entertainment to her?

'I'm sure you remember where we left off last time. So, just carry on from there!'

When did I become a trained seal, faithfully doing tricks for her amusement?

'Can't we talk about something else?'

My therapist's expression darkened a little. She had to work hard to maintain her smile. Something flickered in her eyes. Was that a threat? No, I mustn't start feeling paranoid about my therapist—that's the last thing we need!

'I really admire how bravely you told me about your experiences last time. There's no rush. But there's no point dancing around irrelevant subjects now that we've found the key to your subconscious.'

A violent image flashed across a screen in my mind.

A figure wrapped in a jacket covered in blood spatter was sawing my skull open.

Was my therapist planning on taking a bone saw out of the cupboard and saw her way into my subconscious unless I politely steered her there myself?

Or was the saw in my own hand after all?

I must have been visibly shocked by the image, as my therapist seemed taken aback.

'I'm sorry! I shouldn't have pressurized you! We'll progress at your own pace. What would you rather talk about?'

Arto

I became an author's husband. I still feel sick every time I think of that title. But more than anything, I loathed being a 'muse' to the great author. Now I only existed in relation to my wife. Nobody was interested in what I said or did.

Usually it's the other way around. As the old saying goes, behind every great man is a great woman. I'd never understood how women could simply accept such a fate and even enjoy their role in the shadow of all those great men.

I never got used to the situation. It was as though I didn't really exist. My self-esteem was in tatters and there was no way to sew it back together again.

Entitled *Am I Still Me?*, Marja's debut novel tells the story of an invisible woman called Marja who loves her husband Arto, though this Arto has never actually seen her. It's no wonder every single interview Marja gave started with the same question: was this the true story of our marriage? And every time she was asked, Marja denied it so emphatically that I was left in no doubt whatsoever that it really was about us.

The novel's subplot, at least, was so far-fetched that nobody believed it could be anything but fiction: the couple's daughter turned out to be a serial killer.

Where on earth had Marja come up with such a ludicrous story?

It wasn't long before Marja no longer had time for me or Ida. She was far too busy touring the literary circuit. Everywhere she went, a crowd of adoring fans followed her like zombies—mostly starving anorexic teenage girls who related to Marja's protagonist with a sick devotion.

At around this time, Ida had her tenth birthday and started torturing herself just like Marja's fans.

Marja was dedicated to her fans and didn't see Ida withering away to nothing. Only I saw it happening, looking on from the sidelines as the thread keeping her alive slowly began to fray.

Since Marja's death, the group of zombies has only grown larger. These days I take pity on them. If Ida hadn't been Marja's daughter, she would probably have been one of them.

Clarissa

One might think that revealing a secret is the hardest part of therapy. But no, the truth is that returning to those secrets at the next session is even more difficult. It is a relief to lighten a heavy burden, but processing that secret requires great strength.

Ida and I had reached the most demanding phase of her treatment programme. Now I knew with absolute certainty what the problem was, and I would have to resolve it.

I knew from experience that our therapeutic relationship was under strain. If the solutions the therapist offered weren't to the patient's liking, this might cause the patient to discontinue the course of therapy.

This can even happen when the therapist is right.

I once had a patient who was married to a violent man. As is so often the case, when we began everything was 'fine'. As cautiously as I could, I tried to ask why she had sought help if everything was fine. I didn't get an answer right away but decided not to rush her. Eventually, she told me what the real problem was. Her husband had been beating her.

Obviously, there was nothing else I could do but recommend a divorce. However, for one reason or another, my patient wasn't ready to leave her husband, though on a subconscious level she knew I was right. And so, she decided to resolve the matter by ending our course of therapy.

I knew things with Ida would have to progress very carefully indeed. I needed to convince her she was in control of the situation.

Ida arrived at my office fifteen minutes late, though in the past she had always been the model of punctuality. I'd already whipped myself into a panic imagining all kinds of dreadful reasons why she might not turn up.

In fact, I was already seriously considering calling round the hospitals when the doorbell rang. I rushed to the door. There she stood, paler than ever before. She looked so withered that it was a wonder she could stand up at all.

Impatiently, I guided her through to the couch.

'Remember, we're going at your pace.'

Ida turned to look at me. She looked sceptical. Her expression offended me; I had always respected her wishes!

'You and I are going to get to the bottom of this problem.'

At this, she scoffed. What now? What had I done wrong?

I didn't need to ask; I got the answer without it.

'I don't want to talk about it any more. It was a mistake to tell you about it. I didn't even want to tell you in the first place! You dragged everything out of me without a care for my feelings!'

There was a bitterness in her voice. I didn't understand what she meant.

'But you brought up the subject yourself! I didn't pressure you or force you to say anything!'

'You did! You did! You did!'

Now she was shouting hysterically. I felt utterly helpless. I couldn't for the life of me understand what she was driving at.

'You've torn me to pieces!' she continued screaming.

I couldn't get a word in.

'I thought you cared about me. I thought we had a special bond…'

Ida ran to the door, rushed outside and slammed the door behind her.

Standing by my desk, I suddenly came to.

Ida had left me.

Pekka

It's normal for patients to fall in love with their psychotherapist. It's a phenomenon called emotional transference. The patient focuses the love they felt for their mother or father on the therapist, regardless of the therapist's sex.

It is the job of the therapist to say all the things the parents should have said long ago. It's no wonder patients fall in love with them.

Clarissa had been working as a therapist for so long that she had found herself in a similar situation on countless occasions. What's a therapist supposed to do? It is their responsibility to maintain the professional nature of the patient–therapist relationship. That is, they should continue as if nothing has happened. The patient may on occasion try to seduce the therapist. It is the job of the therapist to establish boundaries. After that, it won't be long until the patient realizes what's good for them.

Still, therapists are only human.

I remember the first patient who fell in love with Clarissa. He was charming and muscular, the kind of man you would be more likely to see on the cover on women's magazines than knocking at a therapist's door.

One beautiful morning the man appeared at the office with a bunch of roses in his hand and swore eternal love for Clarissa. To prepare for the big day, he had dressed in a tailcoat and a top hat like a character in an old silent film.

Clarissa was obviously taken aback, especially since I'd never resorted to this kind of soap-opera stunt when I was trying to woo her.

Over the years there had been plenty of potential suitors vying for Clarissa's attention. Their behaviour was always so comical that I wasn't the least bit jealous. In fact, I rather pitied them and hoped they would one day be able to put their delusional feelings behind them.

Given her training and education, Clarissa understood right from the start of her career that these patients didn't really love her. There was nothing personal about their emotions. The real objects of their affections were other people altogether: parents, partners, ex-partners, relatives.

If Clarissa had ever succumbed to a liaison with a patient who was infatuated with her, she would have lost her licence.

Let us be in no doubt: this would have been an abuse of the power dynamic between therapist and patient.

The therapeutic relationship is not an egalitarian one; to the patient, the therapist is an authority figure. This hierarchy must always be respected. It is a question of professionalism. Every profession has its plusses and minuses.

I couldn't spend my time keeping a jealous eye on Clarissa's comings and goings. All I could do was trust that her behaviour was always moral and beyond reproach.

And hope that, even if the vows she had sworn meant nothing at all, she might at least have the good sense to uphold her own ethical standards.

Clarissa

I tried to get my head around what had just happened at my meeting with Ida. I was afraid of how she might react now. In my mind's eye, I saw a terrifying image.

A bloodied razorblade.

Ida had often described the incredible sense of relief and empowerment she got by cutting herself. As she put it, the brain released a pain that radiated throughout her body, quelling all her distressing thoughts and offering a moment's respite from her malaise. I'd tried to convince her that cutting was every bit as destructive a solution to her problems as drink or drugs. After a moment's relief, those problems would come hurtling back into her mind all the more powerfully.

Still, I'd been wondering whether she might have been right after all. What if by cutting a wound in her skin, she could keep her demons at bay, if only for a moment?

I started examining the cuts and scars winding their way across her arms whenever I got the chance. She always wore trousers, ankle-length dresses or long-sleeved T-shirts, in her own words specifically so nobody would see her scars. But hiding didn't always help. Sitting on the couch, she sometimes crossed her legs so her trousers rose up just enough for me to catch a glimpse of her ankles.

She had cut a long slit along her right ankle, its scar continuing all the way up her shin. Her left ankle was dominated by three large scars right next to one another, as though she'd been cutting notches in her skin to keep count of something.

The scar on her right ankle was fresh. I remember that, when I saw it for the first time, it hadn't quite healed properly. The scars on the left leg were older, maybe cut years ago.

She had plenty of scars on her wrists, some thin and some thicker. A long scar ran the length of the artery on her right arm. She once told me she'd tried to commit suicide three times, a different way each time. I knew without even asking what had happened on at least one of those occasions.

Ida's scars fascinated me. They were like little creatures hiding in burrows, showing themselves only rarely. Whenever she noticed that my attention had been drawn to her scars, she quickly pulled down her sleeve or trouser leg to conceal them.

I learnt to observe her arms and legs and to enjoy even the brief moments when she let her guard down and forgot to cover her secret notebook. Her skin bore witness to her entire history; it was an autobiography that she didn't want me to read.

Our session had ended with Ida accusing me of not caring about her. She had fled the room, as though I was the cause of all her problems.

I was convinced she would never come back to my office again.

Ida

I don't understand what happened to me. I'd dashed out of my therapist's front door as though my very survival depended on it. Once I'd slammed the door behind me, I leant against it, paralysed—the words I'd shouted echoing in my mind: 'I thought you cared about me.' I was afraid.

What did she want from me? Where had I got the impulse to run away from her? Or was I trying to run away from her at all?

No, she meant me no harm.

It was all because of the iron bars.

They usually disappeared and left me in peace relatively quickly. But this time something extraordinary had happened. This time the vision seemed to be getting stronger.

The longer I looked at the window, the more detail I saw in the bars. I had to force myself not to get up from the sofa, walk to the window and grip them. I could feel the rust between my fingers and had an irresistible urge to sniff them. They gave off the unpleasant smell of iron.

And with that I was in the cage once again, alone in the dark cellar; my only company the rusty bars that would not yield, no matter how much I rattled them.

I couldn't get away. I was locked up. My only chance of freedom was to run out of the room in a blind panic and head for the front door.

I leant against the door, trying to catch my breath. I tried to rationalize things and calm myself down. It had all happened years ago. It was over. I was here now, not behind bars in the cage. I was free.

I could still hardly believe I'd told my therapist all about the cage and the Bastard, right down to the tiniest detail. I was gripped by a nagging worry: that, instead of trying to cure my trauma, she would use what I'd said against me.

I managed to pull myself together enough to walk to the bus stop. My emotions finally gave way to reason. What had my therapist done to deserve my suspicions? After all, she was dedicated to the job of rescuing me.

For the first time in my life, there was someone who wanted to help me, and yet I didn't trust her. How could my therapist ever succeed in her mission if I kept sabotaging everything?

This secret had gnawed away at me, eventually severing my relationships with other people. No matter how much I wanted to tell someone about my secret, I just couldn't. And because I couldn't talk about it, I couldn't talk about anything else either. All my other experiences felt irrelevant by comparison, so there was no point discussing them.

Something so enormous had happened to me that, in comparison, the rest of my life felt small and worthless.

But now at least there was one person in the world, besides myself, who knew my secret.

I wasn't alone. As if this fact could make my experiences more real, give them more credibility. You see, not once did my therapist question what had happened. She never claimed I was lying.

Everything I'd told her had really happened.

My therapist was the proof.

When I was telling her about my experiences, she stared at me intently and encouraged me to continue my story. And whenever I paused, she nudged me onwards. It was as though she knew this was by no means the end, that there were still plenty of details to tell her, each more grisly than the last.

And though she wept as she listened, she never flinched, not once. Because she knew it all long before I'd told her a single thing.

The first time I met her, she looked me in the eyes and saw everything. But the truth was, once I'd told her all there was to tell, she was disappointed.

She wanted me to have suffered just a little bit more.

That way, saving me would have been an even greater act of mercy.

Pekka

I didn't know what to think myself. I'd been looking for the thread tying everything together but couldn't seem to find it. Every time I felt as though I was getting close to the answer, I reached a dead-end. And yet the same thought kept popping into my mind.

Clarissa has fallen in love with the Princess.

There, I've said it now.

I was so inextricably mixed up in this mess that I didn't know what was true and what was false. Still, infatuation was the most obvious explanation and the most sensible. Nothing else could explain why Clarissa was behaving like a lunatic.

And what if I was right? Then all my questions would be answered. That was why Clarissa wanted to treat the Princess herself, though she could see the treatment wasn't working. That was why she didn't have the patient sectioned. That was why she always tried to put a positive spin on it. That was why Clarissa tried to protect her.

I'll admit, I've done things I'm not exactly proud of. Who hasn't? But at least I take full responsibility for my actions.

Every relationship has its own crises. Over the years, I'd forgiven Clarissa for all sorts of things, and she had forgiven me too. But there must be a line that can never be crossed. And this time she'd gone so far past that line that a mere apology simply wouldn't be enough.

Do you realize how serious a matter this was? If Clarissa had ended up having a relationship with the Princess, her career would have been over. That I could have dealt with. But Clarissa wasn't just any old therapist. She was a TV personality.

The scandal would have been raked over in the public eye. And I would have got my fair share of crap too.

I could already see the tabloids: *Celebrity therapist in sordid patient–doctor three-way!*

The shame of it.

I promised myself I would do everything in my power to never have to see headlines like that in the local corner shop.

I would make sure Clarissa's reputation remained untainted.

And when I say everything, I mean everything.

Arto

Everything changed when Ida turned ten. My beloved daughter disappeared, and I never truly found her again. And it was all my fault.

That's right. I was the reason Ida ended up with an eating disorder. Nobody else.

And how do I know that?

Puberty was a tumultuous time for me. I was continually arguing with my own father. We could barely be in the same room together before I'd provoke him and whip him into a rage. My father enjoyed going hunting, so I became a vegetarian just to annoy him.

Puberty is a tough time for kids. But Ida's puberty was unique in many ways. Her psychological changes were so visible that nobody could miss them. Overnight, the independent, at times, stubborn little girl turned into a prim, well-behaved girl with an almost obsessive need to ingratiate herself both to her parents and her teachers.

I was idiot enough to think that being good and well behaved was her true character. A good father would have been able to read her better, but for me it was more important to write my masterpiece than spend time with my own daughter. It suited me fine that Ida didn't seem to need my help.

I completely misinterpreted Ida's transformation. I kept thinking that puberty didn't seem to be a crisis for her the way it had been for me, that she would get off much more lightly. If she'd gone around slamming doors and telling me to eff off, I might have talked with her about it and explained that puberty only lasts a short while, then life starts to get easier. And let her know I would always be on her side, no matter what.

But because she never snapped at me, I thought she was fine. I left her to get on with it.

I didn't support her, I was absent.

Ida couldn't manage by herself. And that's why she became ill. She turned into a robot, started to control her life with steely determination.

She dedicated herself to her schoolwork. The word perfectionism doesn't do justice to how she slogged through her homework. But when it came to her eating disorder, she was unflinching.

I soon realized that Ida was seriously ill. Marja disagreed with me because Ida tried to please her in any way she could. Ida no longer had a will of her own and instead followed Marja around like a loyal spaniel. Marja refused to take Ida to see a psychologist, though I considered it essential and unavoidable. We didn't live in Helsinki at the time but in a small provincial town where everybody knew everybody else's business better than they knew it themselves. Marja was worried that our neighbours would find out that Ida needed help. She didn't want anybody to think she had failed as a mother.

Eventually, I took Ida to see a child psychologist in the neighbouring town—behind Marja's back.

The psychologist reached her own conclusions about Ida's condition after just a single visit.

Apparently, there was nothing wrong with her.

Ida told Marja in passing that we had visited a nice lady who had let her play with dolls. Marja thought I must have a bit on the side and that I'd taken Ida with me on one of these dalliances.

There was nothing I could do but tell her the 'nice lady' was in fact the psychologist we had visited.

Marja never forgave me for this betrayal. How could I possibly have told some psychologist about our family problems without her permission?

If a single event is enough to destroy a marriage then, for us, this was it. From then on, Marja remained married to me for one reason only: because of Ida.

Everyone knows staying together for the sake of the children is the worst possible solution for all concerned.

But I didn't realize this until it was far too late.

Clarissa

I spent the weekend lying on the couch in my office with an unbearable hangover. Ida's fit of rage had shocked me so much that, as soon as she'd left, I drank myself into oblivion.

The sound of the alarm clock sent a pain shooting through my head, as though someone had stuck an ice pick through my eyeball and right into my brain. I couldn't spend all day lying on the couch. I decided to go for a walk in the hope that fresh air might make me feel a little better. I looked in the wardrobe for some Chanel. Just as I pulled on my mallow trouser suit, the doorbell rang. I flinched, startled at the thought that with all the drinking I'd got the days mixed up, that it was already Monday, and this was one of my patients.

I had no idea who might be at the door, but I opened it all the same.

No sooner had I done so than I almost got a branch in my eye. On the doorstep were three little girls dressed as Easter witches, waving their wands made of twigs, brightly coloured feathers and crêpe paper, and chanting in chorus.

Two of the girls were in costumes consisting of long dresses and chequered aprons, with bright pink scarves tied round their heads like Russian dolls, the kind of scarves my mother used to wear when I was little.

She used to tie on a headscarf like that every time she was getting ready to leave my father.

She would stand in front of the mirror, that determined look on her face, and tie the scarf in a tight knot. Then she brushed the few strands of hair underneath the scarf and started dragging our two suitcases to the front door. One of them contained her belongings, the other mine. I was never allowed to pack my own suitcase; instead, my mother always threw everything together in a hurry. If I hadn't been watching her, she wouldn't have packed a single one of my toys.

My mother's determination generally lasted only until we reached the front steps. I think the record was the rickety gate where she stopped to steady herself. Standing on the steps, she would stare into the distance and try to gather strength. A moment later, she would come to, as though she didn't know what she was doing. She'd let go of the gate, turn on her heels and come back indoors.

After this she would leave my suitcase by my bedroom door and throw her own on the sofa in the living room. I had to empty the case myself and hide it under my bed before my father came home.

Once my mother had unpacked her own suitcase and checked that I had unpacked mine too, she always made me some hot chocolate.

'Isn't it nice living here with Daddy?' she asked, nervously glancing around her as if my father had filled the kitchen with hidden cameras and she was scanning the room looking for them.

We had performed this same piece of theatre so many times that I knew my lines off by heart.

'I love living here with Daddy,' I said glumly.

In my work, I've noticed it's not unusual for parents to force their children to lie to them because, on the one hand, they can't face the truth and, on the other, they can't keep the truth at bay by themselves.

I'd often thought we should pass a law that anyone thinking about having children must first pass a demanding psychological examination, just as people hoping to adopt a child are put through a series of tests to assess their suitability. And this even though, had such a law existed at the time, I would never have been born.

No, that was wrong.

I didn't want a law like this despite the fact that I wouldn't have been born, but specifically because of it.

I left my reminiscences and returned to the girls standing at my door. The third one was dressed as a cat. Dangling from the bottom of her coat like a tail was a nylon stocking stuffed with cotton wool. The tip of her nose had been painted red like a cat's and she had whiskers drawn across her cheeks.

Longing began to bubble inside me. Why weren't these sweet little girls my children? And as humans so often do, I pushed the anguish away with another emotion: anger.

Why didn't these girls' parents give a damn about them? Didn't they realize that anything can happen to little children if they go around ringing strangers' doorbells? Their blind faith in people's kind-heartedness was leaving their children at the mercy of paedophiles: at day care, school, swimming pools... If these were my children, I would do everything in my power to make sure nothing bad ever happened to them. I would protect them like a lioness.

I snapped out of my thoughts. I rummaged in my blazer pockets, and in among all the badges and dirty tissues, I managed to find three one-euro coins. I hurriedly dropped the coins into the basket of woven bark brandished by the girl dressed as a cat and closed the door on them.

I didn't want to see their innocent faces—faces that at any moment someone might tarnish with their dirty fingers.

Arto

I sacrificed Ida on the altar of our marriage. Like Marja, I used to think divorce was the worst thing that could happen to a child. I thought that if Marja and I could just put up with each other for a while longer, we could give Ida a decent childhood. How wrong I was!

To me, this meant Ida being able to grow up in if not a blissfully happy, then at least a normal home. Of course, the truth was, she ended up having to take responsibility for her parents' unhappiness.

Every time she looked her parents in the eye, she saw the disappointment and bitterness that Marja and I felt at having to forgo our own happiness so that our daughter could be happy.

We placed a weight of guilt on her shoulders that not even an adult—let alone a child—could have borne.

I tried to placate Marja in any way I could, simply to stop our marriage from breaking up. And in doing so I sacrificed Ida. You see, Marja thought there was nothing wrong with her daughter. I didn't dare take Ida to the professionals behind Marja's back a second time. I was sure Marja would find out. That would have been the final straw, and I could have said farewell to our marriage.

And so, I watched helplessly as Ida's condition steadily worsened. I tried to bring up the subject of her illness with Marja again and again, but she refused to see the truth. She told me she used to make herself sick when she was younger to keep in beauty-queen shape and said it was nothing to worry about.

Apparently, I just didn't understand women.

Then whichever greater power determined our mortal fates, be it in Heaven or Hell, decided I hadn't quite had enough yet and that I needed even more shit to deal with.

Marja was diagnosed with breast cancer. The diagnosis came too late. The doctors gave her six months at most.

I dedicated my life to keeping Marja alive and forgot all about Ida. That was when she started trying to starve herself to death.

I can still feel the shame burning in my chest as I tell you this. But I want to be honest with you. Besides, if you're planning your own death, what's the point pretending to be a better person than you really are?

Over the years, Ida's illness got progressively worse. At some point, I had to admit to myself that anorexia would kill my daughter sooner or later. I tried to encourage her to get help. I implored her, begged her, bribed her, threatened her, black-mailed her, manipulated her. But it was no use. She had decided to commit a very slow suicide, and there was nothing I could do to stop her.

And once you've heard what I'm about to tell you now, you'll want to spit in my face.

I gave up.

I visited Ida less frequently. Every time I saw her, her condition had worsened. It was a miracle she was still alive at all.

What if one day I found her lying in bed, lifeless? What if more than anything else, her death felt like a relief? Because Ida wasn't my daughter any more; she was like a walking corpse, the living dead.

Every time I saw her, I felt a deeper sense of anxiety that there was nothing I could do to help her. And so, I started avoiding her more and more.

It was an infernal vicious circle. I felt guilty for avoiding her, but guilt made me avoid her even more. The gaps between our meetings got longer each time. And this in turn caused me even more guilt.

When Marja was still alive, I had tried talking to her about Ida's condition. Ida was ill and needed help, but we weren't doing anything to help her. Marja disagreed. Even when she was terminally ill, my embittered wife was convinced I'd tried to ruin her life by inventing our daughter's eating disorder.

Since Marja's death, the only person I've opened up to about Ida's illness is Irmeli. The night of our team-building seminar, I poured out all my sorrows about how I had caused Ida's condition by not supporting her while she was a teenager.

Irmeli tried to comfort me, but I couldn't help noticing how she too seemed convinced of my guilt. In fact, I don't think my drinking problem was the only reason Irmeli fired me; it was also because of how irresponsibly and selfishly I'd behaved towards my daughter.

But what would Marja and Irmeli have thought if they'd known the whole truth? That I left my daughter when she needed me most?

I missed Ida, but I couldn't bring myself to face her. The guilt was wasting me away.

Instead of taking care of Ida, I sat in the park watching as she stood at the window drinking tea and waiting to die.

Irmeli and Marja would despise me if they knew the truth.

Though not as much as I despised myself.

But rather than Marja and Irmeli, there was one person in this world to whom I had a duty to tell the truth.

Ida.

I suffered for her sake.

I loved her.

And because I was incapable of helping her, I would have to die instead.

Ida

Again, I'd spent the night in the cage. My dreams felt so real that they might have been suppressed memories. And there were blanks in my memory too. I remembered how I was forced into the cage and how I got out of it, but I couldn't remember anything about the five hours I'd spent in there, the five hours that changed my life. By the time I got home that evening, I'd already forgotten all about them.

What sort of things might I be suppressing? I don't know.

In the evening, the Bastard washed me in a bathtub in the corner of the cellar. After this, he took a hairdryer and dried my hair, combed it and plaited it. Then something happened, something I still don't really understand. The Bastard dressed me in my own clothes, carried me out of the cellar and up to the back seat of his car, drove to the very same parking spot in front of the fairground where he'd snatched me earlier that day, lifted me out of the car and placed me on a bench next to the car park, then drove away.

Yes, you did read right.

I didn't have to try and escape.

The Bastard let me go.

I've thought countless times about why he just let me go like that. Was there still a flicker of light in his black soul after all? What if he couldn't bear the thought of what he'd done, of the misery he'd caused his victims? What if deep down he wanted to stop sexually abusing children but couldn't do it on his own? What if he let me go precisely so that I would put the police on his trail?

Of course, the very fact that the Bastard had a cage in his cellar showed he intended to lock someone up down there. But was I the only one or one of many? Had others gone before me, or did they only come afterwards?

Was there a little child locked in the cage right now?

It was clear that, the longer the Bastard continued sexually abusing children, the greater his risk of being caught. You'd think at least one set of parents would believe a child who came home in tears and told them about the cage.

The thought that, after all these years, the Bastard was still doing what he'd done to me was too much to bear.

But if I was wrong and he was still at it, I would have to bear responsibility for every one of those kids. I knew what had happened, but still I did nothing to stop others meeting a similar fate. I couldn't live with that thought. It throbbed in my mind, day after day. I had to do something.

I would have to find the Bastard and kill him myself.

It was my duty.

But as sure as I was about that, I knew I wouldn't be able to face him in the flesh. The very thought made me tremble with fear. I fantasized about cutting him into thousands of little pieces, but I knew that when it came to the crunch, I would freeze.

The murders I'd committed had been nothing but a rehearsal for this one. But no amount of practice could ever prepare me for the duel I was about to fight. Standing in front of the Bastard, I would turn into that ten-year-old girl again, quivering with fear, the girl whose life he had destroyed.

The situation would be exactly the same as before.

A little girl versus a grown man.

Besides, the Bastard would have a home advantage, as there was no way I'd be able to lure him where I wanted him. Our final battle would be fought where it had all started: in the cellar.

Clarissa

I stuffed the decorated twigs the Easter witches had given me into the wastepaper basket in the hallway. I didn't want them there to remind me of the children I could never have. I deserved punishment for my sins, namely for the fact that I'd spent the entire weekend drinking. I decided to get to work. I felt weak, but I sat down at the kitchen table and booted up my laptop.

For a while now, I'd been planning to submit an article to *Psychology Matters*, a personal essay about photography. You see, I had a conflicted relationship with photographs.

Nobody takes photographs of crying children or a violent husband, not to mention the bruises he leaves. People only want to immortalize happy moments. And if there are no happy moments to immortalize, we stage them.

Adults and children alike are always smiling in photographs, no matter what the occasion. Our photo albums are full of lies. They could never be used as evidence of a happy life. Instead, they attest to the desire to live a lie.

A little child smiles brightly behind a birthday cake and a heart-shaped balloon. Because she is truly happy? Or because you're supposed to smile in photographs and Mum has told her to?

When I looked at pictures from my own childhood, I didn't know the answer.

The more I thought about this, the more unpleasant photographs began to feel. And not just my own, but all the photo albums that used to fill our bookshelves and now took up space in our phones' memories.

Once I'd written the introduction to the essay, I decided to look through my own photo albums for inspiration. I took them out of the bedroom cupboard and laid them out on the kitchen table. After leafing through my childhood photos, I decided for the first time in a long while to look at some from my life with Pekka, the few shots where I'd managed to catch him.

I'd put the photos from our wedding in a rose-pink folder that I'd decorated with some beautiful white lace. I'd glued our wedding photo to the first page. The photographer was so pleased with this shot that he'd asked if he could display it in his studio window. I didn't like the idea of our intimate moment being there on a busy shopping street for all to see, so I refused. I opened the album and prepared to admire myself twenty years younger.

The page was empty.

Someone had torn our wedding photo out.

I was startled. I flicked through the album from cover to cover. The pages were full of gaping holes.

All the photographs of Pekka were missing.

There wasn't a single one left.

Ida

I rang my therapist's doorbell and tried to look as neutral as possible. She opened the door and let me in.

I sat down on the couch and silently prayed she wouldn't mention the outpouring of emotion at our last session. My prayers were answered, as she appeared to be bursting with enthusiasm. She suggested we return our attention to dream analysis after the little hiatus. She could hardly wait to start raking through my bleak subconscious again.

'In my work as a therapist, I've noticed that almost all my patients have the same recurring nightmare. I've been having the same nightmare since I was a child. What about you?'

The cage. The cellar. The Bastard. I'd been having that nightmare from the very moment I was set free.

Can I even call it a nightmare? Every bit of it was true.

My musings were interrupted when I noticed how oddly my therapist was behaving. She was so excited that she couldn't sit still and instead stood tottering at the edge of the rug like a little girl in high heels. At times she looked like she was about to topple over but stretched out her arms at the last minute to keep her balance. It reminded me of those American drink-driving tests where a suspect is asked to walk in a straight line without wobbling.

The only explanation for my therapist's behaviour was that she was drunk.

I was so taken aback that I didn't think to stop our session and instead said I was ready to tell her about the nightmare I'd been having ever since I was a child. She bounded over to her desk, snatched up her pencil and notebook, sat down in her chair and kicked off her high heels.

'In your own time,' she said.

The high heels must have been too small for her, because she had a blister on her heel. It had burst, and blood had seeped into her nylon tights.

'I've been having the same dream since I was ten. I'm in the shower. A strange figure appears in the bathroom.'

She smiled at me, but the left corner of her mouth was twitching. Twitch. Twitch. Twitch.

The corner of her mouth was like a metronome to which I could have played the piano.

'The figure has a knife; he's trying to kill me.'

My therapist's mouth twisted into a grotesque grimace.

'Who is he?' she asked eagerly.

I startled.

'I was hoping you could tell me that.'

She scoffed.

'This isn't some kind of all-inclusive service. In explorative therapy, it's the patient who does all the work.'

I shivered. Her tone was positively frigid. As if she'd suddenly decided she was tired of pretending to be nice and pretty, and now, for the first time, she was letting me see her true self.

And the sight terrified me.

'Please, tell me who the man is!'

I stared back at her defiantly and said nothing. I was hoping she wouldn't realize that my expression was just a bluff. Deep inside, I was quivering with fear.

Throughout our sessions together, I'd never seen my therapist get angry like this. It was clear she had no intention of giving in.

She walked towards me and sat down on the couch next to me. Instinctively, I shuffled further away from her. Her perfume smelt familiar.

My mother's perfume. Chanel N°5.

But not even this warm childhood memory could make me feel at ease.

My therapist leant over towards me and looked me deep in the eyes, as though she was trying to hypnotize me. I almost expected her to pull a watch from her dress pocket and start swinging it in front of my eyes.

But instead, she gripped my jaw.

I flinched, both with horror and surprise.

Therapists don't have the right to touch their patients. She had deliberately broken her own ethical code. Instead of trying to wriggle free of her grip, I froze like a hare playing dead in front of a fox.

'Who is that man?'

She held my jaw even tighter, as though she was trying to squeeze a blackhead from my chin.

I was surprised at the power in her fingers.

Close up, her nail varnish looked like blood. The shade could have been called 'Murderous Night'.

My therapist's thumbnail pressed deep into my skin, and I winced with pain.

I wondered whether she was planning to hold on to me until I answered her question. In that case, we'd be sitting on this couch until kingdom come.

I glared at her, as angrily as my fear would allow. My gaze seemed to have no effect on her. Her eyes were still flashing with a rage so intense that I barely thought it possible.

'Tell me!' she snapped.

I gripped her fingers and prised them from my jaw one at a time. She flinched at my touch. We sat there a few confused moments longer, looking at each other as though neither of us could quite understand what had just happened.

She was the one who recovered first. She pulled a tissue from a packet and carefully wiped my chin, as though she didn't want to accidentally leave any fingerprints on my skin. Afterwards, she inspected my jaw from all angles, presumably to make sure she'd achieved the desired result. Then she nodded in approval, carefully folded the tissue in four and slipped it into her dress pocket with a sense of exaggerated calm.

Then she looked up at me, as though nothing had happened, a smile now beaming across her face.

'I think that'll be all, don't you agree?'

Perplexed, I stood up from the couch and walked to the door in a daze. I glanced at her over my shoulder. She waved back at me with that same radiant grin.

At the time, I thought that when she said, 'that'll be all', she was referring to that specific session. I was wrong.

This was to be our final session.

That evening, as I was going to sleep, I glanced at myself in the mirror. Though I was still in shock, the encounter hadn't left any physical marks on me.

With the exception of a small bruise on my chin, precisely the shape of my therapist's thumbnail.

Part Four

THE GAD-7 ANXIETY TEST

Clarissa

We all have our secrets.

Pekka loved American talk shows where members of the audience shocked their relatives with all manner of revelations on live television. What need did these shows fulfil? Was he using them to analyse the darker side of his psyche?

Personally, I couldn't stand watching real people's problems turned into social pornography. To my mind, it was shameless; it was abuse of the lowest kind.

Pekka, however, gobbled up one episode after another with such gusto that I started to think these shows must speak to some secret part of him. Could he too be hiding a secret so monumental that revealing it would make a studio audience ripple with horror?

What does it say about me that I'd never asked him?

Talking is difficult. All couples have their own taboos that it is hard—if not impossible—to talk about. For instance, we'd never properly talked about what our lives were like as children.

Pekka and I were by no means alone in this. You'd be shocked to learn the kinds of things people keep from their spouse. I once had a client who was born to a single mother in the 1930s. My client had never told her husband who her father was. Why would she? He had never asked her.

Would our relationship have been different if we'd been able to talk about things? Probably. But I'm not sure talking would necessarily have made it any better. There are plenty of other ways people can find a connection with one another. And I don't just mean sex.

I'm sure you can imagine an episode of one of those talk shows entitled 'Therapist and patient in lesbian love drama!' Would it ever have occurred to Pekka that Ida and I were in a relationship if he weren't addicted to sensationalist talk shows? Maybe, maybe not; we'll never know.

But that's not the question we should be addressing here.

Pekka tricked you all like a magician who catches the audience's attention by waving his left hand, while pulling four aces out of his pocket with his right.

He wanted to make me a scapegoat so that you wouldn't pay any attention to what he was really doing. You see, he did have a secret, and he was prepared to sacrifice anything to keep it hidden.

Pekka

I've always felt irritated at the way nightmares are portrayed in films. First, we see the character thrashing around in bed, mumbling something incomprehensible. Then they wake up with a jolt, eyes wide open, and sit upright. After this, they sit in bed, bewildered, and catch their breath.

Has that ever happened to you? It certainly hasn't happened to me.

Except on the morning when I finally unlocked the secret of the drawings.

I'd been scrutinizing the sketches every day for months. I found them repellent. Of course, the events they portrayed were repellent too. But that didn't bother me. Instead, I was perturbed that they seemed to be telling a story.

A story I didn't want to hear, though I knew it would be told whether I liked it or not. I knew the solution to the puzzle was close at hand. I couldn't keep it at bay much longer. It was drawing ever closer, inexorably. Perhaps I'd already known the answer for a long time. I just couldn't admit it to myself. People have a habit of rejecting things that it would be too painful to acknowledge.

Ultimately, my subconscious solved the puzzle for me. Clarissa would have chuckled to herself if she'd known I'd gone all Freudian on her. I've always made my disdain for psychoanalysis abundantly clear.

But the answer really did come to me in a dream.

I snapped awake, sat bolt upright and realized that what I'd been dreaming was real all along.

The cellar. The cage. The little girl.

I knew who that girl was.

The Princess.

And I knew who the picture represented.

The man in the suit with the sadistic smile on his face.

That's me.

Clarissa

I can hear your accusations. You think I must have known Pekka was a paedophile. You think I deliberately turned a blind eye, leaving him to carry out his crimes in peace. There's no way he could have hidden it from me, no matter how much he tried to cover his tracks. How can you keep something like that a secret, especially from your own wife?

But the God's honest truth is, I knew nothing.

I swear!

I only found out once it was all over, and by that time I couldn't save anybody. You'll believe me if you think about it. Why would I have waited for him to get caught? What would I have gained by protecting him? Was I too responsible for his crimes?

Pekka ruined our life, a life that we had painstakingly built up over the years. And he has the gall to blame me for it!

If I'm honest, I must admit I always suspected something was wrong. As though a dark, ominous shadow was constantly flickering just out of sight, but when I tried to look at it, it disappeared from view. Maybe I imagined that, if we didn't talk about it, it didn't exist.

But even if I'd had an inkling that something was amiss, I could never have imagined what!

Does Pekka have any remorse for his crimes? I doubt it.

Nobody knows him as well as I do.

And it seems I don't know him very well either.

Pekka

I abducted the Princess ten years ago. I locked her up in the cellar at my summer cottage, sexually abused her, then as evening drew in, I let her go. I'd never been caught for what I did. The Princess certainly wasn't my first victim. And she wasn't the last either.

There's the confession you've all been waiting for. You're welcome!

For many years, the fairground's annual visit was the highlight of my calendar. That year, I'd prepared myself by buying a bag of Turkish peppers.

The fairground opened its doors at ten o'clock in the morning, but I only arrived a few hours later once there was an excited buzz around the place. If I'd been one of the first to arrive, I would have drawn too much attention to myself; after all, I was a man and I'd come alone, without a child. Later in the day, nobody seemed to notice me.

I stood by the ticket office and started looking for a suitable victim.

There were dozens of children at the fairground. But none of them was alone. They were all accompanied by a protective parent or chaperone.

All except the Princess.

She'd come alone.

I waved at her from a distance. If anyone had happened to see us, they would have thought I was the Princess's father, waiting for my daughter at the gates.

The Princess waved back at me.

I walked up to her and offered her the bag of Turkish peppers.

'My favourite!' she squealed.

'What other goodies do you like?'

'Liquorice, biscuits, cinnamon buns. But I like sandwich cake most of all!'

'Sandwich cake, is that right?'

'Yes!'

'Well, now there's a coincidence. You see, I'm a baker. I've got a great big sandwich cake in my car right now. Would you like to taste it?'

'Yes, please!'

We set off towards my car. The Princess wanted to show me how frogs jump. I walked, and the Princess hopped merrily beside me.

'Hoppity, hoppity, hop!' she shouted.

We arrived at the sandy field that served as the fairground car park, and I opened the right-hand door at the back of my car.

'The cake is on the back seat. Jump in and you can have a slice.'

The Princess stuck her head in the door. I opened the boot of the car and took out a camouflage-patterned tarpaulin, then closed the boot as quietly as possible.

'I can't see any cake in here.'

I bundled her into the back seat, threw the tarpaulin over her and slammed the door shut. I opened the front door and sat down behind the wheel. Then I closed the front door and activated the central locking.

I turned the ignition and headed to my summer cottage.

I hadn't told Clarissa I'd bought this cottage. My wife travelled a lot for work, but I wanted a place where I could take my victims while Clarissa was at home too.

Once we arrived, I carried the Princess from the car and down into the cellar. I'd recently taken a course on hypnotherapy and decided to try my skills on her. I would hypnotize her so she wouldn't remember a thing.

I took an old pocket watch out of my jacket. I held it by the chain and began swinging it in front of the Princess's eyes.

'Follow the watch with your eyes and you'll feel better,' I told her.

The Princess obediently did as she was told. It didn't take long until she was fully hypnotized and under my spell.

So, now you know everything, but I managed to string you along all this time.

Clarissa didn't have a clue.

Having said that, I was very careful. I'd never been caught, though I'd had plenty of victims over the years.

But now the Princess had reappeared to mess up my plans.

I recognized her the very first time she arrived at Clarissa's office and I saw her through my office window.

But even if I hadn't recognized her, the drawings revealed everything.

It was hard to believe they were drawn by a ten-year-old.

The Princess had already almost lost her life at my hands. Out of the goodness of my heart, I'd decided to let her live. Now she'd sprung back into my life like a jack you can't stuff back into its box.

I couldn't allow that.

Why had she turned up at Clarissa's office? Could it really all be a coincidence?

Bullshit! She was up to something.

I had to find out what.

It was only a matter of time before the Princess told Clarissa that I had ruined her life. When would Clarissa finally realize that the Princess wasn't the least bit interested in therapy but had gone to Clarissa in an attempt to rat me out?

At first, I panicked and was certain I would be caught. I didn't want to be forced to take responsibility for my actions.

Time passed, but the Princess did nothing.

I felt increasingly anxious. Why hadn't she told Clarissa about my guilt?

After racking my brains, I finally understood what this was all about. The Princess knew more about reverse psychology than most people. Instead of blurting everything out at once, she'd decided to soften Clarissa up a little first.

This was a smart move. If the Princess had told her everything right away, Clarissa probably wouldn't have believed her and would have thought the story was nothing but the deranged fantasies of a lunatic. Instead, the Princess's strategy was to slowly wrap Clarissa round her little finger. Once she had Clarissa in her grasp, only then would she tell her story.

That suited me.

It gave me more time.

But whatever the Princess's plan, I had to react. I could no longer presume she would keep her mouth shut.

There was only one way to make sure she kept quiet.

Clarissa and I would have to get rid of her.

Together.

Ida

That Saturday morning, I woke up to the beep of a text message on my phone. I could hardly remember the last time anyone had sent me a text. To my surprise, it was from my therapist.

She asked me to visit her as soon as I got the message.

I was confused. What could be so urgent that I needed to visit her this very minute?

I decided to reply and ask what this was about. She didn't answer. I called her, but she didn't pick up and didn't call me back. After waiting for an hour in vain, I called her again. This time, the call wouldn't even connect.

Curiosity got the better of me. I set off for her office.

I had no idea what she wanted to discuss, but I never imagined I would be putting myself in danger.

On the bus journey, I wondered what she could possibly want to talk about. Had she made a breakthrough in my treatment? Whatever this was about, I wondered why it couldn't wait until our next session.

I walked from the bus stop towards my therapist's house. It reminded me of the wicked witch's gingerbread house in the old fairy tale. I was sure that, if I'd seen this place as a child, I would have wanted to break off a piece and taste it to see whether it was as good as the gingerbread biscuits my father used to bake at Christmas. I couldn't remember how things turned out in the fairy tale. All I remembered was that someone got bundled into the oven and burned to a crisp.

But was it the witch or Hansel or Gretel?

There are moments in our lives when fate changes direction at the very last minute. I rang my therapist's doorbell several times, but nobody opened the door. I was this close to giving up and heading back home.

What would have become of my therapist if I'd turned around and left? It didn't bear thinking about. But fate, or whatever it is that guides us, had other ideas.

We were both destined to suffer a little longer and much, much more.

Ida

Maybe it's time you finally heard the truth. In fact, nothing I've told you so far is true. Nothing except the cage and the Bastard.

All those murders I told you about? That wasn't me.

And yet, it was.

I can still recall my first compulsive thought. I was ten years old, and the Bastard had kidnapped me a week earlier. I was sitting on the sofa with my parents—my mother Marja and my father Arto—watching the news on TV. I wasn't paying it any attention. I just wanted to sit next to them, safe and secure. I might not be able to tell them about my experiences, but at least I could be close to them.

I was constantly having flashbacks to what happened in the cage. The flashbacks only left me in peace when I was with my parents. It was as though my immature brain still didn't grasp that even they couldn't protect me.

The newsreader was reeling off the ups and downs of the stock market. The litany of numbers came to an end, and she moved on to the next item. She assumed a more compassionate expression and began: *In recent years, the sexual abuse of children has…* She hadn't even reached to the end of the sentence before my father changed the channel.

And it was then that the thought occurred to me.

What if I were to crack my father's head open with a hammer?

The thought distressed me greatly. How could I even think something so sick? And about my own beloved father? Was I losing my mind—or had I already lost it?

I tried to push the thought from my mind, but I couldn't do it. Father. Skull. Hammer. Father. Skull. Hammer. Father. Skull. Hammer.

I saw myself opening the garage door, unlocking my father's toolbox, gripping the hammer by the handle, slowly walking to my parents' bedroom door, opening the door. I saw my parents lying there asleep, watched myself creeping next to their bed, bludgeoning my father on the head with the hammer. I heard the crack of his skull.

I watched the blood seeping into the sheets.

The sight was unbearable.

That couldn't be my thought!

But whose thought was it then? Nobody else could transmit their thoughts into my head.

The next thought was even more horrific. What if I lost my mind and actually did it, though I didn't really want to? What if some strange force had a power over me and compelled me to do it? What if the Devil controlled my body? What if all I could do was silently scream for help and nobody heard me? And once my father was lying in a pool of blood, what if I was accused of his murder, though at the time I'd been unable to control myself?

All these thoughts ran through my mind in a matter of seconds, not minutes. I felt like I could burst with anxiety.

I got up from the sofa so quickly that I knocked the pile of newspapers off the coffee table. My father started gathering them up from the floor. His balding crown was right under my hand.

I pressed the palm of my hand against his bald pate and stroked the faint wisps of hair.

My father turned to look at me, confusion on his face. I couldn't remember the last time we'd touched each other. I ran from the room.

There's only one thing I remember of the weeks that followed: the compulsive thoughts. The more I tried to suppress them, the more mind-space they commanded.

I tried to avoid my father's company as much as possible, so as not to do him any harm. But our family had a habit of eating dinner together, and this was one rule that my parents kept strictly. While he ate, my father used to leaf through the newspapers and didn't seem to notice my odd behaviour. I thought about killing him: sometimes by poisoning his food, sometimes by whacking him round the head with a frying pan. But mostly with a hammer.

I couldn't tell my parents about these compulsive thoughts. I was convinced they would have me sent to a psychiatric unit.

I truly believed I was a danger to others. I should have been behind lock and key. What kind of person is so afraid of themselves that they dare not be in the same room as their own father?

Thinking about it rationally, I realized my thoughts were completely irrational. But to me they were real. I knew perfectly well I didn't have the slightest intention of killing my father, but this did nothing to assuage my fears.

I wanted nothing more than to stop watching this sick horror movie in my mind, even just for a moment. Then I came up with a method that helped—if only for a moment.

Whenever a violent compulsive thought popped into my head, I silently apologized for it. Soon, however, one apology was no longer enough, and I had to apologize three times for each thought. Then five times, and so on. I couldn't concentrate on anything else, because my time was spent thinking compulsive thoughts and apologizing for them.

It was then that I delved even deeper into the realms of magical thought. If I did something wrong, my father would die, but if I did something right, he would live. If I couldn't do my maths homework, my father would have a heart attack. If I walked up the stairwell two steps at a time, my father's life would be spared. Once magical thinking stopped working, my illness developed into compulsive tics. I had to check time and time again that I really had locked the front door or switched off the cooker.

Did this help? No, but there was nothing else I could do. I slavishly repeated my rituals over and over, but I didn't get any better.

Everything started with that hammer.

I was afraid, but at the same time I knew I'd run out of options.

Even at the garage door, I hesitated. Could I really do it?

I remembered where my father kept all his tools.

My fingers were so sweaty that I almost couldn't open the lock mechanism. As I gripped the hammer's handle, I could have vomited.

I still don't understand how I survived. The hammer was as heavy as the gravest of sins. With the hammer in my hand, I slipped out of the garage.

I'd dug a hole in the nearby woods in preparation. I dropped the hammer into the hole and buried it there. Now I couldn't kill my father.

At least, not with that particular hammer.

After this operation, I sat on the floor in my room. I realized I'd never be at peace. Simply hiding the hammer wouldn't be enough—or maybe hiding it had been a mistake after all. I sat on the spot, frozen, and waited for the universe to give me some kind of sign.

Suddenly I was certain of what I had to do.

I stood up and hurried into the cellar. I was afraid I might chicken out, so I dashed to the steps leading downstairs, without even stopping to switch on the lights, and managed to get down the stairs in the dark.

I stood in front of the doll's house and repeated out loud: 'This will help.'

One at a time, I felt the dolls in the doll's house until I found the one I was looking for. I took the doll with me and walked into the garage. Hanging on the wall above the toolbox was a saw.

I took the doll that represented my father and sawed off its head.

Clarissa

There is nothing wrong with the grip on reality of those suffering from generalized anxiety disorder. Such patients are not delusional. They are, one might say, completely compos mentis. Instead, people suffering from generalized anxiety disorder believe they are crazy, though they are perfectly normal.

The notion of intrusive thoughts can best be illustrated using the familiar Pink Elephant Paradox. If someone tells you not to think about a pink elephant, you'll suddenly find you can't think about anything else.

Try it!

Intrusive thoughts work in the same way. It's impossible to reject them.

The dictionary definition of generalized anxiety disorder, or GAD, should include a picture of Woody Allen. Think of all the characters Allen has portrayed in his films—neurotic men who are afraid of anything and everything. What if I choke on the almond in the Christmas rice porridge? What if an asteroid comes crashing down on my head? What if the end of the world is nigh?

Allen's films are comedies, and this is why they never mention the darkest fears of those suffering from GAD. What if I go mad and kill myself or the first person who walks past or my parents?

Or my own children?

There's nothing friends and family can do to calm the mind of someone suffering from GAD. 'You're not going mad and you're not going to hurt anybody.'

'I know it.'

Yes, but what if...?

Ida

In the first few months after the cage, I learnt that you have to distrust everything. It felt like I was split in two, into my previous nice self and my current evil self which was taking up more and more space inside me.

I had no way of processing my traumas, not to mention my reactions to them.

And nobody helped me.

When my biology teacher taught us about puberty and the development of the personality, I assumed my problems must have something to do with the changes taking place in my body. I'd been well behaved as a child, but that wasn't my true nature. It was only now, during puberty, that my real persona started to force its way to the surface.

So, essentially, I was evil.

If something bad happens to a grown-up, they ask: 'Why me?'

But children are convinced that the reason for any misfortune must be inside them.

I was all alone.

There were no adults to talk to. And I didn't even have the words to describe what had happened.

My loneliness was all-encompassing. Gradually, I floated further away from other people, and ultimately from humanity itself.

What happened inside the cage sullied everything else I experienced. It erased all the beautiful memories from my mind. If I tried to recall them, all I could see were flashes of the cellar.

I really believed I didn't deserve anything good any more.

The Bastard had seen right into my soul. I'd always been able to trick other people, but not him. He must have grabbed me with his black fingers because he knew I was so dirty that he wouldn't leave any marks on me.

With hindsight, it's obvious I was angry at my parents. They didn't see my distress, didn't react to it. But I couldn't feel hatred towards them. I had nobody else but them, so I couldn't risk losing them too.

And thus, my rage turned into compulsive thoughts.

At least rage might have cleared the air. Now all I felt was guilt and anxiety.

Did the Bastard know what he was doing to me? Did he know he was tearing my life to shreds? Was I nothing but a toy to him, a plaything that amused him for a day until he decided to throw me away again? Had he spared a single thought for me since that day? Would he even recognize me if he walked past me in the street?

And the worst thought of all: what if I wasn't his only victim?

Ida

I've kept hundreds of newspaper clippings of the violent crimes I've committed. I've put them carefully into folders organized thematically. Most of them are assaults (three folders). There's a thick folder for murders too.

Time has already yellowed some of the earliest clippings. Over the years, the clipping from my first murder has become so smudged you can barely read it. It doesn't matter; I remember it word for word.

I started collecting these clippings when I was fourteen. It was four years to the day since the Bastard had released me from the cage. That's right: I was still counting the days.

At the time, I only read newspapers for the cartoons. This time, however, I was forced to pick up a copy of *Helsinki Today* as my teacher had asked us to find an article that interested us and analyse it at the next lesson.

I sluggishly flicked through the paper and tried to focus on the headlines, but they all sounded so dull. Politics, the budget, bureaucracy, corporate mergers. Some of them I didn't even properly understand. Most of the time I only read the first word, then skipped on to the next headline.

Suddenly, my eyes caught a headline that made me stop in my tracks. 'Man disappears in Salo'. The item told the story of digger operator Martti-Kalervo Katveenluoma, who had disappeared from his home in Salo. A thought flashed through my mind and startled me profoundly.

Had I killed Martti-Kalervo Katveenluoma?

By this point, I'd been living with my compulsive thoughts for four years and I already understood their logic—if logic was an appropriate word to describe something so completely illogical. I realized my compulsive thoughts weren't real.

I hadn't killed Martti-Kalervo Katveenluoma or anybody else. But that didn't stop me descending into a state of abject panic at the thought that I *might* have killed him.

Sense and emotion were engaged in battle in my mind, but emotion could thrash sense any day of the week.

I tried to convince myself that I couldn't have been guilty of Katveenluoma's murder. I'd never heard of the man, let alone actually met him. I didn't even know what he looked like because the short news item didn't include a photograph. And I'd never set foot in Salo. I had no reason to kill Katveenluoma. And so on and so forth.

But no amount of reasoned arguments could calm the maelstrom in my mind. I knew I had nothing to do with Katveenluoma's disappearance, but still I was convinced I must have killed him.

That night, I could barely sleep from the anxiety. I dreamt of killing Katveenluoma: sometimes with a knife, sometimes with a shotgun. In the morning, I woke to the sound of someone knocking at my door. The events of my last dream still lingered in my memory. Katveenluoma was standing in front of me, weepily begging for mercy.

The knocking continued. I was convinced it must be the police waiting behind the door. I'd finally been caught and would be sent to jail for my crimes. But it was my mother who had come to wake me up. I closed the door and dashed to my desk to guzzle up the news report again.

The previous night, I'd read the report so many times that by now I knew it off by heart. But I still had to read it again as soon as

I woke up, because now another compulsive thought had popped into my head, one that wouldn't leave me in peace: the news item mentioned my name.

'In connection with the murder of Martti-Kalervo Katveenluoma, police are looking for a suspect by the name of Ida Haaleajärvi.'

Naturally, the article was exactly the same as it had been the day before.

Soon, I started to believe I was guilty of all kinds of violent crimes. Assault, manslaughter, murder. I imagined slaying a jogger in Tampere on the same morning as shooting a barman in Keuruu. I was constantly guilty of new violent acts, no matter where I was or what I did.

Every moment of my life inexorably turned into a past that I would live to regret.

Guilt, guilt and more guilt.

Nothing could convince me that I wasn't, in fact, guilty of anything. Believe me, I tried everything. Every morning started the same way. I opened the paper and started looking for information about the crimes I'd committed. Often, there would be assaults both in Lapland and in southern Finland. Naturally, I couldn't be in two places at once, but trying to convince myself of this was useless.

I truly believed I was responsible for all the violent crimes committed in Finland after April 2009. Every headline sent me into a blind panic.

All the same, I was compelled to open the paper as soon as it dropped through the letter box and start scouring it for new stories to fuel my incessant guilt.

When I turned eighteen, I moved out of the house and became a hermit almost straight away. I didn't want to be around other people in case my violent impulses got the better of me and I ended up attacking or killing some unlucky passer-by.

Eventually, the only time I ever left my apartment was when I had to go to the shop, and soon this too felt stressful. The people I encountered had no idea of all the terrible things I could have done to them. They walked past me on the pavement, blissfully unaware that I was the most prolific serial killer in the country. They entrusted their life into my hands without having the slightest inkling of how dangerous it was.

If you think a person can get used to compulsive thoughts, you're wrong. They feel just as distressing every day. I've been having some of these thoughts for years. My first such thought— that I would kill my father—still plagues me to this day.

The only way to keep this thought in check is not to meet him.

In a way, it was a relief when my mother died of cancer when I was fourteen. I didn't need to worry about doing her any harm. That was one compulsive thought fewer. And yet, even the sense of relief made me feel damn guilty.

I was constantly tormenting myself about this. Every now and then, the voice of reason would pipe up, telling me I had nothing to feel guilty about. But guilt trampled this voice and snuffed it out. Day after day, I fantasized about torturing and murdering people, and at night I had nightmares about it. There seemed no way of putting these compulsions behind me.

After my first attempted suicide at the age of fourteen, I woke up in the paediatric ward at the psychiatric hospital. There I could rest. I didn't have to pretend to be fit and healthy, I could just lie there. A few months later, I was sitting in my old bedroom again, thinking about slaughtering the people walking past my window.

The years passed, nothing changed. Sometimes I was so exhausted that I dragged myself to the psychiatric hospital, but I was never taken into the ward because I wasn't considered a danger to myself or others. I turned up at the hospital again and again, but the psychiatrist on duty kept sending me home.

Ida

I spent a long time searching for the Bastard. Well, I'm not sure I can really call it 'searching' because I didn't have a single clue to go on. It took ten years. I never gave up, though I knew it might be an impossible task. I might have been a little girl, but I realized I couldn't move on with my life until I sorted this out.

It wasn't a decision, as such; it wasn't based on any moral conclusions. If I killed the Bastard, would I be lowering myself to his level? Would I be a different person afterwards? Would it tarnish my conscience or morals? Would it ruin me, leave me corrupt, immoral, rotten to the core? Or would I be a hero, a saviour of little children? Or something different altogether, irredeemably changed? Would I cease being human and turn into an animal—no better than the Bastard himself? Would anyone be able to forgive my actions, let alone understand them?

I couldn't afford such theoretical contemplation. Every moment I spent mulling over these questions was another moment the Bastard could use looking for new victims. Other people could interpret my actions however they wanted and judge me by their own moral compass. All I could do was act.

At first, everything was a bit haphazard. After all, I was only a little child. I didn't know the Bastard's name and I didn't have any evidence of his existence save for the drawings I'd made. I liked drawing goblins and dragons too, but that didn't mean they really existed. Why would I have shown these drawings to anybody? Who would have believed me?

I didn't know where to start. I remembered what the Bastard looked like and what it was like in his cellar, but that was it. He had kidnapped me from the fairground and bundled me into his car, but I couldn't remember what colour the car was. He lifted me into the back seat and covered me with a camouflage-patterned tarpaulin. The back seat was dotted in white blotches that looked as though Tom Thumb or some other tiny being had fallen ill and thrown up over the seat covers time and time again.

For the first time in my life, I resorted to magical thinking. If I could just huddle under the tarpaulin and not make a peep, all would be well. I tried to lie perfectly still, exactly where the Bastard had placed me. But keeping still was hard because he was an erratic driver. Sometimes he turned or braked so violently that the back of the car shuddered.

He clearly didn't care that he was a danger to other drivers or to me, or that he was putting himself in danger too. Neither did he seem to care that his driving might have attracted the attention of the police.

I noticed there was a small hole in the tarpaulin but tried to avoid looking through it. I thought, if I couldn't see or hear anything, nothing bad would happen to me. I closed my eyes to make sure I didn't accidentally catch a glimpse of the landscapes flashing past. And that was why I didn't have the slightest idea of the route we had taken or where we were going.

The Bastard slid a cassette into the tape player, and the car's speakers started throbbing right behind my neck. I was so startled that I opened my eyes. Through the hole in the tarpaulin, I saw a small pink sequin sparkling in the footwell under the back seat. My best friend Ella had a T-shirt with sequins exactly the same colour.

It had a picture of Winnie the Pooh wearing a sunhat decorated with pink sequins. I imagined Ella sitting next to me on the back seat, squeezing my hand. Lying next to the sequin was a dog-eared passport photo. A beautiful woman, gently smiling at me.

Maybe everything would be all right after all?

I slipped my hand through the hole in the tarpaulin, picked up the photograph and slid it into my pocket.

This woman would protect me from all evils.

Hit me, baby, one more time, Britney Spears sang on the tape. The Bastard started singing along but stopped after one verse, as if suddenly remembering he had an audience.

Over the years, I've often returned to places familiar from my childhood, as unpleasant as it felt to do so. Every time, it set off such a whirlwind of emotions that I still find it hard to compartmentalize my feelings. This was where everything had happened. On the one hand, I was scared I would bump into the Bastard one day, but on the other I was scared that I wouldn't.

As time passed, I realized it was becoming increasingly unlikely that I'd ever track down my old nemesis. Hope dwindled and despair took hold.

But still I walked this familiar route. My childhood home, the nearby sports field where the fairground had been. The car park where the Bastard had snatched me and bundled me into the back seat of his car. That was my last coordinate. The Bastard returned me to the very same car park later that evening.

It's a miracle I ever managed to establish his identity.

Ida

I didn't want to see any more headlines about new murders for which I'd have to take responsibility. And so, I'd long decided I'd be better off not using the Internet at all, not reading the papers or watching TV. I don't know what divine power made me change my mind that particular evening and switch on the television my father had given me for Christmas.

Sometimes, chance can be grotesque.

Clarissa Virtanen was on TV, talking about feminism on *Newsreel*. I still recognized that face, though by now she was ten years older.

The woman whose passport photo I'd taken from the Bastard's car.

I still had that photograph. It was in the same shoebox where I'd kept my drawings. I hadn't touched the box for ten years, so it took a while before I plucked up the courage to open it. I mustered all the bravery I could find and lifted the lid. Lying on top of the contents was the passport photo, faded by the intervening years.

A beguiling, beautiful woman.

Clarissa Virtanen, my guardian angel.

But what was the Bastard doing with her photograph?

I turned the photograph over. I'd remembered right after all. On the back of the photo was a dedication: 'To my dear Pekka!'

Clarissa

I told you earlier on that Riku was the last of my patients to commit suicide. I owe you an apology. That's not exactly what happened.

In fact, it's not even remotely true.

It's been months now. It all happened early one Sunday morning. Pekka was away on a fishing trip in Lapland and I was at home by myself. The doorbell rang. Standing behind the door was a teenage boy I'd never seen before.

He had combed his green Mohican back across his head, and the front of his ripped denim jacket was covered in the patches and insignias of different punk bands.

I was rather startled by his appearance but tried to conceal my shock.

The boy seemed to wonder who I was.

'Is your husband home?'

I couldn't help my prejudice.

'How do you know my husband?'

'You'll have to ask him that.'

The boy looked at me defiantly. He stank of tobacco and old liquor. I felt sick.

'Pekka isn't here right now, so I'm asking you.'

My voice had changed; it sounded feeble.

'Well, if you really wanna know, let me fucking tell you,' he shouted.

I bristled with fear.

'You should know who you're married to. Your husband's a paedo. He raped me last weekend.'

I reacted before I'd even understood what I was doing. I grabbed his denim jacket, dragged him into the hallway and slammed the front door behind him.

The neighbours mustn't overhear lies like this.

'What is it you want?' I snapped, livid with rage.

'Money. Pekka's gonna pay for this. And 'cause he's not here, you're gonna pay for him. Five hundred or I'll tell the cops.'

The boy clenched his right hand into a fist. Was he going to beat me up if I didn't pay him?

Five hundred euros is a lot of money to a teenager, though I could have pulled the notes out of my purse right away. But I was certain that if I gave in, the blackmail would never stop. He could come back and demand another payment any time, and next time he might ask for even more. Pekka and I would be paying him off for the rest of our lives.

I'd never heard of children using baseless accusations of paedophilia to extort money from adults. Perhaps this boy had seen my interviews about sexual abuse and thought I'd be an easy target; after all, it was my job to stand up for victims.

But how did he know Pekka's name? No, he hadn't used the name first. He'd only asked if my *husband* was at home.

I didn't know how I was going to get rid of the boy, so I had to come up with something on the spur of the moment.

'I'm afraid I don't have any cash right now. Can you come back in an hour? I'll go to the cashpoint and take some out.'

The boy agreed and slipped out of the door in a flash. I retreated to my office to refine the details of my plan. I was certain that these accusations had been plucked out of thin air. Pekka and I had been married for over twenty years. I knew my husband so well that he couldn't say or do anything that would have taken me by surprise.

I was the most highly regarded expert on sexual violence and abuse in Finland. I of all people would have noticed if my own husband was a paedophile!

I was convinced the boy was lying and Pekka was innocent. But what if someone took his accusations seriously? Even if the case went all the way to court and Pekka was acquitted, it would already be too late. My husband's reputation would be destroyed.

And if he was branded a paedophile, what would that do to my credibility? My career would be over.

Ida

It's one thing to fantasize about murder and quite another thing to commit one. I was sitting on the sofa, my hands trembling uncontrollably. But it didn't take me long before I worked out how I could engineer a perfectly natural meeting with the Bastard: I would become his wife's patient!

In the past, he had been streets ahead of me, but now I had the chance to catch up with him. There's no way he would recognize me. I used to be considerably overweight as a child. I had a thick head of fair hair and my skin was tanned. These days I was scrawny, and I'd dyed my hair jet black. I barely recognized myself in childhood photos. How could he possibly connect me to the little girl he'd imprisoned in his cellar ten years ago?

My opportunity had finally come, but I was worried I wouldn't be able to take it. The Bastard still had control over me. For the first time in ten years, I was on the verge of giving up.

I decided to sleep on it and make a final decision in the morning. Naturally, I didn't sleep a wink. By morning, I'd made up my mind.

I was ready to die.

I'd whipped myself into such a frenzy that I felt the urge to attack the Bastard right away. Nonetheless, I managed to quell my impatience. I'd been waiting for this moment for over ten years. What was the rush? I could do this slowly.

And I would strike when he least expected it.

With quivering fingers, I googled his wife's name. I could hardly believe what I found out. The whole of Finland seemed enthralled with Clarissa. She was everywhere: on TV, on the radio, in glossy magazines. How was it possible I hadn't paid her any attention until now?

Of course: my self-imposed media blackout.

The search engine directed me to her home page.

Clarissa Virtanen. Psychotherapist. Areas of expertise: childhood experiences of violence and abuse.

I stared at the screen, utterly paralysed. I didn't realize I was crying until I looked down and saw a puddle of tears on the keyboard.

Clarissa

An hour later, I was nervously waiting to see whether the boy would return as promised. When the doorbell rang and I saw him standing on the doorstep, I could sense he was nervous too.

I handed the boy a 500-euro note. He snatched it from me so quickly that it almost ripped in two. Again, he disappeared in the blink of an eye.

I waited a moment, then hurried after him.

He must have been afraid that I might have second thoughts, because he broke into a run. I sped after him, keeping enough distance that he didn't see me. After we had both run a few hundred metres, he suddenly stopped. I hurriedly hid outside an old antique shop, in a doorway that smelt like a public urinal, then peered around the corner to see what he was planning.

The boy shrugged off his backpack, took out his phone and headphones and started listening to music. The volume was so loud that I heard the aggressive opening bars of the Sex Pistols's 'God Save the Queen'.

The boy walked off and continued on his way. I followed him relentlessly. It turned out he was heading to the Central Railway Station. He headed to the escalators leading down into the underground, and I kept right behind him.

He stood waiting for the next underground train, apparently not paying any attention to the warning lines painted at the edge of the platform.

Almost as though he could sense his fate.

It was so early that the platform was empty.

I ran up to the boy. He hadn't noticed I'd been following him. I appeared out of nowhere. He was so surprised that he couldn't defend himself. I pulled him towards me and grabbed his hands through the sleeves of my trench coat. I swung him out over the tracks, still holding him by the hands.

The train came hurtling out of the tunnel.

I let go of Riku's hands and called for help.

It took the guards a moment to run down the escalator. When they arrived on the platform, I was trembling hysterically. The guards called the police, who lifted Riku's body from the tracks back onto the platform.

I looked at him one last time, and then I left.

I was called down to the police station for interview that same afternoon. The police had already watched the footage from the security cameras. A long time ago, I had taken a self-defence course, just in case one of my patients ever got violent. This was the first time I'd been able to use my skills. From the footage, it looked as though Riku was trying to throw himself in front of the oncoming train and I had tried to save him. The police didn't suspect me. I surely wouldn't have waited on the platform until the guards arrived, let alone cried for help if I had killed him.

The officer interviewing me only wanted to establish how Riku and I knew each other. I said Riku was one of my patients. Before the interview, I'd drawn up a document that I now pulled out of my handbag. I explained to the officer that, because Riku was a minor, I had asked him to get his parents to sign a document giving consent for his therapy. Should the police ever show this document to Riku's parents and learn that the signatures were forged, I could always say that Riku must have forged them himself because for one reason or another he didn't want to tell his parents he had reached out to me for help.

Naturally, the police knew I was bound by a duty of confidentiality towards my patients, but because a death had occurred, they said they hoped I would answer their questions as candidly as possible.

I told them Riku had come to me asking for help a few weeks earlier and that I had seen him at my office twice. I had decided to make an exception and offer him treatment pro bono. Initially, I'd been reluctant to take him on as a patient and had instead planned to contact social services and ask them to treat him.

I also told them Riku had appeared at my office that same morning and started pouring out his anguish. He'd seemed depressed, almost inconsolable. I told them I'd decided it was time to confront Riku's parents about their son's problems. I'd managed to convince him to talk to his parents on the condition that I accompanied him. When we arrived at the railway station, Riku had burst into a run and dashed towards the escalators leading to the metro. I'd hurried after him but had slipped, as the station floor had recently been waxed and was still very slippery. I told them I was relieved to see him standing there on the platform waiting for me. I ran up to him, took him by the hands and squeezed as tightly as I could.

I told the officer that I went to the gym regularly and considered myself to be in good shape. But what match was I, a slender woman, for a strong teenage boy? Riku had wrenched himself free of my grip and thrown himself on the tracks, as the security footage clearly showed.

I made sure that, when I pushed him onto the tracks, I'd gripped his hands hard enough to leave bruises that the pathologist would find at the autopsy. They would convince the police that I'd been

323

holding on to Riku with all my strength to stop him jumping onto the tracks.

The officers wanted to know whether Riku had demonstrated suicidal tendencies before. No, I assured them; his suicide had come as a complete surprise.

The police said they were grateful for my help. The interview was over. The case seemed cut and dry. There was no point even considering the possibility of foul play.

This was clearly a suicide.

Pekka

Just so we're clear, Ida wasn't my first victim.

Do you want to hear some more?

I bumped into Riku by accident in the car park at the Central Railway Station. It was only a few months ago. He came up and asked if I would buy him some beer from the shop. He was only fifteen, so he couldn't do it by himself.

Riku was what you might call an alternative kid. But no matter how much he tried to make himself ugly by sticking all kinds of things through his nose and ears, nobody could fail to notice that his face was as beautiful and innocent as a little child's.

He had narrow lips which he accented with blue lipstick, long eyelashes like a newly born foal, and such high cheekbones that I felt almost faint.

Needless to say, I had to lure him away with me.

Luckily, Clarissa was away on business.

It was easy. Riku was already drunk and he couldn't think straight. I told him I had a thing for fine wines and that he could taste some in my wine cellar if he wanted. It didn't take long before we were in my car heading back to our house.

During the drive, Riku spilled out his life story. He essentially lived by himself in his parents' one-bedroom apartment in Kontula on the disreputable east side of Helsinki. His parents were junkies who didn't spend much time at home. He had just managed to scrape enough grades to finish lower school, but only a few months after the hymns from the graduation ceremony had faded, he was down on his luck and quickly falling through society's cracks.

That meant only one thing: nobody would miss him.

We arrived at my house. As I've done this far, I'll spare you the details. But I will tell you that I laced his drink with temazepam, and before long he was in such a state that I could do whatever I wanted with him.

A few hours later, I dragged his comatose body onto the back seat of my car, drove to the car park outside the Kontula shopping mall and left him on a park bench to sleep off his drug-induced slumber.

I assumed he would be so ashamed of what had happened that he would never breathe a word about it.

Ida

Why are you so keen to hear all the gory details of my time in the cage? You don't know me. To you, I'm nothing but letters on a sheet of paper. To you, I'm not a real human being; I might as well be a character in a novel.

Everything I've told you is just social porn; you might as well have been flicking through the tabloids. You gasp in horror at my suffering, but more than anything, you're relieved. Thank God, all those things happened to her and not to me!

You claim to have sympathy for me, but you're secretly disappointed that what happened to me wasn't gruesome enough. It was bad, but it could have been worse, right? It's a pretty good story, but it could have been even more depraved. It's the same disappointment you feel when watching a horror film: more blood and guts, please, more, *more*!

The more I suffer, the more you enjoy it.

I'm nothing but entertainment to you.

Or am I being cynical?

Maybe you do feel sympathy for me.

But that is enough. To you, they might just be words, but every word, no, every thought rips my wounds open again and again.

What use is it to me to tell you all this?

Maybe the more I tell you about the cage, the more you'll trust me. Maybe every drop of blood, every bruise and graze will convince you that it really did happen. Maybe if you saw the scar on my thigh? Or do you want even more evidence? Photographs? Video footage? Medical records? A police report?

Exactly. I've got none of that.

It's just my word against his.

Me against the Bastard.

But why would I lie about being a serial killer, you might ask? Why couldn't I tell you the truth?

I apologize!

I loathe lies because I've spent my whole life trying to hide what really happened during my childhood. To me, nothing is more important than the truth, but I had a good reason for lying. Honestly.

After all, I'm a serial killer—in my mind, that is. For the last six years, I've done nothing but kill people, murder them, in my mind during the day and in my dreams at night. When I called myself a serial killer, I wasn't lying.

At least, I didn't think I was.

Clarissa

The police interview lasted barely half an hour. First, I planned to call Pekka as soon as I got home and tell him everything that had happened. But as I sat on the tram, I realized he had nothing to do with it. I had caused this mess all by myself.

Riku had decided to torment Pekka because he'd seen me in the media and found out that I work with the victims of sexual violence. Pekka had nothing to do with this devious scam.

So, I decided not to tell him anything.

My husband would never accept the murder of a teenage boy, no matter what spin I put on it.

He might even hand me over to the police.

The day's events had exhausted me so much that I decided to go to bed early.

The following morning, a question forced its way into my mind and woke me. How did Riku know I was married? And where had he found our home address?

Our address wasn't in the public domain, so there was no way anyone could have found out where we lived.

Unless Pekka had brought him to our house.

I was consumed with a sense of foreboding.

Riku had been telling the truth.

None of my clients had ever lied about being abused. Abuse is such a shameful thing that nobody would make it up on a whim.

And I had dismissed Riku's claims as lies simply to protect myself and my reputation!

I don't remember anything else about that day. In the past, I used to be quite a moderate drinker, but that morning I drank myself into such a stupor that I blacked out. The guilt was unbearable.

Now I understand why I tried to defend myself against his accusations so aggressively. My psyche couldn't handle the knowledge that my beloved husband was a child molester. I felt the urge to deny it in any way I could, and so I rejected the knowledge in the most extreme way. Subconsciously, I was trying to convince myself that Pekka was the innocent party and Riku was lying, all so that I wouldn't have to face the truth. Once the imminent danger was over and Riku was dead, my psyche gradually began to accept the fact that his story had been true all along.

Having spent my entire career examining the machinations of the human mind, now I learnt that when it came to the crunch, I couldn't even read my own motivations.

The following morning, I woke up with a terrible hangover. Guilt hammered at my subconscious so mercilessly that I was worried I might be losing my mind. All I could do was decide how to live with it for the rest of my life.

What was most important was to prevent Pekka from ever committing another crime. I could only do this if I stayed married to him. My life's goal was now to follow him so closely that he would never be able to act upon his sick impulses again.

Pekka

Had I ever envisaged ten years ago that Ida and I would one day cross paths again? I could have killed her right there in the cage, but I let her go free.

You probably already know that deep down we criminals *want* to get caught—at least, subconsciously. You've read enough crime novels to know this is why we always return to the scenes of our crimes.

I wasn't afraid that by letting Ida go, I would one day be caught. I had no reason to worry about that. In many interviews, my wife had explained that a child's psyche can cope with far less trauma than an adult's. And only a very few adult psyches were resilient enough not to suppress the things I had done to Ida. And so, I was confident that she wouldn't remember anything about her experiences. Besides, I'd hypnotized her to make her forget about everything. I still don't understand why it didn't work.

However, post-hypnotic suggestion, whereby the hypnotist defines a trigger at which the subject will re-enter hypnosis again and again, can work perfectly well ten or more years later.

All those years ago, I had chosen a particular gesture as our trigger. So, I lured Ida to our house with a text message sent from Clarissa's phone, and when she arrived, I gripped her by the shoulders in the hallway. She slipped into hypnosis right there and then.

Ida

On the face of it, it was a flawless plan: I was going to commit my very first murder. I didn't really care if I got handed a life sentence as a result; it couldn't make my life any more miserable than it already was. Instead, I could finally rest in the knowledge that no other little kids would ever fall victim to the Bastard.

I thought I'd fine-tuned my plan to perfection. I didn't want to ruin things by needlessly rushing. I was prepared to go to a lot of trouble to pull this off.

When I rang the doorbell, I knew my therapist hadn't sent the text I'd received. There was a typo in the message, but I'd read the essays on her home page and I knew she had an unrivalled mastery of Finnish grammar. I was convinced that, waiting for me at the door of the surgery, would not be my therapist but the Bastard himself.

The plan was to trick the Bastard into taking me back to their summer cottage, where he'd imprisoned me in the cellar all those years ago. In my bag I had a filleting knife that I planned to use to force him down into the cellar and slit his wrists, so his death looked like suicide.

I'd even written a pre-prepared suicide note in which he confessed to his crimes, acknowledged everything he'd done to me when I was an innocent little girl, said that he realized he'd killed my spirit, that he wanted to ask me for forgiveness, that he could no longer live with the guilt. Blah blah blah.

As if paedophiles could ever feel guilt over what they had done.

Now I realize quite how ridiculous my plan was. It could have gone wrong in so many ways.

And boy, did it go wrong.

As I was standing in the hallway at the surgery, the Bastard grabbed me firmly by the shoulders and stared right into my soul with his devil's eyes. He probably thought he could hypnotize me. But there he was mistaken.

He'd tried to hypnotize me the first time he kidnapped me, swung an old pocket watch in front of my eyes. It was silver and had a skilfully engraved image of a compass rose on it.

We'd just learnt about the cardinal points at school. I made a mental list of them one at a time as the watch swung back and forth: north, east, south, west. North-east, south-east, south-west, north-west.

I kept my eyes firmly fixed on the Bastard's watch but concentrated only on the cardinal points, repeating them in my mind like a mantra. It felt as though my mind was tearing itself apart with fear, but by concentrating on the compass rose, I managed to hold it together.

I'm convinced it was because my brain was focused on the points of the compass that the hypnosis didn't work. Still, I was so terrified that he made the mistake of thinking it had worked. I didn't have the strength to struggle, to fight back. All the energy drained from my body, and I slumped to the ground like a marionette whose strings had been snipped. It's no wonder he thought he finally had me in his power.

Ten years later I was standing in the hallway at the surgery and the same thing happened again. The Bastard grabbed me by the shoulders, and I slumped to the floor.

I tried to cry out, but my vocal cords wouldn't obey me, and I didn't make a sound. I felt something wet on my cheek, and when it trickled into my mouth it tasted salty.

I knew this was my last opportunity to flee.

I should have stood up, taken the filleting knife from my bag and thrust it deep into his chest. I imagined the blade sliding into his flesh and scraping his sternum so that the bone gave a dull wail.

Blood would start gushing from the wound, less and less with every pulse, until he was dead.

I knew what I had to do in order to stay alive, but suddenly I was rendered incapable of doing anything.

The Bastard lifted me from the floor like a sack of potatoes and threw me over his right shoulder. He opened the front door and carried me to the red car parked outside. I tried to look around, to see if there was anyone to witness this, but there was nobody in sight. The neighbouring garden was empty.

The Bastard lifted me into the back seat of the car, and I couldn't fight back. He threw the camouflage-patterned tarpaulin over me, the same one he'd used to cover me the first time he'd kidnapped me. The car still stank of ingrained sweat and tobacco smoke. The upholstery was still covered in splotches of Tom Thumb's sick.

I knew exactly where we were heading.

I managed to pull myself together enough to check whether I could open either of the back doors, but the Bastard had locked them both and removed the handles. I didn't have the strength to do anything else. I was like a lamb being led to the slaughter.

I felt indifferent, almost as though my own fate didn't interest me in the least.

I knew the game was up.

I sunk back into memories from my childhood.

I'd always been Daddy's girl. My most cherished memories were of spending time pottering in the basement with my father. We used to carve wooden dolls for my doll's house. We painted them carefully, right down to the smallest details of the face. We carved so many dolls that we had to add new storeys to the doll's house to accommodate them all.

When I think of my childhood, there's nothing I yearn for more than those hours spent with my father in the basement. My father's cheerful whistling, the floor quickly covered in wood shavings. The look of concentration on my father's face as he painted the dolls' lips with a tiny paintbrush. And his proud smile when I showed him another doll I'd finished.

At those moments, I was sure my father loved me, though he never said it out loud.

After my time in the Bastard's cellar, I couldn't be in any under-ground space. The stuffy smell in the basement reminded me of the Bastard and the cage. I'll never forget how disappointed my father looked every time I refused to spend time with him.

I'm actually surprised at how persistently my father kept asking. But I couldn't set foot in the basement any more. And I couldn't tell him the reason why. He started spending more and more time in the basement, but now that I wasn't there, it was the bottle that kept him company. It's my fault he became an alcoholic.

That's not a compulsive thought.

It's the truth.

The Bastard's car turned onto a smaller, unsurfaced lane. I was thrown uncontrollably around the back seat, painfully banging my elbow against a pot of paint sloshing in the footwell. I didn't care about the pain. There was only one thought in my mind, and that was guilt.

Tears welled in my eyes.

The cottage stood at the far end of an untended garden, hidden from view under a large maple tree. It was impossible to tell how old the cottage was. The paint had flaked off years ago and the roof tiles looked so precarious that the wind could have blown them off at any moment. The chimney stack was about to collapse. The grass in the garden came up to my knees; it hadn't seen a lawnmower in years. The building must have stood empty for a long time.

The Bastard stopped the car, opened the back door and snatched me into his arms.

I was there, but I wasn't there.

The Bastard could do with me as he wished.

My soul was already elsewhere.

Ida

I don't know how long I was in the cage. The cellar looked the same as it had ten years ago. There was no furniture in storage, no piles of junk or old newspapers. The only things down there were the rusty cage and the old bathtub.

The acrid smell of mould warned me that the heart of the house was rotten.

They say that, when you revisit the places you knew as a child, everything suddenly looks smaller. I couldn't lie down or stand up in the cage any more, I could barely even turn around. I huddled and tried to stretch my legs, which were numb from crouching in such an uncomfortable position.

The cellar floor was covered in a thick layer of dust; cobwebs dangled here and there across the ceiling. It looked as though nobody had been down here for a very long time. Ten years, maybe. Could my worst fear really have been in vain? What if I really was the last victim to be locked up in here?

The floor inside the cage was lined with the same white rug as before. The rug was covered in a layer of ingrained dirt. I knew that beneath all the filth there was a pattern that hadn't given me a moment's respite. I pulled down the sleeve of my father's old hoodie to cover the palm of my hand and scrubbed the rug as hard as I could until the pattern started to come into view.

A butterfly drawn in blood.

My blood.

I remember as a child imagining a pink butterfly hovering above my head in the cage and keeping me company throughout the hours I spent locked up there.

I didn't have to be alone. The butterfly fluttered around me until I was finally set free.

I snapped out of my reverie and returned to the here and now.

All of a sudden, the cellar was filled with butterflies.

Apollos, with sets of blood-red eyes on their white hind wings. Female Arctic blues, their wings as grey as freshly dried concrete. Orange tortoiseshells, the blue speckles along the edge of their wings painted as skilfully as my father used to paint my wooden dolls.

The butterflies were heading towards the cage. They landed in my hair, on my shoulders, my face.

And on the rug, right in front of me, there suddenly appeared a whole swarm of pear-tree swallowtails.

The pear-tree swallowtail isn't native to Finland. It's only been sighted here a handful of times.

The drugs were starting to take effect.

Once the Bastard had locked me in the cage, he disappeared for a moment. Soon afterwards, he came back down the ladder into the cellar, clattering on his way as if to warn me of his arrival. He was carrying a plate of porridge. He opened the cage door and started force-feeding it to me. I tried to fight back, but he had bound my hands and feet, so struggling was futile. He was stronger than me and managed to force most of the porridge down my throat. It had a bitter aftertaste.

He must have laced it with drugs or poison in an attempt to sedate me.

I tried to convince myself this was all a hallucination. The butterflies didn't really exist. I screamed as loudly as I could.

'None of this is real!'

'Real! Real! Real!' came the echo from the bare cellar walls.

I was starting to feel drowsy. I tried to force my eyes open, but they kept drooping shut. I knew that if I gave in now, I would die.

I was a butterfly.

And then I flew off.

Arto

I sat down at my desk and started drafting my suicide note for the umpteenth time. Nothing I'd ever written throughout my thirty-year career could have prepared me for this. I wanted to find exactly the right words for Ida: I wanted to talk about love, regret and guilt.

My emotions had been pent up inside me for so long that putting them into words felt impossible.

In the course of my journalistic career, I'd written some very personal articles, including a piece entitled 'My year as a widower', where I talked about the loneliness I experienced in the aftermath of Marja's death. Now it felt as though words were beyond my reach.

The sentences I sketched out felt flat and empty. Words were nothing but words. I couldn't imbue them with enough emotional charge, though it was with these very words that I needed to convince Ida I'd never loved anyone as much as I loved her.

The greater the emotion, the fewer words there are to express it.

I stared at the screen and deleted yet another draft. I started again but couldn't get beyond the first few lines. I'd been writing in a professional capacity my whole life, but it seemed I hadn't learnt anything. I failed at everything I touched; I couldn't even write a decent suicide note.

The cursor blinked at the top of the empty document. I swallowed back the tears. There was only one thing I wanted in this world.

It wasn't too late.

I wanted to save Ida.

Pekka

All those years, I'd had the upper hand, so I admit I was surprised the first time the Princess turned up at Clarissa's office. I would have put money on her not having told anyone about me, neither at the time nor later on. People would have talked about it in the media, and I would have been hunted down, both by the police and the press. But now she had decided to tell Clarissa everything, and I had to make sure that didn't happen.

I needed a carefully laid plan. How could I destroy her without leaving a trace? I prepared everything one step at a time. And only once I was certain my strategy was watertight did I finally put it into action.

Everybody should have at least one doctor in their circle of friends. Clarissa's mentor Harri Kuikkasuo was a dull old sod who could bore anyone to death, and usually his gibberish went in one ear and out the other. Time had passed him by decades ago. Freud this, Freud that—the man was like a broken record.

But right now, I needed him.

When I told him I'd suffered from years of debilitating insomnia, Harri took pity on me. He was worried about how I would cope and wrote me generous prescriptions for sedatives, mostly temazepam. It was these sedatives that I used to drug Riku. And the Princess.

It was much harder to get the Princess locked in the cage the second time around. It was too small for a grown adult. But I managed it, then went upstairs to the kitchen to make some porridge.

When I opened the pack of temazepam, I realized I'd taken the tub with too few pills left in it. I would be able to drug her with this smaller dose, but it wouldn't be lethal. There was nothing else for it; I had to go home and fetch the full tub of pills.

Clarissa

That Saturday morning, I was due to head to Kuopio where I was to spend the weekend with my good friend Minna. In the morning, I realized I'd overslept, and now my whole schedule had gone out the window. We had a table booked for twelve o'clock at my favourite restaurant, the Fisherman's Hook. I would have to drive for four and a half hours straight, ignoring the speed limits, and there was still no guarantee I'd get there in time. I could feel a stress-induced headache beginning to throb in my temples. I quickly packed a few things, said goodbye to Pekka and jumped in the car.

I'd already driven for two hours without a break and had almost reached Mikkeli when I remembered I ought to call Minna and warn her I might be a little late for lunch. I turned off the motorway, pulled into a petrol station and began rummaging in my handbag for my mobile, but couldn't find it anywhere. I tipped the contents of my handbag onto the passenger seat: hairbrush, chewing gum, a few coins, a card holder and a couple of used tissues, but no mobile phone. I cursed my own absent-mindedness.

I couldn't spend the whole weekend without my phone. I had several patients whom I'd promised could call me at any time of day. I couldn't remember all their phone numbers, and some of them did such top-secret jobs that they had unlisted numbers, so there was no way I could have found them, not even through directory enquiries. What's more, one of them—an artist, whose name I obviously can't disclose—was currently in the middle of a terrible crisis. Only that past week, the artist in question had called me several times a day and sounded utterly inconsolable. I couldn't just turn my back.

I was so upset about losing my phone that it didn't even occur to me that, once I arrived in Kuopio, I could call Pekka on Minna's phone and ask him to list my patients' numbers so that I could call them and tell them they could contact me at Minna's number over the weekend.

Instead, I turned the car around and headed back to Helsinki.

I arrived home a few hours later. I opened the front door and gave a start. The hallway was filled with the piercing shriek of an alarm: the smoke detector had gone off. My head was so sore that the sound was almost unbearable. There was the smell of smoke in the hallway. Without taking off my shoes, I ran straight into the kitchen. The cooker was switched off.

I spun around and ran into my office. Smoke hung in the air by the door. I ran across the room to open the window. Standing in the middle of the rug was my tin bucket, full of burnt papers. Next to the bucket was a half-burnt scrap that must have fallen out of the bucket. It was as though someone had performed a suicide-note ceremony in the room, and everything had gone horribly wrong.

I picked up the scrap. Someone must have tried to extinguish the fire by stamping on it; there was a footprint on the paper. A man with a wicked smirk had lost his torso in the flames. Now all that was left of him was his head.

It was one of Ida's charcoal sketches. I took the remaining scraps of burnt paper from the bucket and quickly looked through them. Pekka had torn all of Ida's sketches to shreds and tried to burn them. I stared at the mess in dismay. What on earth had come over him?

My first impulse was to take a photograph of the bucket and the charred remains of the sketches. I needed evidence of what had happened, so there was no way Pekka could deny it. I instinctively slid my hand into my handbag and fumbled for my phone. Only then did I remember I'd come home specifically because I'd forgotten it.

I turned towards my desk but noticed my phone wasn't in its usual place there either.

I backed out of the room, still in a state of shock, and walked through into the kitchen. My phone was on the kitchen table. I'd received a text message. It was from Ida.

What's so urgent that we need to meet right away?

I stared at the screen in stunned silence. I hadn't asked Ida to come today. I clicked through to my outbox to see the messages I'd sent.

We need to meet. Now. We have to talk. This cant wait.

Why would Pekka send Ida a message like that?

I ran around the house in a panic, going through every room, even the cleaning cupboard. I went out to the patio and peered around the garden.

There was no sign of Pekka. Or Ida.

I found myself back in the kitchen. I called Ida. The number I had dialled could not be reached.

It was only then that I noticed a set of keys on the kitchen table. A key ring with three rusty keys, two of them identical. I guessed that the larger key would fit the door of an old house, but I couldn't imagine what the smaller two were for. I turned the key ring in the palm of my hand for a moment until it all dawned on me. The smaller keys must be for a padlock.

Hanging from the key ring was a dirty square of cardboard. Written on the card, in Pekka's jittery handwriting, was an address:

Kanttarellinkaarre 5. The address meant nothing to me. I keyed it into my phone. The location was half an hour's drive away in the remote village of Lurikkala. Why did Pekka have keys to a property in a village I'd never even heard of?

I ran out to my car, sat down in the driver's seat and brushed a few strands of hair from my eyes. I glanced at myself in the mirror. There was a rusty smear on my face, like a butterfly wing.

I typed the address into my satnav and set off for the village of Lurikkala.

Clarissa

I felt faint. I'd eaten nothing but a light breakfast all day, but my light-headedness could have been a result of the fear. I was afraid of what lay in store for me at Kanttarellinkaarre.

With a feeling of determination, I put my foot on the accelerator, but something within me was reluctant. I could still drive to Kuopio and return home on Sunday evening, just as Minna and I had agreed. After getting home, I could breezily greet Pekka and ask how his weekend had gone, adding that I hoped he'd remembered to relax and hadn't spent the whole weekend huddled over his laptop. I could even pretend to believe his answer, as he appealed to my sympathies by lying, telling me he had worked all weekend and hadn't left the house once, not even to fetch a pizza. I could massage his shoulders and try to convince myself I had a wonderful, faithful husband whom I could trust wholeheartedly.

But I couldn't live a lie any longer. Ever since Riku's death, I'd been keeping up appearances, I'd managed to convince myself I hadn't separated from Pekka so that he wouldn't have the opportunity to abuse a child ever again. Only now, sitting behind the steering wheel in my car, did I have the courage to confront the truth head-on. How could I have prevented Pekka's terrible acts? It was impossible! I couldn't have followed him, shadowed him all day long. And as the sketches, torn and burnt and left at the bottom of the tin bucket, revealed, I didn't have the faintest idea what he did when I wasn't there.

With my patients.

I realized I'd sunk so far into my own thoughts that I'd taken a wrong turn. The satnav told me to make a U-turn. I followed the instructions and turned the car onto a road full of potholes. A crooked signpost read Kanttarellinkaarre. The satnav told me I had arrived at my destination. At the end of the lane was a small cottage.

My phone rang.

Pekka.

I knew I would live to regret it, but I gave my husband one last opportunity to explain himself.

He didn't even bother to say hello.

'There was a set of keys on the kitchen table. Where are they?'

I barely recognized his voice. He sounded threatening, as though the mask had slipped to reveal his true face.

I said nothing.

'Clarissa, listen to me, this is important! I need those keys.'

I remained silent.

'When did you get here?' he continued. 'I only nipped to the shop, and when I got back the keys were gone.'

I hung up, but before I could end the call, I heard him shouting: 'I'm coming, Clarissa. I'm already on my way.'

Clarissa

I parked my car and ran towards the cottage. The front door was locked. I took the set of keys out of my handbag and pushed the larger one into the lock. I had to yank it and twist it, but eventually it gave way. On the front step there was a basket full of firewood with an axe propped against it. I picked up the axe. It was only as I tried to get a firm grip on its handle that I realized I already knew exactly what awaited me inside the cottage.

I quietly pushed the door open and peered in. The cottage was dark. I couldn't see anybody. Very cautiously, I stepped inside. Sunlight struck a metallic hook on the floor, glinting briefly. It was a sign. I gripped the hook with my left hand, still holding the axe in my right, and pulled open a hatch. The thought occurred to me: I can still back off, turn around and run away. But I couldn't. Not now.

Beneath the hatch there was a rickety ladder leading down into a cellar. I kicked off my high heels and climbed down the ladder. I stood quietly at the foot of the ladder and held onto it to steady myself as I tried to take stock of my surroundings. The first thing I could make out was a rusty old bathtub. Then I saw the cage.

It was right at the back of the cellar. And it wasn't empty. But though I knew there was someone in the cage, my mind tried to play tricks on me one last time, tried to fool me into believing there wasn't anyone there at all. Then I heard it. A shrill howl, like that of an animal that knows it is dying. The sound boomed through the cellar, growing in strength as it echoed across the mouldy brick walls. I quivered with fear until I realized that the source of the howl was me.

I hurried towards the cage. Ida was lying on the ground inside it. She muttered something to herself, as though she was talking to someone else. Suddenly, she turned towards me and said:

'I knew you would come.'

It looked as though she could see right through me, as though there was someone standing behind me.

I didn't know who she had been expecting.

Ida

The cellar started glowing, bathed in white light. A beautiful, spellbinding figure appeared before me. All the figure had to do was point a finger at the cage, and the bars dissolved.

A set of snow-white wings unfurled and pulled me into their embrace.

An angel.

My guardian angel.

The angel had beautiful long hair and she was wearing a pink dress. Her face was calm; her expression promised that she would take care of me.

I'd dreamt about this angel as a child. In my dreams, she had whispered a secret to me, 'We will meet again.'

The angel's fingers squeezed my arms. Her nails sank into my bare skin, making my arms bleed. She lifted me from the floor of the cage, helped me to my feet and slapped me across the face with the flat of her hand. Once. Twice. Three times.

The angel walked ahead of me to the ladder, an axe swinging in time with her steps. I climbed the ladder after her and found myself in the cottage kitchen.

'I'll kill you!'

I heard the shout, but I didn't know which of us the shouter meant.

The axe made a whooshing sound as it flew across the kitchen.

I'd never heard the sound of someone fighting for their life before. The scream was raw. I pressed my hands over my ears and dashed out of the cottage door.

I thought I'd managed to escape the cage for good, but, of course, I was wrong.

Arto

They say alcoholics only start to get better once they've reached rock bottom. For me, rock bottom was when I heard that my daughter had been sexually abused as a child, and at the time it happened, she didn't trust me enough to tell me about it.

What kind of man does that make me? What kind of father?

For the first time in my whole life, I looked myself earnestly in the mirror, and I didn't like what I saw. For all the questions I asked myself, there was only one real answer: it was time to kick the booze once and for all.

I insisted on hearing Ida's impact statement in court.

I still don't know how I had the strength to listen to the statement in its entirety. Emotions swirled within me. Disbelief, anger, sorrow. To think of everything my little girl had had to endure! And yet the same question still plagued me: what kind of father did that make me?

I can't bring myself to look at Ida in the same way as before. It's as though that man is always standing next to her, casting his shadow across her face.

Pekka Virtanen.

Or, as Ida calls him, the Bastard.

Ida

When I woke up in the hospital the following morning, I heard it was my therapist who had brought me there. I didn't remember anything about the journey as I was still in a drug-induced haze. I also learnt that my therapist had called an ambulance. The axe had struck the Bastard in the thigh, severing an artery. His injuries were serious, but he was expected to make a full recovery.

At the trial, the Bastard claimed that my therapist had been an accessory to the kidnapping. Apparently, she'd planned to kill me and had come to the cottage to see out her plan but changed her mind at the last moment, just as she was about to bring the axe crashing down into my chest. My therapist pleaded guilty to all charges.

At first, I couldn't believe any of these claims were true. All along, I'd assumed she genuinely wanted to help me. But I've never been a very good judge of character. If I was, I'd never have ended up in the cage in the first place.

And now they were both caged up, in a psychiatric prison.

I believe at least one of them is planning to escape.

Ida

Can an estranged father and daughter ever wipe the slate clean and start again? Well, we're trying, at least. I moved back in with my father so we can take care of each other. He attends AA meetings and is desperately trying to kick the bottle. I really hope he can do it, but I doubt he will. Now he has more reasons to drink than ever before.

My father and I have never spoken about anything. He doesn't want to. He wants to give the impression of being open-minded, but the truth is he avoids anything remotely difficult. I don't suppose he's told you anything that would push him over the edge. I bet he hasn't even mentioned my suicide attempts.

My father asked to hear my impact statement in court, but I should never have agreed to it. He didn't deserve to hear the truth. He is an idealist, a hippie, a tree-hugger. In his world, there is no such thing as absolute evil.

When I told the court about the Bastard, I saw disbelief flicker across my father's face, though he tried his best to hide it. I was a riddle he'd been trying to solve: why had his beloved daughter's life gone so far off the rails?

The pieces of the jigsaw were beginning to slot into place, and he had no other option but to believe me. He had to turn his back on everything that was dear to him: his values, his world view and his morals. The world wasn't the way he had imagined it.

My father, who used to be a staunch opponent of the death penalty, can't console himself with anything but violent fantasies now. The Bastard has destroyed my father's life too. He'd never say it out loud, but he wishes I had died in the cage that day. My very existence reminds him of what happened to me. If I'd died, he would have been able to place all his pain in the coffin and bury it alongside my body in the bosom of the earth. Now there's no respite from the agony. I can see it in his face. He can't look me in the eyes any more.

I'll never be able to forgive my father for not protecting me when I was a child. He is perceptive enough—or he feels such a profound sense of guilt—that he doesn't even expect me to forgive him.

The Bastard twisted me into a knot, and my father can't help tugging at the threads, though this only pulls the knot tighter. As a coping method, he comes up with all kinds of things he thinks might cure me. Would hypnosis help? What about meditation? I have to get better, no matter how I do it!

It's hard being so ill. But the fact that my father can't accept my illness makes it all the harder. I'm responsible for his woes too.

It's a burden I don't have the strength to carry.

And so, recently, my thoughts have been returning to pills, razorblades and nooses, to all the things I could do to take my own life, so that all this might finally be over.

Until I received a letter from the Bastard.

Ida

My father had fetched the post and left the letter on my desk. He didn't know that the careful handwriting was the Bastard's or that it was sent from the prison hospital. The lettering curled across the surface of the envelope like vines waiting to wrap themselves round my neck and strangle me.

I wanted to chuck it straight in the bin, but I knew I couldn't do it. The Bastard had such a strong grip on me that I couldn't resist the bait he'd thrown me. The letter was like a bomb that would continue to tick until I opened it.

It was best to get it over and done with, because I couldn't think of anything except the vitriol bubbling inside the envelope, the words whose only intention was to poison my mind.

The letter contained a single sentence:

You are mine.

I read it a second, a third time, before tearing the paper to pieces. It was only then that I understood something I should have realized years ago. The truth had been right under my nose for years; I just hadn't seen it.

When I was a child, I had something the Bastard did not.

My innocence.

He wanted to tarnish me, trample all my purity under his feet and stamp the life out of it, tear it, rip it, cut it up and saw it into pieces, crush it and smash it smithereens.

And he had succeeded—almost. But though he'd wiped his

grimy hands on me and though I would forever be covered in his black fingerprints, I still had something that he craved.

My life.

It wasn't much, it wasn't a lot, and maybe it was worthless, but the Bastard still longed for it. And I would not let him have it.

I scrunched up the shreds of the letter, threw the ball of paper into the bin and, as if to test myself, said: 'Never.'

I realized I'd just made the greatest decision of my life.

I had to learn to live.

I owed that to the little girl locked up in his cage ten years ago.

There and then, I swore I would find a way out of the cellar, a way to rescue little Ida.

Clarissa

As I drove Ida from the cottage to the nearest hospital, I could think of only one thing. The punishment I had meted out to myself was nowhere near sufficient. It wasn't good enough to try and serve as Pekka's conscience and prevent him from committing more crimes. I needed to be properly punished for my own crime: Riku's murder.

In court, Pekka claimed that he and I had planned everything together, tried to murder Ida together. I had no idea that Pekka had abused Ida or that he was planning to kill her. But that didn't stop me wanting to be punished for his crimes.

I was certain he would be sent to a psychiatric facility. If I admitted to having a part in his crimes—though I wasn't in fact guilty of them—I would end up at the same address.

There could be no more fitting punishment for me than to spend the rest of my life with the paedophile whose innocent victim I had killed.

But I had no intention of admitting to Riku's murder.

Especially not to Pekka.

I don't ever want my husband to know I was so keen to protect him that I was even prepared to kill his victim.

The first weeks in hospital passed in a blur. I sat in my room and listened to the rain lashing against the window. I'd been in hospital at least a month when another patient was admitted: a young woman dressed in black with a thick bandage tied around her right wrist.

At supper, the woman sat down opposite me at the table in the corner where I used to sit by myself. In a fragile voice, she asked me to pass the sugar. She couldn't look me in the eyes. I handed her the sugar bowl, and almost without noticing brushed my thumb against her forefinger.

I felt a connection between us.

Fate had brought us together.

My life had a meaning again.

This one I would save.

MEET ME IN THE DARKNESS

Acknowledgements

Many, many thanks to everybody at WSOY: Anna-Riikka, Hanna, Lea, Reetta, Samuli, Satu-Maria and Tuuli. You're the best!

Thank you to Elina Ahlbäck and the Elina Ahlbäck Literary Agency, who have successfully sold the translation rights for this novel to twelve countries and counting.

Thank you to David Hackston for the excellent translation.

Special thanks to Pushkin Press, particularly Adam Freudenheim and Daniel Seton, who believed in Ida and in *Follow the Butterfly*.

Thank you to Otto Virtanen for my photo.

I would also like to thank Aija, Jenna and Susanna for their valuable contributions.

And finally, the most important thank you of all. Writing my first novel took four years. Throughout that time, I often regaled my husband with problems related to the novel. Six months before it was due to be published, in a brief moment of clarity, I asked him if he was already bored of listening to my complaints. 'Ages ago,' he said. I solemnly swore to keep my mouth shut. 'There's no need. The point of a relationship is to listen to each other's worries, even when you really can't be bothered.' How can I ever thank you? I have only one word: Strontium-90.

AVAILABLE AND COMING SOON
FROM PUSHKIN VERTIGO

Jonathan Ames

You Were Never Really Here
A Man Named Doll
The Wheel of Doll

Simone Campos

Nothing Can Hurt You Now

Zijin Chen

Bad Kids

Maxine Mei-Fung Chung

The Eighth Girl

Candas Jane Dorsey

The Adventures of Isabel
What's the Matter with Mary Jane?

Margot Douaihy

Scorched Grace

Joey Hartstone

The Local

Seraina Kobler

Deep Dark Blue

Elizabeth Little

Pretty as a Picture

Jack Lutz

London in Black

Steven Maxwell

All Was Lost

Callum McSorley

Squeaky Clean

Louise Mey

The Second Woman

John Kåre Raake

The Ice

RV Raman

A Will to Kill
Grave Intentions
Praying Mantis

Paula Rodríguez

Urgent Matters

Nilanjana Roy

Black River

John Vercher

Three-Fifths
After the Lights Go Out

Emma Viskic

Resurrection Bay
And Fire Came Down
Darkness for Light
Those Who Perish

Yulia Yakovleva

Punishment of a Hunter
Death of the Red Rider